LETHAL DREAMS
Anne Patrick

Lethal Dreams
Copyright © 2010 by Anne Patrick. All rights reserved.
Cover art by Karen Michelle Nutt
ISBN:
ISBN-13:
Licensing Notes:
This book is protected by Federal copyright laws. All rights are reserved and it is illegal to copy, scan, or in any way mechanically or digitally reproduce this book except for brief passages used in reviews and related articles. Requests for other uses should be directed to the author or publisher for written permission.

Lethal Dreams is a work of fiction. Names, characters, and incidents are the products of the author's imagination and are either fictitious or are used fictitiously. Any resemblance to actual events or persons, living or dead, is entirely coincidental.

Chapter One

Erin Jacobs paused outside the emergency room, slipped on her backpack, and stared up at the threatening clouds. The distant rumble of thunder alerted her that she didn't have much time. With any luck, she could make the six blocks to her sister-in-law's homeless shelter before the rain started. She hustled to the nearby bike rack. At two-thirty on a Sunday morning, hers was the only bike there.

"Looks like we're in for a wicked storm."

Erin glanced up at the familiar voice of Dr. Thomas Duncan. "Hey, Tom. How was the fishing trip?"

"It could have been better. Candice was seasick most of the day. You should be glad you didn't go."

Erin chuckled. She felt bad for her friend and former college roommate, who was now the morning charge nurse. "Tell her I said she should have listened and taken the Dramamine along."

"I'll let you tell her yourself. Anything exciting happen tonight?"

"A pileup on the expressway. Thankfully no fatalities, but plenty of customers. I'm surprised they didn't page you." As the head of Orthopedics, he was always in big demand.

"I left strict instructions not to unless it was a national emergency. Is that why you're here?"

"Yeah, they were shorthanded in the ER. Morton and Jensen are out with the flu, and Thornton is still on vacation." She glanced at her wristwatch. "If I'm lucky, I can get four hours of sleep before my actual shift starts."

"Well thanks for filling in."

She hadn't really done much. Checked vitals, started IV's. As a Doctor of Physical Therapy, her skills would come later when she helped the patients recover from their injuries.

A flash of lightning, followed shortly by a clap of thunder, warned her that she needed to get moving if she hoped to beat the rain. "Any time. I'll see you in a few hours."

"Hey, where's the helmet Candice bought you?"

She grinned sheepishly. "On my kitchen table."

He shook his head. "Be careful, Erin. I want you back here in one piece."

Erin was within a few blocks of Safe Harbor Homeless Shelter when the first drops of rain began to fall. She inhaled the delicious scent and blinked as droplets peppered her face. She loved thunderstorms. Shifting gears, she started down the hill, figuring to take the alley as a shortcut.

Two loud pops echoed from the surrounding buildings.

Gunshots!

They sounded close, but in the maze of tall buildings, she couldn't tell what direction they'd come from. She slowed down in order to make the left turn into the alleyway and heard the squeal of tires coming from the alley to her right.

A pair of headlights sped toward her.

She hit the brakes hard, hoping to avoid a collision. *Aw man, this is going to hurt.*

The bike skidded on the wet pavement and she leaned sideways to lay it down. She winced as her left side made contact with the concrete, gravel and dirt penetrating the tender skin of her thigh and forearm.

The black SUV crossed underneath the streetlight. The driver looked down at her and his dark eyes widened. Both irritated and angry, she stared at the guy. "Jerk," she hollered as the SUV sped away.

A second pair of headlights in the alley caught her attention. The car was just sitting there. Its passenger door opened. She immediately recalled the gunshots just prior to the SUV exiting the alley.

Oh, no!

Erin jerked her backpack off and ran to the car. She spotted the passenger on the ground, saw a leg move, then looked at the driver who was completely still. Going for the driver, she jerked open the door and froze at the sight of the gun and badge pinned to his belt.

Cops.

Erin stared at the crimson stain spreading across his chest. A wave of nausea washed over her. She shook off the reaction and checked for a pulse with one hand while unbuttoning his shirt with the other. He had a chest wound, but his pulse was strong.

She got on the car radio, gave their location, and reported officers down and in need of immediate medical attention. She then gave a description of the SUV and driver.

"Can you repeat the description, ma'am?" the female dispatcher asked.

"Early to mid-twenties, tall, stocky build...athletic, black hair, mustache, black t-shirt, diamond stud in his left ear. There was a passenger, but I couldn't see them. I don't know if it was a male or female."

"Can I get your name, please?"

"Addison," a male voice spoke from the other side of the car.

Erin hung up. The voice sounded weak. She ran around to the passenger side of the car. He'd managed to sit up and was leaning against the front wheel. She opened his shirt. He had a bad shoulder wound, but would live. "Sir, I need you to lie back down."

"My partner, is he..."

"He's going to be fine. So are you." She looked around for something she could use to elevate his feet. She spotted a wooden crate near a dumpster and dragged it over. With her arms wrapped around him, she eased him back down, then lifted his legs onto the crate. He started to stir again. "Please, you must lay still." Grabbing the keys from the ignition, she went to search the trunk for a first aid kit and blanket.

<hr />

LOGAN DRIFTED IN AND out of consciousness. His shoulder felt like it was on fire. He never imagined getting shot would hurt this bad.

"It's not a serious wound. You...you're going to be fine."

He looked up at his rescuer. Moments ago, she'd sounded so calm and collected as she'd given a detailed description of the driver over his police radio. She was far from that now. Even her hands shook as she applied pressure to his wound. Though she avoided looking at him, he had seen the tears glistening in her eyes.

She had a gentle touch, soothing even. And she was beautiful. The rain had drenched her green scrubs, and her dark, shoulder-length hair was matted to the sides of her face and neck. She was wearing credentials. The photo ID turned so that only *Mercy General Hospital* could be seen. "Are you a nurse?"

"No."

He heard sirens drawing near. "A doctor?"

She started to stand, but he tightened his grip on her hand. "Where are you going?"

"I'm sorry. I've gotta go." The words seemed ripped from her lips. As if she had no choice.

Logan watched her run awkwardly the length of the alley. *She was hurt.* Had she been shot too? She stooped over, picked up a backpack, then slipped it over her shoulder. His eyes narrowed. He saw a bike lying on its side. Relief swept over him. She hadn't been shot, only wrecked her bike. He recalled the description she'd given of the shooter—so much detail. If she'd gotten that good a look at the shooters, then they had gotten an even better look at her. As he watched her disappear into the darkness, he prayed the Lord would watch over her until he was back on his feet and could find out who she was.

"HOW IN THE WORLD DID you manage this?"

Erin smiled at her sister-in-law's question. It was four-thirty in the morning, and for the last forty-five minutes, she'd been picking gravel out of Erin's left thigh and forearm. Erin had hoped to slip into the shelter and crash on the sofa in the recreation room until it was time to start serving breakfast, but Emma had somehow gotten word of her accident and had come over from the parsonage to check on her. "Some jerk pulled out in front of me. It was either chance road rash or a concussion. I'm thinking I should have gone with the concussion."

"Not without a helmet you don't. Please tell me the bicycle was totaled."

Erin looked up at her sister-in-law. There was only a year's difference in their ages, but in the last two years, Emma had taken on more of a mothering role in her life than a big sister. "That's mean."

"Is she decent?"

Emma quickly covered Erin's bare thigh as Bobby entered the recreation room. "She's lucky to be alive, that's what she is."

"Sorry, Erin, no sign of your bike."

"That figures." She glanced up and saw Emma smile.

"I didn't say a word."

"No, but you were thinking it. You do realize that bike is my transportation?"

"I'm sure Bobby will be happy to give you a lift wherever you need to go. And the two of you do work the same shift at the hospital." Emma gathered the tweezers and bloody towel and stood. "Go soak in the tub now, and use some antiseptic spray afterwards. You don't want to get an infection."

"Yes, Mother."

Emma yanked the pillow out from underneath Erin's head and hit her with it. "And don't even think about helping with breakfast. We've got more than enough help."

Erin started to protest. Working at the shelter was one of the highlights of her day. But, since she was due at the hospital in two and half hours, she didn't argue. Two hours of sleep was better than none.

She waited until the door of the recreation room closed before turning to her friend of six years. "You just had to call her."

He looked up from the over-stuffed chair he was sitting in and grinned. African American, mid-forties, and ex-army, Bobby had been a friend of both her and her late husband. After almost losing his leg in Iraq, he'd returned to the states to find out his wife and son had up and moved to California with another man. One thing had led to another and the man had given up all hope and was living on the streets when her husband had found him. At the time, Bobby hadn't cared if he lived or died.

"Emma was right; I'll be happy to give you a lift wherever you need to go."

"Don't think I won't take you up on that offer. Some of my patients live all the way across town."

"Just let me know where and when."

She wrapped the sheet around her, rose gingerly from the sofa, and leaned over to hug him. "You're a good man, Bobby."

She started to pull away, but he grabbed her hand. "What really happened in the alley, Erin? And don't tell me it was just a minor accident. The cops are still searching the area for a witness."

She eased herself down on the arm of his chair. Just as Emma had appointed herself a mother figure in Erin's life, Bobby had appointed himself a protector. Not just of Erin, but of everyone at the shelter. "Promise me you won't say anything to Emma or Andy?"

He slowly nodded.

Considering the fact he'd already ratted her out once this morning, she hesitated. But she knew the danger she'd placed herself in earlier. She was a witness in the shooting of two police officers. In all likelihood, those responsible could come looking for her. If that was the case, Bobby needed to know. Emma and Andy were the only family she had left. Their safety and the safety of their children was the only thing she cared about. "The cops are looking for me; I'm the witness they're searching the area for."

"You saw the cops get shot?"

"No, but I saw one of the shooters as they pulled out of the alley. That's how I wrecked my bike. I was trying to avoid hitting them."

"There was more than one?"

She nodded. "I didn't get a look at the passenger, only the driver. I called the shooting in on the car radio and gave a description of the guy. I imagine that's why they took my bike, to try and lift my prints." She smiled. "It's a good thing I don't have a record."

"Forget the cops. It's the shooter you should be concerned about. Did he get a good look at you?"

"I don't think so." She stood and gathered her backpack. "It was dark, and he wasn't expecting to see me there."

"I hope you're right, Erin."

"So do I," she said quietly.

"ANY LUCK WITH THE BIKE?" Logan asked his captain. Two days had passed since the shooting. The pain in his shoulder was nothing short of tolerable. Surgery had gone well; the doctor had been pleased with the results. He recalled their conversation barely. He'd mentioned pins in the collarbone, torn muscles, and six months of physical therapy before complete recovery could be expected. It was unacceptable. He couldn't be off the job that long. He had to find out who the shooter was and why he had chosen him and his partner as his victims.

Captain Connelly took a seat beside Logan's bed. "We lifted several prints, but no matches. Whoever your mystery woman is, she doesn't have a record."

He wasn't sure if he was glad of that. At least if she had they would be closer to finding out who she was and what she was doing in an alleyway at three o'clock in the morning. "Did you ask around the hospital?"

He nodded. "No luck. If they do know her, they aren't saying. Are you sure the ID said, 'Mercy General'?"

"I'm positive." She was about the only thing he remembered after the shooting.

"If the guy was wearing a ski mask, how did she give such a good description?"

"That's a good question." He wished he had the answer. The license plate on the SUV he'd run had come back to a local elderly couple that later reported it stolen. Late for a meeting with an informant, he and Addison had flipped to see who got out of the car to check the suspicious vehicle sitting in the alleyway. He had no sooner gotten out of the car when the passenger side door opened on the SUV and the masked gunman opened fire. Neither Logan nor his partner had time to draw their weapons. "The only thing I can think of is the driver wasn't wearing a mask."

The captain let out a sigh as he ran his hand back through his salt and pepper hair. "This informant you were supposed to meet, is he reliable?"

"No way is he responsible for the shooting." Logan trusted Frankie Purcell almost as much as he did his partner. The recovering drug addict had done a one-hundred and eighty degree turn since Logan had busted him six months ago. Had entered a drug program, gotten a job, and had even turned his life over to the Lord. He'd never seen anyone turn their life around the way Frankie had.

"You said you were meeting him in connection to the counterfeit bank cards?"

"Yeah. He said he had a pretty good idea who the inside source was." The thieves had, so far, managed to swindle thousands of dollars from area banks and Logan suspected they weren't armatures.

"Any chance this mystery woman could be involved?"

"She was wearing scrubs and an ID badge for this hospital," he reminded. Besides, he didn't know of too many thieves who'd come to the aid of a cop.

"Maybe she works at the bank part time," the captain suggested.

"No. My gut tells me she was just in the right place at the wrong time."

"Well, if she's got nothing to hide, why isn't she coming forward? The request has been in all the local papers and news channels."

In Logan's opinion, that had been a foolish move on the captain's part. The woman's life was already in danger. Why broadcast it? At least he hadn't given her description or mentioned the fact she worked at the hospital. "My guess is, she knows she's in danger and is smart enough not to come forward, knowing the shooter is probably watching."

"The longer she stays hidden, the more danger she's placing herself in."

"Which is why I need to get out of here." Logan hated the thought of something happening to the woman, especially after she'd helped save their lives.

"You just concentrate on your physical therapy. We'll handle the rest. You're due to start tomorrow, aren't you?"

"Yeah." And he wasn't looking forward to it. Getting shot was bad enough, but being cooped up in a hospital while the jerk who put him there was still on the street was pure torture. Oh well, the sooner he finished his physical therapy, the quicker he could go back to work.

"Well, I better get out of here and let you get some rest," the captain said as he got up from the chair.

"If you stop in and see Addison, tell him I said hi and that I'll come see him tomorrow."

"Will do. Get some rest, and good luck with your therapy."

"Thanks."

ERIN FROZE AT THE NAME on the file. *Detective Logan Sinclair.* It'd been all over the news for the last three days. He was one of the cops that had been shot in the alley near the shelter, the one that had been conscious according to the photograph on the ten o'clock news. She'd lost count of how many times in the last three nights she'd woke with that face imprinted in her memory. It wasn't his gorgeous, sandy-blonde hair and light green eyes that she remembered the most, but the blood saturating his shirt. She'd tried not to look at him because every time she had, she'd seen her husband's face, and his motionless body lying on a gurney.

Rats! Of the three hospitals in the area, they had to bring him here.

She could go to Dr. Duncan and ask the chief orthopedic surgeon to assign another PT, but she knew that would open up a can of worms she didn't really want to deal with. Or she could do the cowardly thing. Go home, faking the flu for two or three days. He was due to be released on Saturday. She'd never have to see him again. Or, there was always the possibility that he wouldn't remember her. It had been dark, after all, a nearby security light and the dome light of the car the only light sources. She went with the latter, hoping she wouldn't regret the decision.

"ARE YOU FEEDING THE cats like I asked you to?" Logan inquired of his mother. Reluctantly, she had agreed to drive out to his place once a day. He knew it was big sacrifice on her part. Normally she wouldn't be caught dead on a farm.

"Yes, dear. You really should consider adopting some of them out. I lost count at seventeen."

"That sounds about right. And I don't want to get rid of them. They're good mousers."

A soft knock sounded at his door. Both he and his mother turned as the door crept open. His eyes widened at the sight of his mystery woman.

"Good morning, Detective Sinclair. I'm sorry to intrude. I'm Erin, your physical therapist." She stepped forward and offered her hand.

He took it, smiling. He never thought he'd see her again. *Erin.* It was a beautiful name. It fit perfectly. "Good morning. Erin, I'd like you to meet my mother, Marilynn Sinclair."

His mother stood and offered her hand across the bed. "It's a pleasure to meet you, Erin."

Erin smiled and placed her backpack on the end of the bed. She had a lovely smile, uninhibited, carefree. "It's nice to meet you, Mrs. Sinclair."

"Oh please, call me Marilynn." She turned Erin's right hand over. "What a beautiful ring."

Logan glanced at it. Interlocking gold hearts surrounded an oval sapphire. "Thank you. It was an anniversary gift from my husband."

"Well he has very good taste."

Logan glanced at her left hand and frowned at the presence of a gold wedding band. *Just my luck, she's married.*

His gaze lingered on her hands. They were slim and deeply tanned, as were her arms. She no doubt spent a lot of time in the sun. Her right arm still bore signs of road rash, small patches of skin not yet scabbed over, particularly around her elbow. It looked painful.

"I better go, dear. You be good and listen to what the doctors tell you."

"Yes, Mom. And don't be giving away my cats while I'm in here."

"As tempting as that sounds, I wouldn't dream of it. Erin, I hope to see you again."

Erin smiled. She was much taller than he remembered, at least five-eight. "It was a pleasure meeting you."

He watched his mother leave the room, then shifted his eyes to Erin. "So we meet again."

She tossed him a coy smile. "I suppose you've been wondering why I took out of there so quickly?"

He nodded. "Your husband must have been pacing the floor when you got home."

"Well, I assure you, I haven't any warrants out on me. But then I'm guessing you already know that."

He grinned. She was smart and beautiful. She was also disturbingly cheery. "So are you going to tell me why you took off in such a hurry or am I going to have to guess?"

"I'm very sensitive. Blood always upsets me. I know that sounds ridiculous given my profession, but there you have it."

"And are you always this cheery in the morning?"

"Afraid so." She took a pad from her backpack and sat in the chair next to the bed. "Before we begin I need to get your medical history."

He sat up on the side of the bed and looked over at her as she began to make notes. For the next twenty minutes, he answered her questions about previous injuries, sports activities he participated in, and his duties in the field.

"You said you played high school football. What position did you play?"

"Tight end."

"And you were never injured?"

"Just the usual bumps and bruises; nothing serious. What sports do you play?"

"Basketball mostly. I also bike and run."

"That reminds me, a buddy of mine is in the process of repairing your bike for you."

She glanced up from her pad with a generous smile. "Thank you."

"It's the least I could do." He glanced at the badge hanging around her neck. Her last name was Jacobs. For some reason, the name struck a familiar cord. "What's the DPT stand for?"

"Doctor of Physical Therapy." She stood and placed her pad on the end of the bed. "Can I get you to slip off your gown, please?" She pulled the curtain around the front of the bed to provide privacy.

He did as she instructed. Thankful for the pajama bottoms his mother had brought from home. "So tell me, Doc, how long before I get the full use of my shoulder back?"

"That depends largely on you. The time and effort you invest in your therapy program will help you to enjoy the best possible outcome."

"How about giving me a ballpark figure?"

"Three to six months."

The doctor had said six; he liked her optimism.

She stepped forward and removed the sling from around his neck. "Let me see what you can do with your right shoulder so I can establish a base line of normal movement."

He went through a series of exercises while she jotted down notes. When finished, she laid down her tablet and stepped in front of him. "Okay, we're going to test your resistance. If you feel any pain, tell me and we'll stop. With your elbows at your side, ball your fists, turning them toward one another. I'm going to place my hands at the back of yours and you're going to push against my hands."

She was very focused in her work. He liked that. "How long have you been doing this, Erin?"

"Eight years. Now externally." She placed her hands on the inside of his, the back of them against his knuckles. "Very good. Now we're going to start with five post-operative exercises. They shouldn't cause you pain so, if they do, be sure and tell me and we'll stop. Okay?"

"Okay."

She rolled the tray table over, turning it length ways toward him, and spread out a towel. "I want you to place your palm face down at the end of the towel, and then, while keeping contact by the heel of your hand, crumple up the towel into a ball inside your hand."

He did as she instructed, conscious that she was watching his every move. "Have you always lived in Florida?"

"Yes. You?"

"On and off."

She jotted down a few notes and then rolled the table back. "Now with your arm at your side, bring the elbow up so that your fist is almost touching your shoulder. Then, slowly allow your elbow to relax so that your arm, from the elbow down, lowers towards the floor. Just like you did with your right arm a while ago."

He followed her instructions. "Is your husband in the medical profession too?"

"I lost my husband two years ago."

He looked at her. Her face was void of any expression. "Let me guess, you wear the ring to ward off unwanted advances?"

She smiled. "That, and to avoid annoying questions."

"I'm sorry for your loss, Erin."

"Thank you." She stepped to her backpack at the end of the bed. "When you were a kid did, you play with silly putty?"

"Is this a trick question?"

She smothered a smile. He grinned. "A few times."

She opened a small plastic container and dumped a ball of putty into his hand. "I want you to work this in your hand whenever you're not asleep."

"Okay." He watched as she gathered her notepad and pen, slipping them into her backpack. Was she leaving already? "What about the other exercises?"

"Excuse me?"

"You said there were five. We only did three."

"We'll do the others tomorrow. In the mean time, do the ones I showed you as often as you feel comfortable with. But remember, if it starts to hurt, stop."

"I've upset you. I'm sorry."

"No. You didn't upset me. It's just that if I don't leave now I'm going to be late for my other job."

"Erin, before you go, we need to talk about the other night. You gave a very good description of the shooter, which makes me believe he got just as good a look at you."

"You think my life may be in danger?"

He didn't want to frighten her, but she needed to know. "It's a very good possibility. The passenger was the shooter, but he was wearing a black ski mask. For some reason, the driver wasn't, and you're our only witness."

Her eyes leveled on him as she considered his words. "Whose idea was it to broadcast that there was a female witness to the shooting?"

If she was scared, she showed little sign of it. She seemed more irritated than anything. "That would be my captain, and I'm sorry about that."

"So what do you want me to do, a composite?"

Either she was familiar with the procedure, or she watched a lot of TV. "It would be helpful."

She twisted her bottom lip to one side, nibbling at it. She had perfect teeth, straight and pearly white. "Have a sketch artist meet me here Saturday morning at nine; I'll be free until noon."

He considered suggesting it be done at the station, but figured she'd be more comfortable in her own environment. Plus, he wanted to be there.

"Thank you, Erin. And thank you for the other night. If you hadn't made that call, my partner may not have made it."

"You're welcome. I'll see you tomorrow."

He was looking forward to it.

Chapter Two

"You're late."

"So fire me," Erin bit out. Derrick Rydell, star quarterback for the Florida Cougars, was presently her most important patient. Having fractured his elbow at the end of last season, the doctors were only giving him a sixty percent chance of playing his senior year. Rumors were already circulating that he may never play again, which was why his parents had hired her instead of going with the paid athletic trainers at the university.

"Don't tempt me. Rough morning at the hospital?"

"You could say that. How'd practice go this morning?"

"I only completed thirty percent of my passes, Erin. I'm not getting any better."

She offered a sympathetic smile. Having missed most of spring practice, the doctors were just now letting him suit up.

She followed him into the weight room his parents had built for him his senior year of high school. Working private duty with top named athletes over the last eight years, she'd been in many mansions just as nice, if not nicer, than the Rydell's. The only difference being, most of those were professional players. The pressure Derrick was under to fight his way back to full mobility was working against him, and she wasn't sure how to deal with it. His parents, both in real estate, were only part of the problem. Derrick was losing his confidence, and as of late, was easily discouraged.

"Is it true you helped Marcus Wheeler get back in the game after his knee injury?"

Erin didn't usually talk about other clients, but thought in this instance it might inspire him to try harder. "Marcus fought his way back against all odds. Everyone had given up on him, even his teammates."

He looked up at her from the weight bench. "Everyone but you."

The anguish she saw in his eyes tore at her heartstrings. She had to find a way to move him past this obstacle. "I can have all the faith in the world in you Derrick, but what it comes down to is the faith you have in yourself." She pulled up a chair and sat down next to him. "Let me ask you something...why do you play football?"

"Because I love the game."

"Are you sure? Or is it because you don't want to disappoint your parents and friends?"

"I guess it's a little bit of both."

She appreciated his honesty. "That's why you're not getting any better, Derrick."

He sat up. "What do you mean?"

"You don't want it bad enough, and until you do, you won't get any better."

"You're wrong, Erin. I do want to play again, and not just because my parents and my friends want it, but also because I've dreamed of playing professionally since I was six years old and threw my first football. The odds are stacked against me, though. Do you know how many black quarterbacks there are in the NFL?"

"What difference does that make?"

"Plenty when you're injured. Come draft day, the first thing they're going to look at is my injury. The second thing they'll look at is the color of my skin. That's two strikes against me right there."

"That's your father talking, Derrick, not you. You say you want to play again. Then prove it to me. Get off the self-pity wagon and start showing me some heart. Stop worrying about starting the season or making the draft, and concentrate on right now. Think back to when you were a little kid, the love you had for the game, and use it as motivation. Because in the end, none of the other matters. It's your love of the game that got you where you are, Derrick, and what's going to get you into the pros."

He grinned. "You really think I still have a shot?"

"If I didn't, I wouldn't have said it. Now come on, I'll spot you."

ALMOST THREE HOURS later, Erin entered the office of Home Health Unlimited.

"You look tired. Tough day?" Patsy McGraw asked from her desk in the reception area.

"I just spent the afternoon with Derrick Rydell. I'm about ready to strangle his parents. Is Wade around?"

"He's due in any minute. Have a seat; I'll get you a soda."

Erin stretched out on the sofa. After helping serve breakfast at the shelter, working her morning shift at the hospital, and an afternoon of private duty, she was beyond tired. She'd just shut her eyes when the office door opened.

"Why is it I get a call from Rydell's parents after every one of your visits?"

She opened one eye and smiled at her friend and mentor of ten years.

"Did you really call them rotten parents?" Wade asked.

"Only because they are."

"My office...now."

Erin sighed and rose from the sofa just as Patsy returned with her soda. "You might want to hold his calls; I have a feeling we're going to be awhile."

"Erin!"

"Good luck," Patsy offered.

Erin closed the door and flopped down on the leather couch, propping her feet up on the coffee table. She glanced over at the man sitting quietly behind his desk. It wasn't the first time he'd called her onto the carpet and she knew it wouldn't be the last. They were both very passionate about their careers, but often clashed in the way they achieved their patient's goals. Wade Adams was the reason she'd chosen this field of medicine. He had taught her things that couldn't be learned from textbooks or in clinical work. In his late forties, he'd started Home Health Unlimited after losing his wife to Cerebral Palsy.

"Need I remind you that this business is my livelihood? And that you work for me, not the other way around."

"I've had it with them, Wade...they counteract everything I do. Derrick is a mess. Last week he was throwing forty-five percent completion rate, this week he's down to thirty. If they don't back off and let me do my job, I'm quitting."

"You've never quit anything in your life." His eyes narrowed on her. "You're serious?"

"I'm really worried about Derrick. He's under enough pressure without his parents breathing down his neck. He's either going to end up hurting himself more, or he'll give up and just quit trying all together."

His expression softened. "What happened today?"

"When I arrived, he was disappointed about this morning's practice. We talked. He was in good spirits, had a good work out. And then his dad comes in bashing him about his performance. Wade, the kid is a basket case."

"Are you sure you're not exaggerating?"

She stood, frustrated, and began pacing. "He's being pulled in so many different directions he's not sure what he wants. He has the heart, I know he does, but he needs to quit worrying about the future and concentrate on the present. His parents aren't letting him do that. They're so concerned about him making the pros that nothing else matters. They forget he's got another year to play."

"Can you get him ready before the season starts?"

She turned and met his troubled gaze. "If you can get his parents off my back, I can. Otherwise, they'll have to get someone else, 'cause I'm not putting up with them any longer."

"Do you think he'll go number one in the draft next year?"

"At one hundred percent he will."

"All right, I'll talk to his parents. But Erin, could you maybe keep your opinions to yourself next time?"

"I'll try," she promised. "Now, can I get a lift home?"

"No word on your bike?"

"It's being repaired." She hadn't planned on telling Wade about the shooting, but when he'd noticed her limp Monday, she'd had no choice. Both having lost their spouses, they had a tendency to look out for one another.

"Erin, you have a brand new Jaguar sitting in your garage. Why don't you drive it?"

She smiled. It'd been a gift of appreciation from Marcus Wheeler. She'd spent the last four months trying to talk him into taking it back. But he was as stubborn as she was. "I don't know. I don't feel right keeping it."

He walked with her to the door. "It was a gift, Erin, not a bribe. That torn ACL three years ago could have easily cost him his career. But thanks to you, he's playing better than he ever has."

She smiled at the compliment, knowing most of the credit belonged to Marcus. He had worked hard, had forced himself beyond normal limits to reach his goal to play again. All she had done was irritate him to the point where he had to recover just to get rid of her. "I guess I could drive it till I get my bike back."

"We still on for dinner tonight?"

"I made reservations for seven at Rizzoli's. Patsy's picking me up. We'll meet you there." What neither of them knew was she had prearranged to be paged away at seven-fifteen on a non-existent emergency. She'd been trying for months to set up her co-workers on a date, but one or the other had always backed out at the last minute. Tonight she wasn't taking any chances. They were going to spend the evening together whether they liked it or not.

He paused at the door, tossing her a wary look. "This isn't one of your matchmaking antics is it?"

She skirted around the truth. "Would you relax? It's just dinner."

"I thought she was still dating the hockey player. What's his name?"

She noted a hint of jealousy in his tone. "Bruce Parks. They haven't gone out in months." Though he wouldn't admit it, Wade had had eyes for Patsy ever since she'd come to work for him four years ago after losing her husband in a car accident. The mother of a teenage boy, Wade had stepped in as a role model for the troubled teen, but had never gotten the nerve to ask the single mother out. And Patsy, just as timid, refused to admit her own attraction to a man she had grown to admire and respect.

"This better not be a set up, Erin."

"With Tommy away at college, she's suffering from empty nest syndrome. She needs her friends. It's not like you have anything better to do with your evening."

Wade opened the door for her. "You're one to talk. When was the last time you went out on a date?"

She smiled smugly. "I went to the movies with Miles Friday night."

"If you're talking about the X-ray technician, he doesn't count. And neither does Marcus."

He was right. She and Miles were just friends, had been since college. Wade was the big brother who liked to fix the things wrong in her life, and Miles and Marcus were the ones she called when she needed someone to have a good, safe time with. Together, the three of them were the perfect man for her. Together, they equaled what she'd had with Ben. "Are you going to give me a ride home or not?"

He laughed. "Just what I thought."

ERIN'S HOUSE SEEMED emptier than usual. After tossing her keys on the counter separating the living room from the kitchen, she took a seat on one of the bar stools and checked her messages. Marcus had called to remind her of the rain check she'd promised after being paged the last time they'd gone out. And Candice phoned to remind her of the wheel chair games scheduled for Saturday afternoon, and asked that they meet for coffee in the morning to discuss last minute details.

Erin thought about calling Marcus to set up a time to have dinner. She was still set on giving back the Jag, even if it wasn't a bribe to get her to go out with him. Though he was one of Sheridan Springs's most attractive and eligible bachelors, neither seemed interested in taking their relationship to the next level. Instead, they had settled on being very good friends. It was a friendship she cherished. With only a couple of years difference in their age, and with similar backgrounds and tastes, the two never lacked for conversation.

She kicked off her shoes and picked up the cordless phone, deciding that, after she ducked out on her friends, she'd spend the evening with Marcus.

ERIN LOOKED ACROSS the candlelit table to her dinner date. The last hour had been spent enjoying a delicious meal in one of Sheridan Springs's finest restaurants. As usual, the proprietor had respected the celebrity's wish for privacy and had seated them at a table that offered seclusion and the best service available. The handsome wide receiver had rewarded his thoughtfulness with a very generous tip.

"I want you to take back the Jag, Marcus."

"I'm not going to do it, Erin."

"I'm selling it then."

"Do what you want, it's your car."

She smiled. "You won't be mad at me?"

"I won't be mad. I promise." He tucked a stray lock of dark curls behind his ear. The shoulder-length hair had been a trademark since the beginning of his career, reminding her of Samson in the Bible.

He reached across the table and wrapped his hand around hers. "Erin, you've no idea the impact you had on me when I was recovering from my injury. You motivated me to recapture a dream that I thought had been lost when I went down on that field. That car is just a small token of my appreciation."

"A forty thousand dollar car is no small token of appreciation, Marcus."

"It is compared to what you gave me. Football is my life, Erin. It's the only thing I know how to do. It terrifies me to think what's going to happen a few years down the line when I'm forced to give it up."

She gave his hand a gentle squeeze. "You'll cross that bridge when you come to it."

The waitress appeared to refill their tea glasses. Once she'd stepped away, his eyes leveled on her again. "Let me guess, you're going to donate the money to the shelter?"

"Actually, it'd go toward opening the youth center." It'd been a dream of hers for over three years now. Not only would it give the kids a place where they felt they belonged, she hoped to offer programs that would benefit their futures. "The bank has approved me for a loan. All I have to do is come up with a down payment."

"Tell me something, Erin. You being an orphan, is that why you donate so much time, energy, and money to the shelter?"

"I wasn't in the system as long as you were, but I was in it long enough to appreciate a good home. Walter and Julia literally saved my life." At thirteen, she'd been on the brink of going to juvenile detention as a habitual runaway. The Brannon's, friends of the judge she'd gone before, had graciously invited her into their home and their hearts. She just wished they were still around so she could show them her appreciation.

"The foster homes you were in, were they pretty bad?"

"Some of them were."

"Is that why you kept running away?"

Marcus was one of the few people who knew about her childhood, and whom she felt comfortable talking about it with. She knew he'd been there, and from the stories he'd told her, he'd had it just as bad as her, if not worse. "Let's just say I was very fortunate the Brannon's took me in when they did."

"Do you have any memories of the fire that killed your family?"

"I barely remember my family, much less the fire."

"You lived with an uncle for a while afterwards. Do you remember him?"

"Not really. The only memory I have of around the time of the fire is when I was in the hospital and had been told that my brother and sister, as well as my parents, had been killed." She took a drink of her iced tea, meeting his empathic gaze. "A shrink told me once that I blocked that part of my life out because it was too painful. He said someday I might remember, but to be honest, I hope I never do. As far as I'm concerned, my life began when the Brannon's adopted me."

"Are they the ones who introduced you to Christ?"

"Yes. They were like a guiding light in my dark world. It was their faith in me that got me to where I am today."

"God has big plans for you Erin," Marcus said with a gorgeous smile, "I just imagine this youth center you're talking about opening is part of it."

She shifted uncomfortably in her chair. God was the one subject she wasn't comfortable talking to Marcus about. He knew that, and had always found a way to slip Him into their conversations. Like her, Marcus had come through a lot of obstacles in his life, but accepting Christ into his heart had made him a new man.

"I have a huge favor to ask of you, Marcus," she said, hoping to change the subject.

"Just name it."

She hesitated, met his smile, and knew he was sincere. During the last three years, a special bond had formed between them, one of respect and admiration. While battling back from what could have been a career ending injury, she had seen him at his lowest, and he had been there for her during one of the roughest times in her life. She'd given him the motivation to play again, and he had given her the hope that she could recover from the devastating loss of her husband and move on with her life.

"So, are you going to tell me what this favor is, or do I have to guess?"

"I need some advice. I'm working with a kid. A quarterback, who is a probable first round pick in next year's draft. He's fixing to start his senior year, but is really struggling under the pressure of starting the season after an elbow injury."

"Derrick Rydell?" he guessed.

She nodded. "His parents have been relentless, especially his father, about his performance, which seems to be getting worse instead of better. I'm afraid he's losing his confidence, and I'm running out of motivational speeches." Keeping her patients inspired was often the toughest part of her job.

"Have you shared your own experience?"

"No." She thought of the car accident she had college, and the pain of re-learning to walk again. It had been one of the worst experiences in her life.

"Do it. It helped me," he said before taking a drink of his iced tea. "Or if you want, I could maybe talk to him."

She smiled. She'd hoped he would offer. "He is a fan. You wouldn't mind?"

"Of course not. I'd be happy to. Just tell me when and where."

"Thanks, I appreciate it." Hopefully, the visit from Marcus would boost Derrick's moral enough that he'd get his mind back where it belonged—on his therapy.

Marcus leaned back in his chair, crossing his arms in front of him, and smiled. "Now let's get back to the subject of the car. I want you to keep it. I don't like the idea of you wheeling around the streets of Sheridan Springs on a bike, especially when you refuse to wear a helmet."

Chapter Three

"So, how'd it go last night?" Candice asked on their morning coffee break.

The last minute details of the wheel chair games had been debated, leaving barely enough time to discuss their matchmaking antics. Candice, her co-conspirator, was the one that'd paged her for the non-existent emergency at the hospital. Borrowing Patsy's car, she'd gone to meet Marcus, leaving Wade and Patsy alone. It was dishonest, and it was dirty, but she had no regrets.

"I don't know yet. They both looked pretty perturbed when I left, and when I returned Patsy's car just after ten the lights were off, so I just stuck the keys in her mailbox."

"They would make a good couple. They have so much in common, and they're both very active in church. Speaking of church, we've missed you."

Erin took a drink of the lukewarm coffee. Up until now, her friend had avoided the subject of church, knowing Erin was going through a spiritual crisis. Since Ben's death, she'd been a fair-weathered Christian, only attending church on the holidays, and only then at the persistence of her in-laws.

"How long are you going to stay mad at God, Erin?"

She looked at her friend. "Until He gives me some answers."

"He can't give you answers if you aren't willing to listen."

"I'm not the one who isn't listening," she retorted. She'd been pleading to God for two years, desperate to know why He had taken away the only good thing to ever happen to her. "I've got to get back to work." She grabbed her backpack. "I'll see you later."

Candice grabbed her hand before she managed to escape. "I'm here if you ever want to talk about it."

"I know you are. Thanks." Erin tossed the backpack over her shoulder, dumped the Styrofoam cup of coffee into the trash receptacle, and headed toward the elevator.

"GOOD MORNING, MRS. Sinclair," Erin greeted the detective's mother as she exited his room.

"Good morning, Erin. I'm afraid my son's a bit of a bear this morning. I don't think he slept well last night."

"Thanks for the warning. Any suggestions as to how I might cheer him up?"

She smiled. "Turn the TV to the comedy channel. He loves cartoons, especially Road Runner. Just don't tell him I told you."

"It'll be our secret."

Erin entered cautiously and deposited her backpack on the end of the bed. "How're you this morning?"

"How do you think?" Logan barely looked at her, his eyes glued to the magazine in his hand.

"Oh come on, snap out of it. The sun is shining, the birds are singing, you couldn't ask for a more beautiful morning."

He shot her an annoyed look before returning his attention to his magazine. She smiled, reached for the remote, and turned on the TV. It was already on the comedy channel. Bugs Bunny and Elmer Fudd danced across the screen. She couldn't help but be amused that the detective was a cartoon lover too.

"You can turn it if you want."

"This is fine. Road Runner comes on in twenty minutes."

He glanced at her briefly, but said nothing.

She grabbed her pad and pen from her backpack. "How'd you sleep last night?"

"Okay." He finally laid down his magazine. "You?"

"Like a baby. Any pain this morning?"

"It's tolerable."

She glanced at his breakfast tray. He'd barely touched it. According to his chart, he hadn't eaten much yesterday either. "Not much on hospital food I take it?"

"I wouldn't exactly call it food. My cats eat better than this."

She recalled the conversation he'd had with his mother yesterday about his cats. She hadn't met many men who were cat lovers. "How many cats do you have?"

"Seventeen."

"Outdoors, I hope."

Her humor won her a smile. "All but one."

She pulled the curtain around and waited for him to sit up on the side of the bed. She then carefully removed the sling from around his neck. "How's your partner doing?"

"Good. I heard they had him sitting up yesterday."

"He's a lucky man. Why weren't you two wearing your vests?"

"Didn't think we'd need them. We were meeting a trusted informant."

She was tempted to query further, but didn't. She set his breakfast tray on the counter near the sink and pushed the table closer to the bed for his first exercise. He didn't wait for instructions; he went right into them. She grabbed her pad and jotted down his progress.

When he was done with those, she pushed back the table and lowered the head of the bed so that it lay flat. "Okay, I'm going to have you lay on your stomach with your left arm hanging over the side."

Erin waited until he was comfortable and began massaging his left shoulder, careful of the incision. She couldn't help but notice that he had the body of an athlete—well toned and muscular.

"So, what's your other job?" he asked.

"I do private duty in the afternoons. Any pain?"

"No. What kind of private duty...you mean guys like me?"

"Athletes mostly."

"Anyone I know?"

"Probably. What about now...any pain?"

He jerked. "Yeah."

"Sorry." She eased up on the pressure. "On a scale of one to ten, how severe?"

"Maybe a seven. I suppose you work weekends too?"

"Usually."

"Doesn't leave much time for a social life."

"No, it doesn't." She had a feeling where he was heading and definitely didn't want to go there.

She heard the familiar *beep, beep*, and turned up the volume.

"I can't believe you're a fan of Road Runner."

It'd been her favorite cartoon since she was a kid. "Isn't everyone?"

"They should be."

"Any leads on the shooter?" she asked, glancing over her shoulder in time to see Road Runner barely escape Wile E. Coyote's ingenious trap.

"Not yet. You have great hands, Doc."

And he had great muscle tone. It was obvious he worked out on a regular basis. "How long have you been a cop?"

"Eleven years, mostly in Atlanta. I grew up here, but moved away after college. I transferred back a year ago."

"Atlanta's a beautiful city."

Logan raised his head slightly. "You've been there?"

"I spent a couple of months there on business last year." Her career often took her on the road, which was fine with her. The busier she was, the less time she spent dwelling on the past. Plus, she was able to make a decent living at it.

"Where else has your work taken you?" he asked as he rested his chin on his right forearm.

"Dallas, Denver, Oakland, Seattle…"

"You were serious when you said you worked with athletes?"

She leaned down and met his surprised expression. "Did you think I was lying?"

"No. I just didn't think you meant professional athletes."

"I specialize in sports medicine, but not all are professional athletes."

"Wait a minute." He rolled over on his side. "I remember reading an article about you a few years ago in *Football Review*. You're the one that helped Stuart Granger recover from his shoulder reconstruction and go on to win the super bowl."

She smiled. The article had sparked calls from all over the country, and had made Home Health Unlimited very popular among injured athletes.

"And Marcus Wheeler recover from his torn ACL three years ago," he added.

She padded his bare back. "You can get up now." She picked up her pad and noted the tenderness below his clavicle. "You know, if you're having trouble sleeping, just mention it to your nurse. All she has to do is phone the doctor to get you something that will help."

"Or you could come back and give me another massage. That seemed to do the trick. I'm totally pain free."

"I'm glad." She shoved the pad and pen back into her backpack.

"Aren't you going to stay and finish watching Road Runner?"

She glanced up at the TV screen. "Nah, I've seen this one at least a dozen times. Enjoy. I'll see you tomorrow."

"Get some sleep, Erin. You look beat."

She glanced back and smiled.

***

ERIN DECIDED TO CUT through the park on her way to the office. As she neared the basketball court she caught sight of one of the kids from the shelter. She was within a few feet of him before he saw her. His eyes widened. "Don't even think about running," she warned.

"I'm not." He dribbled toward the goal post.

Erin dropped her backpack and snuck in to steal the ball from him. She dribbled the ball around her twice, trying to entice him to go for it before making a basket. "Running a little late for school, aren't you?"

He caught the rebound and quickly turned away from her, using his left arm to block her advance. "I suppose you're going to tell on me?"

"Depends on how good your excuse is." She leaned to her right to get him to turn the opposite way. When he did, she reached out with her left hand to knock the ball away, then twisted around, her back to him, and regained control of the ball. A good three inches taller, she was able to make the basket with ease.

"I hate school, Mrs. J. I have nothing in common with any of the kids. My only friends are the ones who hang out at the shelter."

She empathized with the boy. In the system since he was six, he'd spent the last nine years being bounced around from one foster home to another till Andy and Emma had taken temporary custody of him six months ago. "This is your first year going there. You have to be patient, Joey, let them get to know you."

"It's not that easy for me. I'm not as outgoing as you are."

"Believe me, Joey." She took his hand and led him to a nearby bench, "I know what it's like to be an outsider, to feel you don't belong. I was in and out of so many schools in the Sheridan Springs area that when someone asks me where I went to grade school I can show them the yellow pages and tell them to pick one, I've been there."

He smiled. "Did it ever bother you because you were different than the other kids?"

"Joey, the only difference between you and them is geography. Yes, they may have a set of parents and a couple of siblings, but you have a whole shelter full of people who love you and think of you as family. I know that doesn't ease the hurt. But what you have to realize is that, as bad as things seem right now, life is all about change. Right now you have no control over your circumstances, however, there'll come a day that you will. Eventually, you'll step into a place where you'll feel that you belong."

"So what do I do in the mean time?"

She smiled. This wasn't the first heart-to-heart talk they'd had. Out of all the kids that came and went from the shelter, Joey held a special place in her heart. In the six months they'd known one another, a strong bond had formed between them. He was almost like a son to her. "You do the best you can, Joey, and remember that the past doesn't dictate your future."

He grinned. "I think I can do that."

"I know you can." She glanced at her watch. "If you leave now, you should be able to make your afternoon classes."

"Will you write me note?"

"Are you gonna be skipping classes anymore?"

"No."

"All right, but if Andy or Emma get word of this you're dead meat."

He leaned over and hugged her. "Thanks, Mrs. J."

LOGAN WATCHED BOBBY place his lunch tray on the table. He guessed him to be in his late forties, his skin a dark charcoal, and he stood well over six foot with very muscular arms. There was an air about him that screamed military and Logan suspected he had seen a lot of action during his time. According to one of the other nurses, he was a close friend of Erin's.

She'd been on his mind ever since that first night. The gentleness of her voice that soothed away the fear at being shot, the compassion in her eyes as she tended to his wound, the heart-stopping smile that graced her lips almost every time her saw her. He'd met a lot of women in his life, had dated many of them, but none had ever occupied his thoughts as much as Erin Jacobs had. And this morning, the way she'd breezed in here and lifted him out of the sour mood he was in, had been very impressive. The fact she was a Road Runner fan had all but clinched it. He had to get this woman to agree to go out on a date with him.

"Word has it you know Erin Jacobs pretty well?" Logan finally got the nerve to ask.

"Yeah, I know her. Why?"

"I'm curious. She's responsible for saving mine and my partner's life. How long have you known her?"

"A few years. Her sister-in-law runs the homeless shelter where I live."

"You live in a homeless shelter?" It shouldn't have surprised him. It was a sad fact that the shelters housed a lot of veterans. Duty to their country had often cost them their homes and families.

"I help out there for room and board."

He recalled there being a shelter just down the block from where the shooting had taken place. Had she been on her way there? "Does Erin live there too?"

"Look, man, Erin's my friend and I don't know you. You want to know any more about her, you'll have to ask her yourself."

"Hey, I'm a cop. I only wanna send her some flowers or something to show my appreciation."

"Well, I wouldn't send flowers if I were you. She doesn't like them much."

Logan's eyes narrowed at his comment. What kind of woman didn't like flowers?

ERIN POKED HER HEAD in the office door, glanced around, and saw Patsy at her desk. Suppressing her smile, she strolled in. Patsy glanced up and smiled. Erin took it as a good sign that she wasn't in the doghouse. "How was dinner?"

"Very nice. We missed you. How'd things go at the hospital?"

"Okay. Did you guys do anything afterwards?"

"We caught a movie. It must not have been much of an emergency since you had the car back before eleven."

Erin suppressed another smile. "What movie did you see?"

"The new Tom Hanks one. So, what was the emergency? Another pile up?"

Erin grinned, unable to keep up the pretense any longer.

Patsy's eyes widened. "I knew it. You dirty rat. If I hadn't had such a good time, I'd be mad at you."

The smile that spread across her friend's face eased what little guilt she had for setting them up. "You had a good time, then?"

"I think we both did, or at least that's what I gathered since he suggested we do it again sometime."

Erin took a seat on the sofa, basking in her victory. "You see, I knew you two would hit it off."

"He's so shy. I'm not used to guys being that shy."

For some reason, an image of Logan popped into Erin's mind. For the life of her, she didn't know why. He was anything but shy. She quickly shook the image out and looked at her friend. "Give the guy a break. He doesn't get out much."

"I didn't say I didn't like it. I just said I wasn't used to it. I'm thinking of inviting him over for dinner Saturday night. What do you think?"

Erin shrugged her shoulder. "I think it's a great idea."

"Would you come?" Patsy folded her arms as she leaned back in her chair.

"Patsy, you don't need a chaperone."

"He might."

"You know he's only timid around you because he likes you so much. He's had his eye on you ever since you started work here."

Patsy looked at her suspiciously. "Really?"

"I thought you knew that?"

"I had no idea." She leaned forward and shifted through some papers on her desk. "Listen, I was planning on wearing my yellow and blue chiffon dress, what do you think?"

Erin laughed. The last date she'd gone on had been with her husband. "You're asking me for fashion advice? Oh honey, you are desperate."

"I am, aren't I?" Patsy got up and filed the papers in a nearby cabinet. "Maybe I should just wear a nice pair of jeans and my pink cashmere sweater."

Erin pictured the two outfits in her mind. "Go with the dress. It'll make a better impression."

"You're right. Any suggestion on what to fix for dinner?"

"He likes Mexican."

"Perfect. I have a deep dish Mexican casserole recipe I've been dying to make."

"There you go."

The office door opened. Wade entered, looked at the both of them, smiled sheepishly, then quickly disappeared down the hall to his office.

Erin laughed. They were like two high school kids on the Monday following the prom.

"Will you please come Saturday night?" Patsy pleaded, adding a pout.

"All right."

"And you better not get a page and disappear on us."

"THE CAPTAIN SAID YOU located the mystery woman?"

Logan glanced over at his partner. It was good to see him up walking around. Even it was just to the bathroom. In the last year, the two had become good friends and he hated to think how it could have ended that night.

"Her name is Erin Jacobs. Douglass is meeting with her tomorrow to try and come up with a sketch of the driver."

The color drained from his partner's face. "Erin Jacobs is the one who found us."

"Yeah, why...you know her?"

"She's the widow of Ben Jacobs...the cop that was killed two years ago in the school shooting over at Westmore High."

The words came like a sucker punch, sweeping Logan's breath away. He thought back to the night they'd met. She'd known they were cops immediately, probably seen Addison's gun and badge. He recalled the comment she'd made about the sight of blood freaking her out. Had she been working the day they'd brought her husband in? It explained the tears he'd seen in her eyes that night. No wonder she ran away.

Logan remembered the story his partner had told him only a few months ago when they'd gone to the school to question a witness in an assault case. Ben Jacobs had gone to the school that day as a spokesperson for the department and had been two doors down from the cafeteria when the fifteen-year-old boy began his shooting rampage, killing two students and injuring three others. Ben had managed to get off two deadly rounds, but not before the teenager had fired the bullet that struck his neck, causing him to bleed to death before the paramedics could reach him.

The investigation that followed determined that Ben had, in his heroics, managed to save countless lives as the boy had been armed with enough ammunition to kill at least fifty students. It had earned him the department's prestigious Medal of Valor.

Logan sank further back in the chair, ignoring the pain it brought to his shoulder. The possibility of ever getting to know the woman who'd visited his thoughts throughout each day since the shooting just flew out the window. Erin Jacobs had paid the ultimate price of being a cop's wife. He had no right to even consider asking her out now.

"DERRICK, I BROUGHT someone I'd like you to meet." Erin stepped aside so Marcus could enter the gym. She smiled as a grin spread across the young man's face. "I'll leave you two alone while I go grab some juice." She paused in the doorway, watching as Derrick stood to greet the pro wide receiver.

"It's a pleasure to meet you, Derrick."

"The pleasure's mine, sir. I'm a huge fan."

"Please, call me Marcus."

Erin's cell phone rang. She answered on the second ring.

"Erin, you busy?"

Recognizing Emma's voice, she glanced back at the two athletes. In return, of the favor Marcus had made her promise to keep the Jag. It was a huge price to pay, but she knew it would do wonders for the kid's confidence. "No. What's up?"

"Can you help serve dinner? Andy has to make a couple of hospital visits, which leaves me to work the fundraiser...unless you want to take over for me."

"No thanks, I'd rather help cook." Begging for money from a room full of people was about as far down on her list of favorite things to do as having a root canal. They had four fundraisers a year to bring in money to support the shelter, and thankfully, Andy was a gifted speaker both in and out of the pulpit.

She thought of the money the Jaguar would have brought. It would have made a nice installment toward the future youth center. She couldn't go back on her word, though. She was just going to have to find another way.

"Give me an hour. I'm with a patient."

"Great. Do you need Bobby to pick you up?"

"No, I've got a ride. Good luck tonight."

"Thanks. If I don't see you tonight, I'll see you in the morning."

***

AN HOUR LATER, ERIN glanced over at Marcus. A smile still lit up his face. "I really appreciate you talking to Derrick. I'm sure it'll be a big help in his motivation."

He turned, his smile widening. "I was glad to do it. He's a nice kid. Nothing like his reputation suggested."

"Since his injury, he's changed a lot."

"Desperation has a way of humbling the best of us."

She sifted her gaze out the passenger side window. Since his conversion to Christianity three years ago, his life had changed dramatically. What was so ironic was that she had been the one to lead him to Christ before straying from the church a year later.

"If you have time, I'd love a tour of the shelter."

"Really?"

"Since I blew off the day's agenda, I've nothing else to do."

She tossed him another smile of appreciation, knowing he'd canceled several important appointments to do her the favor. "I must warn you, you're liable to be bombarded. I have several youths that help serve the evening meal. I'm sure they'll recognize you."

"I don't mind if you don't."

As suspected, they barely made it through the doors before Marcus was recognized. Within seconds, a dozen teenage boys and girls rushed forward to greet them. Knowing he was used to the attention and could handle himself, Erin disappeared into the kitchen and began preparing to feed between 225 and 250 people, thankful tonight was spaghetti night.

"Who's the hunk you brought in?" Margo asked, peering over Erin's shoulder.

Erin had been watching Marcus fill the water and iced tea glasses, amused by the green apron he wore. *If only his teammate's could see him now.* She turned to the head cook, smiled, and moved back to the stove to stir the large pot of meat sauce. "A friend."

"A boyfriend?"

"Just a friend." Margo, the only paid employee at the shelter, had worked there since it opened eight years ago. She was a notorious gossiper.

"Have you read the paper today? There was another piece on the shooting that took place up the block. They still don't have any suspects."

"I'm sure the police are doing all they can." She thought of the sketch she was supposed to help with tomorrow. She wasn't looking forward to it, but was thankful Logan had agreed to allow her do it at the hospital and not at the station.

"HOW LONG HAS THE SHELTER been here?" Marcus asked at the conclusion of a brief tour of the facilities.

At 6'5" Erin had to look up to meet his gaze. "Eight years. Ben and Andy were best friends since college, and together they opened Safe Harbor shortly after Andy became the pastor of the church down on the corner."

"Andy is married to Ben's sister, right?"

"Emma. It was during the building stages that they met and fell in love. Two years later, Ben injured his knee at the police academy. I was his physical therapist. And the rest, as they say, is history."

They reentered the huge dining room. Many of the night's guests had lingered to catch one last look at the celebrity. "You know, you coming here is going to make me a very popular person in the community."

Marcus laughed. "I suspect you were already a very popular person in the community. You're doing good work here, Erin."

"It's not just me."

"The homeless are here because of your sister-in-law and her husband; the kids are here because of you." He leaned over and kissed her cheek. "You're a special lady, Erin. I'm blessed to know you."

She elbowed him. "Knock it off," she said with a smile. He was making her blush and every eye in the room was on them.

"Don't take this the wrong way, but I'm glad we never dated. This...what we have now, it's special, and I wouldn't want to do anything to jeopardize it."

She looked up at him, quick to notice the seriousness of his tone. "Are you all right, Marcus?"

"Yeah." He slipped his arm around her shoulder. "I'm just feeling a little humbled is all."

Visiting a homeless shelter could do that to a person. "Thanks again for helping out with Derrick. You're a good man, Marcus."

"It was my pleasure."

Chapter Four

Logan's hospital room door opened and Erin stood in the doorway. He barely recognized her without her usual scrubs. Instead, she wore a pair of well-faded blue jeans, a Florida Cougars t-shirt, and her russet locks of hair was bound in a ponytail sticking out the back of a Dolphin's baseball cap. She looked great. He glanced down at his watch; it was barely eight. "You're early. Douglass isn't coming for another hour."

"I got bored waiting at home." She moved further into the room. He noticed both her hands behind her back as if she were hiding something. She glanced up at the TV screen and caught him watching his cartoons. "Did you get any sleep last night?"

He couldn't lie. "Some." It wasn't so much the pain that kept him from a peaceful sleep, but the nightmares. Reliving the shooting over and over was beginning to take its toll. "What'cha got behind your back?"

"Breakfast burritos." She smiled, set a brown paper sack on the tray table, then buried her hands in her back pockets. "I got you both hot and mild sauce to go with them."

Stunned speechless by her generosity, he only looked up at her.

"You don't like breakfast burritos?"

"No, it isn't that." He wasn't sure what to make of the kind gesture. "How much do I owe you?"

"Don't worry about it. I stop every morning for coffee and a bagel. I'm such a loyal customer they give me a discount. Is it the pain keeping you from sleeping?"

"Not exactly."

"The nightmares will go away eventually." Instead of sitting in the chair, she sat on the end of the bed so she could see the TV monitor.

He looked at her; saw her grin at the cartoon showing. "Is that experience speaking?" He regretted the question the moment it left his mouth, fearing the nightmares she spoke of were of her husband getting killed.

"I was in a bad car accident in college and had nightmares about it for months. They eventually went away, though. Yours will too. Try listening to music as you fall asleep. It'll help."

He found it somewhat annoying that she wouldn't face him as she spoke, her attention still on the cartoon. "What kind of music works for you?"

"Instrumental. Piano, flute, the harp, they're all soothing." She glanced at her wristwatch, then back to the TV screen.

He wondered if the woman ever relaxed. "Is that the only type of music you listen to?"

Finally, she turned and looked at him. "I like all kinds as long as it doesn't have profanity in the lyrics." She reached for the sack and opened it, handing him the burritos. "Come on—eat—before they get cold."

"Will you join me?"

"I already ate. I could go for another cup of coffee, though. You want one?" She stood and headed to the door.

"Black, no sugar."

She returned with two cups, handing him one of them. In her absence, he'd managed one of the burritos and was working on the second one. "These are great. Thanks."

"You're welcome." She glanced at her watch again, then walked to the window.

"Does your balloon ever land?" he asked. She glanced over her shoulder, smiling. "I don't think I've ever met anyone so wound up."

"Life's short," she said. "I don't like to waste a moment of it."

He sensed there was more to it. "You're nervous about doing the sketch," he guessed.

"A little," she admitted.

He'd hoped she wouldn't be. That was why he'd agreed to do it here at the hospital, on familiar ground. "Erin. There's nothing to be nervous about."

"You said I was your only witness. I don't want to mess up."

He hadn't realized the pressure he'd placed on her. Being a cop's wife, she knew police procedure and the importance of reliable witnesses in solving crimes. He wadded up the empty paper and stuffed it into the bag. "You won't mess up, Erin. Just do the best you can."

She nodded, glanced up at the TV screen, and chuckled.

Much to his delight, she finally relaxed. Moving to the chair beside his bed, she positioned it so she could see the screen. For the next half hour, she laughed along with him at the cartoons. It was a quarter to nine before she began showing signs of anxiety again.

Logan watched as she paced back and forth from the windows to the bed, glancing up every so often at the TV screen. She was making him nervous just watching her. "What are your plans this afternoon?" he finally asked, hoping to get her mind off the sketch.

She stopped long enough to look at him. "What?"

"I asked what your plans were this afternoon. This is your day off, isn't it?"

"Oh yeah, it is sort of...the hospital staff and Home Health Unlimited are having our annual cookout and wheel chair games. I'm on the planning committee, among other things."

"Cookout...you mean with real food?" His question won him a beautiful smile.

"Hotdogs, hamburgers, chips, the usual. You're welcome to come. It's next door in the main parking lot. Just have one of the CNA's wheel you over."

"Hopefully I'll be released by then and can come over on my own. I'm sick of hospital beds and wheel chairs."

She seemed about to speak when the door opened and Douglass entered, carrying his laptop. "Mrs. Jacobs?"

She slowly nodded, her eyes fastened on the crisp blue uniform the officer was wearing. She continued to stand in the same spot, as if frozen to the floor, not even blinking.

Logan wished now he'd thought to ask the officer to come in plain clothes. But then he hadn't expected this type of a reaction. "Erin." When she didn't answer, he said her name again, only louder.

She blinked and looked over at him. "I'm sorry. I just need a minute. There's an empty room across the hall. I'll meet you there."

She scurried from the room, leaving both him and the young officer staring at one another in bewilderment.

Logan pressed his call button. A minute later, Bobby stuck his head in the door. "Do you have a long lab coat that will fit this officer?" Logan asked.

Bobby glanced at Douglass then back at him. "Yeah, I'm sure we do somewhere."

"Get it. He's here to do a composite sketch with Erin. His uniform is making her uncomfortable."

"I'll be right back."

ERIN WIPED AWAY ALL traces of her tears, embarrassed by her reaction to the officer's uniform. The flashback had been so vivid, so raw. She remembered being paged to the ER that morning and the nausea that hit the minute she saw the police Chaplin's face as he approached her. They had tried to prevent her from going into the examining room; she'd fought off two police officers. Refusing to believe Ben was really gone...refusing to believe that God would take him from her. She'd known by the massive amount of blood loss he was dead long before they got him to the hospital. He never had a chance. He'd died alone on the cold tile floor of the high school cafeteria.

"Erin, it's Candice. Can I come in?"

Erin stepped to the door, unlocked it, and stepped back.

"Bobby told me what happened. Are you okay?"

"Yeah. Do you have any makeup on you?"

Candice emptied her pockets onto the counter. Erin smiled at the array of assorted makeup. "Please tell me you don't carry this stuff in your pockets all the time?"

"Of course not. I stopped off at my locker; I thought you might need a quick cover up."

"Thanks. I feel so embarrassed. I don't know what happened. I've seen cops in uniform since that day. They've never affected me this way before. I actually had a flashback of being in the emergency room."

"I just imagine the shooting played into it."

Erin glanced up.

"Bobby told me. I wish you had."

"I didn't want to worry you."

"Nonsense," She took Erin by the arm and led her to the mirror. "Come on. I'll help."

Moments later, she inspected the results. "Now all I need is a hairbrush."

"Can't help you there. You want me to get yours from your locker?"

"I don't have one here. I lost it."

"The one I gave you from my trip to Hawaii?"

Erin met her dejected look. "It's a hairbrush, Candice." She thought back to the last time she'd seen it. It had been the night she'd been paged from her dinner with Marcus, the same night Logan had been shot. It must have fallen out of her backpack when she'd wrecked her bike. "Who buys a hairbrush as a souvenir anyway?" Then, seeing Candice checking out her own reflection, she said, "Never mind, stupid question."

"I APPRECIATE YOUR COOPERATION, Mrs. Jacobs, and I'm sorry to have upset you," the police officer said.

"Don't worry about it. I hope the sketch helps."

"I'm sure it will. You have a keen eye for detail."

She smiled, watched as he left the room, then turned and walked to the window. She looked down several stories to the parking lot below. Smoke billowed upward from the two huge grills. The crowd had doubled since she'd looked out earlier.

The door opened with a swooshing sound, and she turned to find Logan leaning against it. He was dressed in street clothes—blue jeans and a dark blue t-shirt. "You okay?" he asked.

She nodded. "Thanks for having the officer put on the lab coat. It helped." It was a nice gesture on his part, one she appreciated very much. "Have you known all along who I was?"

"No. I only found out yesterday."

"I guess now you know now why I didn't want to hang around the night you were shot."

"Yeah. I'm sorry Erin."

"Just when I think I've put the hurt behind me, it jumps out and grabs me by the throat."

He stepped toward her, and for a brief moment, she thought he was going to hug her. Her heart fluttered at the thought. Instead, he shoved his hands in his pockets, his gaze steady on her. "You know earlier when you were talking about the nightmares eventually going away? Grief has a way of working the same way. It just takes time."

A smile crept to her lips. "Are you ready for a hotdog?"

"No hotdog, I want red meat."

"Then we better hurry. The hamburgers tend to be the first to go."

THEY MADE IT IN TIME for burgers. Afterwards, Erin introduced him to some of her patients. Most of them were children and teenagers who were confined to wheel chairs, walkers or crutches. Their faces literally lit up at the sight of their physical therapist.

With each introduction, Logan saw just a little bit further into the life of Erin Jacobs. And he was very impressed. "I admire your passion. You genuinely care about your patients."

She paused and met his gaze. "I worry sometimes that I care too much."

"What do you mean?"

"Well, part of my job is inspirational. When a patient reaches what they feel is their limit, I have to motivate them to push harder, to reach deep inside themselves for that hidden strength. When they can't, I have a tendency to blame myself."

"I doubt that happens very often. Speaking from experience, you're pretty motivational. Which brings me to a personal question."

Her lips curved into a beautiful smile. "Where do I get my motivation?"

"Yeah."

"I suspect the same place you do. Come on, I want you to meet Jaedin. She's a real sweetheart. She's eleven and has MD."

He followed Erin through the crowd of children. Slipping up behind the child with flowing blonde hair, Erin hugged her from behind before whispering something in her ear.

The little girl, bound in an electric wheel chair, swung the chair around quickly, her face glowing as brightly as her long blonde hair in the bright sun light.

Erin squatted down beside her chair. "Logan, this Jaedin, a very dear friend of mine."

She offered Logan her tiny, crooked hand. "Are you a doctor?"

"No. I'm a police officer. A detective," he answered.

"Really…where's your gun and badge?"

"Back at the station. I'm off duty for awhile."

"You don't look like a cop."

Erin laughed. "What does he look like he does for a living?"

"I don't know, but he doesn't look like a cop." The little girl reached for Erin's hand. "Are you going to stay and play with us?"

"Are you kidding? I wouldn't miss it." Erin leaned over and hugged her. "I'll see you in a little bit, okay."

"You really are very good at what you do, Erin," Logan commented as they moved toward the bleachers.

She glanced over at him. Her smile was infectious. "Thank you. As hard as it is sometimes, I love my job."

"It shows." Even her body language, which reminded him of the Energizer Bunny, expressed the passion she had to help others. "So, what made you want to be a physical therapist?"

"I didn't. It just sort of happened." She made a sweeping gesture with her hands. "I wanted to be a cardiologist."

"What changed your mind?"

"It's a long story. Come on, there's a couple more people I want you to meet. You can sit with them while I go have some fun."

LOGAN WATCHED IN AMUSEMENT as Erin wheeled her way down the parking lot toward the end zone marker. Seemingly, on instinct, she turned and glanced over her shoulder just as the ball reached her. With steady hands, she yanked the ball down to her lap and continued to roll past the end zone with barely a hesitation in momentum. Raising her hands in victory, her laughter drifted toward the bleachers as she was greeted by her teammates, all toting strips of purple material sticking out the back of their wheel chairs.

"She sure knows how to handle a wheel chair," Logan commented to the man and woman seated next to him.

"She should, she spent almost two years in one," the woman said, leaning forward to meet his gaze.

His eyes widened at the news. "Why was Erin in a wheel chair?"

"Car accident when she was in college," the man named Wade informed. "She was broadsided by a drunk driver, which resulted in numerous fractures, including a fractured disc in her lower back. The doctors were able to repair most of the damage, but she spent an agonizing two years relearning to walk."

He turned back to the parking lot where Erin was teaching two pre-teen boys how to do wheelies with their chairs. It was hard to imagine this vibrant young woman confined to a wheel chair. He recalled her brief mention of the car accident she'd had in college. She'd described it as just a bad accident, hadn't mentioned the fact it had put her in a wheel chair. "She looks perfectly healthy now."

"Most days she is," Wade said.

"Most days?"

"She continues to battle chronic pain."

Erin rejoined them, minus the wheel chair. "Hey, why the gloomy faces? Didn't you see my touchdown?"

Wade held up his hand for a high five, his expression changing to a deep smile. "You did great, kid."

Logan smiled at her enthusiasm. Only someone in a close relationship with the Lord could withstand the trials she'd gone through and still have this kind of zest for life. His attraction for the woman just broke the scales. He had to get to know her better.

"I'm going for another burger," she announced. "Anyone interested in joining me?"

Though he was tempted, Logan declined. He hoped for a word alone with her boss.

The brunette, introduced as Patsy, stood. "I'll join you. I could use another soda."

Logan watched as the two women made their way across the parking lot.

"How's the shoulder?" Wade asked, turning on the bench.

"Actually, I was hoping to talk to you about that very subject."

"YOUR COP FRIEND IS cute. Not as cute as Marcus, but still cute," Patsy said as they moved to the front of the line and Erin got her burger.

Erin rolled her eyes at her friend before reaching for the mustard. "He's a patient, not a friend, and Marcus is strictly a friend." She squirted a big glob on top of the bun, added half a dozen pickles, and then pressed it against the other half of the burger.

"I get the message. Unlike you, I don't meddle in the love life of others. Speaking of which, don't forget dinner tonight at seven."

"I haven't forgotten. I doubt I'll be able to eat anything, but I'll be there as promised."

"Good. How'd the police sketch go today?"

Erin could have done without the reminder of her temporary melt down. Just as disturbing was her body's reaction to the thought of Logan giving her a hug. She shook the memory from her mind and forced a smile. "The cop said I had a keen eye for detail. I hope he's right. People at the shelter are starting to get nervous at the fact the police don't have any suspects."

"I don't blame them. The shelter is only a block and a half from where the shooting took place."

Erin finished her hamburger, grabbed another soda, and headed back to the bleachers with Patsy. Logan was standing and shaking Wade's hand when they reached them. "Are you leaving?"

He shoved his hands in his pockets and smiled at her. "As much as I hate to, I need to get going."

"Is your shoulder starting to hurt?"

"Some. Will you walk with me back to the hospital to meet my ride?"

"Okay." She handed Wade her soda.

As they began walking, he turned to her. "I had a nice time today. You've nice friends."

An alarm sounded deep inside Erin. There was a reason he wanted company on the walk back to the hospital, and she had a hunch as to what it was. "Thanks. You said you have a ride?"

"The captain is dropping by to pick me up."

"I've been meaning to ask how your partner is doing," she asked hoping to distract him. *If he asks me out on a date, what am I going to say? Yes, I'm attracted to you, and yes, I'd like to learn more about you. But I just can't.*

"He's doing great."

They continued to walk. Erin wished now she hadn't come with him.

"Listen Erin, I'd like to call you sometime if that's okay?"

She kept in touch with a lot of her patients, but she had a feeling he was hoping for something more. She stopped in her tracks and looked at him. He was only a couple of inches taller, their shoulders almost even. "Why?"

He grinned. "Do I need a reason?"

"If it's to keep me posted on your recovery, no...otherwise, I don't date cops." *There, that was simple!*

"I had a feeling you were going to say that."

He began walking again. She was tempted not to follow, to say goodbye there, but she didn't. If she didn't like him, she wouldn't feel the need to explain. The problem was, she did like him. The morning spent watching cartoons together, the afternoon spent talking about the work she did with kids...He'd made an impression on her that made it difficult not to want to get to know him better.

"It isn't that I didn't enjoy today, Logan. I did...very much. The problem is, I can't get this image out of my head of my husband lying on a gurney in the emergency room covered in blood. I remember seeing that badge pinned to his chest and wanting to rip it off." She paused to catch her breath, and to wipe away a tear that managed to escape. "My husband was a hero for what he did, and I'm very proud of him. But I don't want another hero in my life. My heart can't take it."

Logan stopped and took her hand. She glanced down, unnerved by the physical contact she hadn't expected. "Thank you for your honesty, Erin. You didn't have to explain, but I'm glad you did. Just keep in mind that I won't always be a cop."

"You may not always wear the badge, but in your heart, you'll always be a cop."

"I hope you'll change your mind. I'd really like to get to know you."

"Goodbye, Logan. And good luck with your therapy."

He smiled. "See you later, Erin."

"WHAT CAN I GET YOU to drink?"

"Iced tea is fine." Erin glanced back into Patsy's dining room to the white linen tablecloth and three place settings of undoubtedly her finest china. "The table looks nice."

"You think I went overboard?"

"No." Erin accepted the glass of tea she offered. "Are you nervous?"

"I past nervous two hours ago. I hate first dates."

"Actually, this is your second date."

Patsy grinned. "I already tried that. It's not working." She pulled the Mexican casserole from the oven and set it on top of the electric stove. "So, are you going to tell me what took you so long walking Logan back to the hospital?"

Erin moved to the small kitchen table with two chairs. "He asked if he could call me sometime."

"I thought so. What'd you say?"

Erin shrugged her shoulder. "That I don't date cops."

Patsy turned, placing a hand on one hip. "He's a detective, Erin. It's not like he places his life on the line every time he goes on duty."

"He just got out of the hospital with a gunshot wound to the shoulder. A couple of more inches and he would have died."

Patsy's eyes narrowed. "Are you sure you're not just looking for excuses not to move on with your life?"

"What, are you psychoanalyzing me now?"

Patsy leaned against the counter and folded her arms in front of her. "Look, the way I see it, you're an attractive woman with a career that places you in contact with some very eligible men. Yet, you haven't been on a date since your husband died."

"That doesn't mean I'm not moving on with my life. It just means I don't date former patients."

Patsy started to reply, but the doorbell rang, hopefully putting an end to any further discussion about her love life. Erin knew on some level her friend was right. Her rule of not dating former clients was mainly a ruse to protect her from any potential heartache. No one had ever come close to making her reconsider that rule until recently, which was why she needed to avoid Logan Sinclair at all costs.

Chapter Five

"You missed another good sermon this morning, Erin."

Erin glanced up from her textbook to see her nephew, Ryan, and niece, Sammy Jo, coming toward her, their father right behind them.

With everyone gone to church, she'd enjoyed the peaceful solitude of the recreation room for the last two hours. That was about to change. Another ten minutes and the room would be filled with teenagers fighting over the three pool tables and jukebox that played only Christian music. "I'm sure I did, your daddy's a wonderful preacher."

"What are you reading?" Andy asked.

Erin shifted her gaze to her brother-in-law. "An old textbook."

"Brushing up on your skills?"

"Never hurts."

"You wanna see what I colored in Sunday school?" Sammy Jo asked.

"Sure I do." Erin set the textbook aside as the four-year-old climbed into her lap. "Who is that man with the beard?"

"It's Jesus, silly."

Erin smothered a giggle. "So it is...and the woman?"

"His friend, Mary Magdalene."

Ryan, two years older than his sister, turned to Erin with a serious expression. "You need to start coming to church, Aunt Erin."

Andy laughed. "She knows who they are, buddy. She used to teach Sunday school."

"Really?" the children asked in unison, their little eyes fixed on her.

Great! "Thanks, Andy."

"Sorry. Why don't you guys go see if your mom needs any help setting the dinner table?"

Each of the children gave Erin a hug before leaving her alone with her brother-in-law. Fearing a religious discussion coming on, Erin picked up her textbook and stood.

But he prevented her escape by stepping in front of her. "I'd like to talk to you, Erin."

"Not now, Andy. I'm not in the mood for another lecture." She tried to go around him, but he blocked her path again.

"I heard what happened yesterday at the hospital. Are you okay?"

She let out an aggravated sigh. "I'm fine. Bobby, on the other hand, won't be when I get my hands on him."

"Bobby didn't say anything. Now, will you answer my question?"

She met his glare, trying hard to stay calm. She hated it when people butted into her private life, and family was no exception. "I said I was fine; it was no big deal."

"Being a witness to two cops getting shot is a very big deal, Erin. Were you even going to tell us?"

"I figured Bobby would sooner or later," she snapped. "Seems I was right."

"He didn't say anything. Detective Sinclair called last night. He was worried that you hadn't said anything. He felt we should be apprised of the situation."

So it wasn't Bobby who had the big mouth. It was Logan. She considered the circumstances. In all honesty, Andy had a right to know. After all, the shooters could have doubled back and seen her enter the shelter. "Okay, so I was wrong. I should have told you about the shooting. I'm sorry."

His expression softened. "Why do you insist on shutting yourself off from us?"

"What are you talking about? I'm here all the time."

"For the kids. But Emma and I, you distance yourself from. We're your family, Erin. We love you."

Tears stung her eyes as she realized there was a lot of truth to his accusation. "I know, it's just that…well, whenever we're together it makes me miss Ben even more."

"Oh, Erin." He stepped forward, placing his hand on her shoulder. "We miss him too."

"Not like I do."

He squeezed her shoulder gently. "I know. I wish I could ease your pain, but the truth is, only time can do that. But you're not alone. Jesus is with you."

It was like she'd been sucker punched in the stomach, prompting raw anger from deep inside. "You mean like he was for Ben?"

"Erin..."

"Tell Emma I'll see her in the morning."

"Stay for dinner, Erin...please."

INSTEAD OF WALKING home, Erin walked to the hospital. After stopping off at the children's ward, she took the service elevator to the roof, where she found the makeshift basketball court empty. She'd hoped for a competitor. Laying the textbook on a nearby bench, she picked up the lone basketball and threw it at the hoop. It caught the backboard and bounced off the rim. She chased the ball down and returned to the free throw line. Tried again. The ball came up short, landing in the potted bushes beyond the goal post.

"You look a little rusty."

Erin glanced over at the male voice and was surprised to see Logan Sinclair standing only a few feet away. *Oh, great!* "What are you doing here?"

"I was visiting Addison. Saw you get on the elevator. Thought you might like some company."

"Well, you were wrong."

"Okay. Sorry to have bothered you," he said, and walked off.

Erin turned and launched the ball. It went in cleanly. Ignoring the pain in her lower back, she followed up with seven others back to back, each from farther away. For ten years, the nagging pain had been a constant reminder of how much a person's life could change in the blink of an eye. The pain she could live with; it was the numbness that terrified her. She thought back to the accident that had nearly ended her life. For almost an hour, she'd laid pinned against the seat of her car, unable to feel anything below her waist.

"Are you sure you don't want some competition?"

She looked over and saw Logan sitting on the bench, looking through her textbook. "I thought you left."

"I'm having too much fun watching you work up a sweat."

She leaned over, hands on her knees, and caught her breath.

"C'mon, you look like a person who strives on competition."

She rose, placing her left hand on her hip. "You can't participate in contact sports for six months."

"How about a game of HORSE? There's no contact in that."

She gave in, bouncing him the ball. "Okay, but if you bust your stitches, I'm not sewing you up."

"And you call yourself a doctor. You should be ashamed."

"Just shoot the ball."

He did, and missed. "That was a practice shot."

She retrieved the ball and bounced it back. He tried again. Missed.

"You only get one practice shot." She chased the ball down and exchanged places with him. Made the shot cleanly.

"You do realize I'm handicapped."

She returned with the ball. "You're the one that wanted to play."

She bounced him the ball. He caught it one handedly and turned to shoot. The ball bounced off the board and through the net. "Did you see that?"

"I saw." This time, he retrieved the ball and bounced it to her. She bounced it back. "Let's see you do it again."

"Care to make a friendly wager?"

"How friendly?"

"Dinner?"

"Out of the question."

"Lunch?"

"Still out of the question."

"Coffee then?"

She fought off a smile. "Either shoot the ball or give it back to me."

He aimed, shot, and sunk the ball. Erin was glad she hadn't taken the bet, suspecting she was being hustled.

He chased the ball down and bounced it to her. "You come up here often?"

She caught it, leaped in the air, and made the basket. "A couple of times a week. It beats going to the gym."

"Being a physical therapist I would think you practically lived in a gym."

"Sometimes I do, which is why I prefer not going on personal time."

The familiar sound of a helicopter flooded the roof. Erin glanced up to see Life Flight coming over the top of the radio tower. Snagging Logan's shirtsleeve, she pulled him back from the edge of the helipad. He yelled something she couldn't make out, and she nodded toward the steel door several yards away from the elevator. He shook his head, nodding back to the helicopter that landed squarely on the huge 'H'. Her legs throbbing, she moved to the bench and sat down. He joined her.

A crew of two exited the side of the helicopter and removed a gurney just as the elevator doors opened. Candice was the first to step out, followed by two male nurses. The men ran to meet the crew of the chopper while Candice held the elevator. "Erin. What are you doing here?"

Saving her voice, she joined her friend in the elevator. "Shooting baskets. I thought you were off today."

"I got called in. A three alarm fire with multiple injuries."

"Need any help?"

"If we do, I'll page you."

Erin stepped out as the orderlies ran toward the elevator with the gurney. She glanced at the unconscious man strapped to it. He was fitted with a neck brace and was strapped to a spine board. The outline of a facemask and black soot indicated he was a fireman.

Cops aren't the only heroes.

She reached for her pager fastened to her jeans to make sure it was on.

"Who's winning?"

Erin turned in recognition of the paramedic's voice. "Hey, T.J." She stepped in for a hug. "Neither. We're just shooting hoops."

"I thought you only played for blood?"

"Not always."

"Drop by the station sometime. We got a new court."

"I'll do that. You still work twenty-four on, forty-eight off?"

"Yeah."

"I'll drop by next week."

"Great. The guys would love to see you." He reached in for another hug.

"Be careful, T.J."

"Always. See you next week."

She watched as he ran back to the helicopter.

"An old boyfriend?" Logan asked once the helicopter had taken off.

She shook her head, joining him on the bench. Surprisingly, she was glad he had stayed. The friendly banter on the court had gotten her out of her sour mood. "Remember the car accident I said I had in college? He was one of the paramedics that cut me out."

"It must have been a really bad one if you had to be cut out."

She crossed her legs underneath her and met his gaze. "I was trapped for almost an hour. The guy who hit me was in a dual cab. Parked himself right on top of me, rupturing the gas tank in the process. Fearing an explosion, the extrication took twice as long."

"Wade told me you were in a wheel chair for a while."

She nodded. "It took seven operations and eighteen months of therapy before I could walk with a cane."

"I can't imagine what it must have been like for you." He leaned back on the bench, but his eyes never left her.

"Lying there in that hospital bed, not knowing if I'd ever walk again, were some of the darkest days of my life," she admitted, somewhat surprised at how easy it was to talk to him. "But Wade got me through it. He was my PT. He pushed me so hard I hated him at times. Sometimes, I hurt so bad that all I could do was cry, but that didn't phase him. He kept pushing, demanding more."

"I sensed you two were close. Now I know why."

"He's my best friend, and sometimes, my worst enemy."

He smiled at her. "He's also the reason you entered this field of medicine, isn't he?"

She smiled back. "Yes."

"No wonder you're so good at what you do. You've been there, felt the pain, know the struggle. A struggle you're still going through, I suspect?"

She wondered if he had come up with that assumption on his own or if Wade had helped. She suspected the latter. "Though the doctors were able to pin and bolt me back together, some of the nerve damage was irreversible. Occasionally, I still have problems. It's a small price to pay considering the alternative."

"Being paralyzed?"

She nodded slowly as she met his gaze. He had kind eyes, the sort that put a person at ease, which was probably why she had revealed so much about herself. "What about you? What did you feel the night you were shot?"

"We're not going there, Erin." For the first time, he looked away from her, his gaze shifting to the empty basketball court.

She touched his arm briefly. "Please, Logan. I need to know if it was as bad as I've imagined." Though his wound wasn't nearly as bad as Ben's, she suspected he had been just as scared.

He looked at her searchingly. She knew he didn't want to answer her question, but she hoped he would. Whether or not Ben had been frightened was only one of the many questions she had demanded God answer.

With a sigh, he closed his eyes for a second, as if to summon the courage to talk about it. "When I was lying there in the alley, I didn't know where I'd been shot because my whole chest hurt. But I knew I was losing a lot of blood, and I knew that couldn't be good."

"You shouldn't have sat up."

He grinned. "I thought I was going to die. I didn't want to miss anything. I was waiting for my angel of mercy. And then she came."

Erin chuckled. "Some angel of mercy. I ran away." She still felt guilty for abandoning him that night.

"Not before assuring me that both my partner and I were going to be okay. That meant a lot, Erin."

"Were you afraid?" she asked quietly, fearing his answer. She'd often imagined Ben lying on that cafeteria floor, bleeding to death—all alone.

"I'd be lying if I said I wasn't. But deep down I knew that, no matter what happened, I was going to be okay."

She blinked away tears, relieved by his admission. "Thank you, Logan."

"Ben was a Christian?"

"Yes."

"I'm glad," he said with a smile.

"So am I." Even through the bitterness and anger, it meant a great deal to know that Ben had that same peace of mind, and that he was now in the presence of his Lord and Savior.

IT TOOK SOME PERSUASION, but Erin finally accepted his offer of a ride home. He planned on using the opportunity to change her mind about going out with him. "Would you at least let me buy you dinner in appreciation for what you did the night of the shooting, and for the three days of physical therapy?"

Erin turned in the seat to face him. "You've already thanked me for the night of the shooting, and you'll get a bill for the other."

"It doesn't have to be a date. We can call it a nice dinner between friends."

"You can decorate it up all you want. I'd still know it was a date. The first step in a direction I have no intention of venturing."

"Fine. Will you at least invite me in for a cup of coffee?"

"You just had coffee at the hospital."

Her stubborn streak was maddening. "A drink of water then? Come on, Erin, another half hour of my presence isn't going to kill you." And hopefully, it'd be just enough time to change her mind.

"All right. Fine. Thirty minutes, and then I'm kicking you out."

Her neighborhood consisted mostly of older homes with well-manicured lawns and palm trees that lined both sides of the street. It was charming, with a Norman Rockwell appeal to it. Within walking distance of the campus, hospital and shelter, it was the center of her world. He followed her up the half dozen steps to the tan, single story home, noticed the next door neighbor looking out the window, and smiled. He wasn't going to miss living in the city.

"Keep in mind, I wasn't expecting company," she warned as they entered the front door.

Vibrant colors filled the large living room. Light green walls, maroon curtains, and cream-colored shag carpet. A tan sectional couch sat against one wall, facing a large, flat screen TV and entertainment center. Matching tan recliners sat opposite one another, facing the same direction.

Next to the couch he noticed an 8X10 photograph of an older couple who looked to be in their sixties. He picked it up. Neither looked like Erin. "You're grandparents?"

"Parents."

"Are they still living?"

"No."

He waited for details, but she gave none. "I'm sorry," he said.

She smiled. "Thank you."

Across from the living room was the kitchen, separated by an open counter with mahogany bar stools. Oak cabinets lined one wall enclosed around a large, stainless steel refrigerator. Across from it were a modern electric stove, dishwasher, and double sink. The walls were painted the same color as the living room with yellow drapes hanging on double patio doors. To the left of the patio doors sat a small oval table with four oak chairs. He glanced out the glass doors. The redwood deck curved around to the back of the house, as did a six-foot privacy fence.

He stepped out of the kitchen and pointed to the hallway. "Do you mind?"

She shrugged her shoulder, a smile tethering on her lips. "The bedroom at the back is off limits." He glanced back, curious. "I didn't make the bed."

He had yet to see any evidence warranting the warning she'd given upon entry. For someone not expecting company, she was a very tidy housekeeper. The two bedrooms that sat across from one another were small, one containing a full sized bed and dresser; the other had been converted into an office and library. Huge bookshelves covered two walls, with a roll top desk between them. A large bathroom with an antique claw foot tub separated the converted bedroom and master bedroom, across from it the laundry room.

His curiosity satisfied, he returned to the kitchen. "You have a lovely home, Erin."

"Thank you. Iced tea?"

"I'd love some."

He stepped outside on the deck and circled around back. The backyard was spacious with both an orange and grapefruit tree growing at opposite corners of the yard. Judging from the two picnic tables, gas grill and large array of patio furniture on the covered deck, she liked to entertain. Taking a seat in the porch swing, he glanced at the double patio doors. The bedroom that was off limits, he guessed. He fought his curiosity and stayed put. He was glad he had seconds later, as Erin rounded the corner of the deck.

She handed him a glass of iced tea before taking a seat at the picnic table closest to him.

"You have your own fruit trees."

She tossed him a beautiful smile. "It was one of the main reasons I bought the place."

He took a drink of his tea, pleased that she'd added just the right amount of sugar. "How long have you lived here?"

"Not quite two years. I bought it shortly after Ben was killed." She lowered her eyes to the glass in her hand, as if trying to avoid his gaze.

"Where did you live before?"

"We had a house near the ocean. Ben loved to fish and sail."

She didn't, he guessed, or she probably wouldn't have moved. "I see you like to throw parties?"

There was that infectious smile again. "Occasionally," she answered as she glanced at him. "Most of the people I work with live in condos or apartment complexes, so my place usually gets voted in for birthday parties and showers."

"Your sister-in-law and her husband, do they have their own place, or do they live at the shelter?"

"The parsonage next door." She took a drink of her tea, then looked at him. "I wish you hadn't called Andy."

Logan suspected that was some of the aggression she'd been working out on the court earlier. "I'm sorry, but with the sketch airing, I knew the shooter would be likely to revisit the neighborhood."

"Is that why you were so persistent in giving me a lift, and searching my home?"

He chuckled. She didn't miss a beat. "That's one of the reasons. For the next couple of weeks, you'd be wise not to go out alone."

She bit down on her lower lip as she considered his warning. "Do you think they might go to the shelter?"

It was a possibility he had hoped to avoid, knowing she'd be worried for her family. It was the reason he'd phoned Andy. "I suggested Andy not let anyone they were unfamiliar with stay at shelter just in case."

She gave a dry laugh. "I'm sure that went over well."

"He wasn't very keen on the idea, but I told him that not knowing what the actual shooter looks like is going to make things difficult. Even if we are able to locate the driver, it's unlikely he'll be very cooperative."

"I'd never be able to forgive myself if someone at the shelter were to get hurt because of me."

"We're going to do everything in our power to make sure that doesn't happen," he said, hoping to ease her fear. "We're increasing the patrols in the area for starters."

"You mentioned meeting an informant that night. Have you talked to them? Did they see anything?"

"There's a good possibility he did. He's gone underground since the shooting. I haven't been able to locate him yet."

She went silent. Her soft brown eyes fixed on the empty yard. He wished he knew what was on her mind. He was usually good at reading people, but not her. The bits of herself she'd offered so far only tweaked his appetite. He wanted to know more. Lots more. It was going to be interesting unraveling the intricate pieces that made up her persona.

"You need a cat," he suggested moments later.

"Excuse me?"

"I said, you need a cat. To keep you company."

She smiled. "Logan, I'm never home. If I'm not at the hospital or with a client, I'm at the shelter."

"That's exactly my point. If you had a cat, or a dog even, it'd give you reason to come home."

"I don't stay active only because I want to, Logan, but because I need to."

He wondered if that need arose because she was still mourning the loss of her husband, or if it was due more to her lingering health problems. He was about to query further when she grabbed her empty glass and stood.

"Aw man."

He lowered his gaze to the tear in her shirt and the nail sticking out the picnic table that she'd snagged it on. "I'm no good with a needle and thread, but I'm great with a hammer," he offered.

"I'd appreciate it. There's a tool box in the garage. There should be one in it."

WHILE LOGAN WENT IN search of the hammer, Erin refilled their glasses. She returned to the sound of banging. His actions today, especially upon their arrival, were endearing, to say the least. Not only had he managed to get her out of her sour mood, she found herself relaxing her guard, offering more about herself than she had to anyone in a long time.

The job completed, he returned the hammer and rejoined her on the deck. "Who's Jag is that sitting in your garage?"

She handed him his tea. "It was a gift from a former patient."

"What, you'll accept a Jag, but you won't accept a dinner invitation?"

"It was forced on me. I was blackmailed into keeping it."

He grinned, reclaiming the porch swing. "Blackmailed how?"

"The guy that gave it to me, I asked him to give me a hand with another patient, and as payment for the favor, he made me promise to keep it."

"Why aren't you driving it?"

She'd come up with several ingenious excuses to give to others who had inquired, but it didn't feel right deceiving him. She smiled sheepishly. "I don't have a driver's license. I forgot to renew it."

Logan broke out laughing.

Chapter Six

"I appreciate you letting me use your car to take the test," Erin said to Wade as they pulled away from the Department of Motor Vehicles Thursday afternoon. She was now a fully licensed driver.

"You're welcome. I hope this means you're giving up riding the bike and are going to start driving the Jag?"

"Only temporarily. I miss my bike."

"You're going to get yourself killed on that bike."

"I am not." She loved Wade, but sometimes he drove her batty with his over protectiveness. At times, he was worse than Emma.

"I've seen the way you ride, Erin, darting in and out of traffic. It's a wonder you haven't wrecked it before now."

She ignored his comment. "You can drop me off at the fire station. I promised T.J. I'd drop by and shoot some hoops."

"Let's stop for coffee first. There's something we need to talk about."

"NO, WADE...NO WAY."

"He's requested you, Erin."

"I don't care. I'm not interested."

"Since when do you get to pick and choose your patients?"

If it'd been anyone except Logan Sinclair she wouldn't dream of declining a patient. She thought back to Sunday. After he had practically laughed himself out of the porch swing, she had counter-offered his invitation to dinner, had ordered pizza, and spent the rest of the afternoon with him watching old Alfred Hitchcock movies. Much to her surprise, she had enjoyed his company immensely. It wasn't until his pager went off that she remembered he was a cop. From that moment on, she hadn't felt comfortable.

She wished things were different.

She liked everything about Logan. He was sensitive, caring, and had a great sense of humor. He liked football, cartoons, old murder mysteries, not to mention the fact that he was very handsome. But he was also a cop. "I'm sorry, Wade. I can't do it. You're going to have to get someone else."

"Come on, Erin. You've always liked a challenge."

"Physical ones. Not emotional ones."

"I know it's a tough position to put you in. I mean, him being a cop and all, but you're the best around. He knows that. That's why he requested you."

She doubted that was the only reason. He'd already left two messages on her home phone, pestering her to have dinner with him. And she was determined not to go down that road again. Her heart had yet to recover from the last cop that had broken it.

"It's a minor shoulder injury, Erin. A few months tops. Please."

He sounded desperate. And she was a professional.

She reconsidered his request. It would mean an hour a day, three days a week. She mentally checked her client list. She had two that were being released from her care the coming week. She could fit him in if she had to. But it would have to be strictly business.

"Consider it a personal favor to me."

Her eyes narrowed on him. He didn't beg often. "All right, I'll give him four months...beginning Monday. And remember, afternoons only."

"Great. Give Patsy a copy of your schedule and I'll give him a call. Unless you'd like to deliver the good news yourself?"

She shot him an icy glare. He was going to owe her big time for this.

ERIN GRABBED THE REBOUND and spun around, passing the ball off to T.J. Two of his buddies moved in to dog him. Erin came to his rescue. Dodging the giant guarding her, she moved to mid-court just as he bounced her the ball. Grabbing it left handed, she shifted her right hand underneath, and leaped for the three point shot. She was mid-air when the giant collided with her, sending her to the cement on her rear end. The shockwave riveted up the center of her back, forcing her to lay back. She turned her head toward the goal and smiled as the ball sunk through the net.

"You're one crazy dame, you know that?" The giant offered his hand to help her up.

She gazed up at the man nicknamed Cosmo. "Give me minute, I'm basking in our victory."

"Well you only won by one so don't gloat too much." He shook his head. "I should have suspected something was up when T.J. suggested two on three."

"Yeah, I think we were just hustled." Mark Becker joined his teammate.

"Don't even think of weaseling out of the bet, Becker. Dinner's on you." T.J. sat down beside her. "I want pepperoni and mushroom on my pizza."

"Same here...with extra cheese," Erin said.

"You realize we'll have to buy for the whole shift," the other paramedic reminded.

"You're the one that wanted to bet Rychek."

"All right. Come on, Cosmo, let's go phone it in."

"You need a hand getting up?" Becker asked, moving to the other side of Erin.

"I'm afraid so," she admitted, the pain in her lower back still lingering.

T.J. on one side and Becker on the other, they gently raised Erin to her feet. She stood on wobbly legs. "Man, am I gonna to pay for this tomorrow."

"You should be more careful, Erin. I don't want to see you back in a wheel chair."

She winced at the thought.

"He's right, Erin, that was pretty careless," T.J. added.

"Relax, boys. I'm fine. My last checkup, the doctors assured me that all the added parts were in tip-top shape. The only thing I have to be concerned about is making it through metal detectors."

"Erin Jacobs. Rychek said you were out here."

She turned as a burley, gray-headed man grabbed her in a bear hug. "Hi, Captain. It's good to see you."

"Gosh you look great."

"I feel great." *Thanks to these two.* She owed them her life.

"The pizza will be here shortly. Come on in and say hi to everyone."

She followed the captain into the firehouse and was quickly bombarded by firemen and paramedics she hadn't seen in months. By the time the pizza arrived, they'd seated her in the kitchen with a glass of the captain's homemade lemonade.

"Rumor has it you're working with Rydell?" one of the older guys inquired.

"Come on, Jack, you know I can't answer that."

"Rumor also has it he won't start the season, and that Lincoln Phelps is now projected to go number one in next year's draft," TJ added.

She smiled. Phelps name had only recently been added to the list of hopefuls. His sports agent, Gage Washington, had had his eye on Rydell up until a few months ago when Erin warned Derrick not to sign with him. "Who is this Phelps, anyway? I've never even heard of him before."

"Quarterback with Texas A&M. He was a backup to Jackson till he got injured. He threw no less than three touchdown passes in his last eight games. They're dubbing him the next Cody Marshal," Mark informed.

"No doubt Washington christened him with that honor," Erin said.

"What do you have against Gage Washington?" T.J. asked, refilling her glass. "He's made millionaires out of a lot of kids."

"He's also broken a lot of hearts. The guy is a conniving snake in the grass who'd sell out his own mother for the right contract."

TJ seemed about to speak when the station alarm sounded. "Sorry, Erin."

"Don't worry about it. Go. I'll clean up the mess. You guys be careful."

"It was good seeing you again, Erin."

"Take care, Erin."

"Don't be such a stranger."

"I won't," she promised, watching the men scatter to their vehicles.

Erin had just finished cleaning up when her pager went off. She recognized the number from her answering machine at home. It was Logan Sinclair. She took out her cell phone and dialed his number. "Erin Jacobs, you paged me?"

"Wade said it'd be okay. I just wanted to make sure you had the address to my apartment."

He sounded pleased with himself, which was very irritating. "I'll get it when I go by the office on Monday. I thought you lived in the country."

"Actually, I'm in the process of moving. My gym equipment is still in the city so I thought, at least for the next several weeks, we could meet there. I figured it'd be more convenient."

"Whichever is best for you?"

The dispatch radio covered his reply. "I'm sorry, I missed that."

"I said the apartment was fine. Is everything okay?"

"I'm visiting friends at a fire station. That was dispatch you heard."

"Ah. So who won the game?"

"TJ and me. We got pizza out of the deal."

"Pizza, huh? Hey, that reminds me. I had a nice time the other day. Thanks for letting me stay. It's good to know I'm not the only one that still appreciates Hitchcock."

She smiled, wishing, once again, that he wasn't a cop. "You're welcome. You could have mentioned you were interested in hiring me."

"I was afraid you'd decline. Forgive me?"

"Just so you know, I agreed only as a personal favor to Wade. So if you have any other motives besides your rehabilitation, I suggest you forget them."

"I consider myself forewarned. And just so you know, the main reason I requested you is because I heard you were the best."

She smiled. "I'm glad we got that settled."

"So am I. I'll see you on Monday."

"Goodbye, Logan."

"SO, DID YOU DO ANYTHING exciting this weekend?" Bobby asked.

Erin finished tying the trash bag containing the remnants of Monday's breakfast. Since there were plenty of weekend volunteers, she took that time to regenerate from her usually hectic schedule. "Candice and I took some of the kids from rehab fishing yesterday afternoon." She stepped back and allowed him to remove it from the large, green barrel.

"I bet they enjoyed that."

She held the door for him and watched as he deposited the bag in the dumpster. "We all had a great time."

"Hey, that gives me an idea. How about next Sunday you come with me to church? Afterwards we can treat the kids to pizza."

She grinned. When Ben was killed, she'd asked Bobby to take over their teenage Sunday school class and youth group. She had meant it to be temporary, but the longer she'd stayed away; the harder it was to return. "Nice try, Bobby. However, I do like the pizza idea. I'll meet you there. It'll be my treat."

He walked past her back into the kitchen. "The kids really miss you at church, Erin."

He was playing dirty and she didn't like it. "It's been two years, Bobby. Most don't even remember me."

"You never forget a good teacher."

She avoided his gaze. She did miss working with the kids. She hoped the new youth center she was planning on opening would help her to reconnect with them. A few from the shelter she still saw, but most were from other communities and she hadn't seen them since Ben's funeral. "Andy told me you were a wonderful youth leader."

"You're much better with them than I am. You have a gift, Erin. You're able to enter their world on their level. I haven't been able to do that."

"You will. It just takes time to gain their trust."

"Oh, I almost forgot, some guy came by looking for you yesterday."

She immediately thought of Logan. "Who?"

"Said he was a friend of a friend. He left an envelope. I put it in your desk in the library."

"Thanks, Bobby."

Erin went into the library. As she flipped on the lights, she glanced around the room at the shelves of donated books. They were running low. She made a mental note to make a few calls to the area churches seeking donations. She then sat down at the desk and took out the envelope addressed to her in care of the shelter. Inside was a cashier's check for fifty thousand dollars made out to her, and signed by Marcus Wheeler. She laughed and immediately reached for her cell phone.

"I'm sorry I missed your call. You know what to do."

"Marcus. It's Erin." She tried to contain her excitement, but wasn't succeeding very well. She took a deep breath and was about to continue when she heard a click on the other end.

"Erin?"

"You're a good man, Marcus Wheeler." She wished he were there in person so she could hug him. He'd just made her dream a reality.

"I know you'll put it to good use."

"I will. Thank you." She leaned back in the chair and took another deep breath to calm herself.

"You're welcome. Oh, and if you're interested, I talked to a couple of teammates who are willing to serve up meals or something if you want to do some type of fundraiser for the youth center."

"Are you serious?"

"Just pick a date. It'll have to be in the evening, of course."

"I don't know what to say." She had wanted this so badly for so long.

"You don't need to say anything. We'd be glad to do it."

Many of the athletes she knew gave to charity, but this was going far and beyond the usual charitable donation. "You're a good man, Marcus."

He laughed. "You already said that. Listen, I've gotta run. As soon as you have the details, give me a call."

"I will. And thanks again."

"You're welcome, Erin. Talk to you later."

She closed her cell phone and shoved it into her backpack.

"Erin, you got a minute?"

She glanced up and saw Andy in the doorway. "Sure. What's up?"

"Joey came to me last night. It's probably nothing, but you should probably mention it to Detective Sinclair. He said a guy stopped him yesterday afternoon asking about you."

Her smile faded. "Did he say what the guy looked like?"

"He said he was an African American, over six feet, and very muscular."

The man she'd seen leaving the scene of the shooting had been Caucasian. Maybe it was Marcus's friend he'd spoken to. "Did Bobby already leave for the hospital?"

"A few minutes ago."

"Okay, thanks. If you're not busy this evening, I'd like to talk to you about the youth center."

"Did you decide to sell the Jaguar?"

"Marcus made me promise not to. Instead, he gave me this." She handed him the check.

He grinned. "Congratulations. Have you started looking for a site yet?"

"Not yet. I'm hoping for something close by." She slipped the check into her backpack. "He also has volunteered, along with a few of his teammates, to do a fundraiser." Things were finally starting to come together.

"That's great, Erin. I'm sure the center will be a real blessing to the community, but have you given any thought to how you're going to manage it along with a career that you love?"

She hadn't thought that far ahead. She knew he and Emma would help all they could, but they had the shelter to run.

"I'm sure the Lord will make clear his will."

"Yeah." She just hoped giving up her career wasn't part of it.

As soon as Andy left, she put another call through to Marcus. Reaching his voice mail, she left a message asking him to call her as soon as possible. She then called Logan.

"It's Erin Jacobs. The guy you saw the night you were shot, was he an African American?" She tried not to sound too worried. In all probability, it was nothing to get worked up about. But on the other hand, it could be the shooter trying to track her down.

"I couldn't tell. It was too dark, and he was wearing a ski mask and long sleeves. There was a slight hesitation on his end before he asked, "Why?"

"Someone approached one of the kids at the shelter asking about me."

"The kid said he was black?"

"And over six feet, and very muscular. He may have been a friend of Marcus Wheeler's, but I'm not sure. I left a message for him to call me back."

A rustling sound came over the line, as if he was resting the phone against his shoulder, followed by another short pause. "Why would a friend of Marcus Wheeler be asking about you at the shelter?"

"Marcus had him deliver something to me," she answered nonchalantly.

"Another Jaguar?" he retorted.

She smiled, recalling their conversation about the gift. She hadn't mentioned any names. He was fishing. "No. It wasn't another car."

"What was it?"

"Does that really matter?" she asked, smiling to herself. She couldn't help but be flattered by his interest. He was a handsome and successful man, who under any other circumstances, she'd be more than tempted to go out with.

"Are you dating Marcus Wheeler, Erin?"

The thought of lying to the man just to put a stop to his advances never even occurred to her. Instead, she gave him an honest answer. "We have dinner together every now and then, but we're just friends."

"A friend that gives you a Jag?"

She couldn't help the chuckle that slipped out. "Is that jealousy I hear in your voice?"

He sighed. "Be honest, Erin, is it really because I'm a cop that you won't go out with me?"

She suddenly felt guilty, as if she'd led him on. "I don't play head games, Logan. I generally say what I mean."

"All right. So, where are you?" he asked in a more serious tone.

"At the shelter."

"How long before your shift at the hospital?"

She glanced at her watch. "It started fifteen minutes ago."

"Stay put. I'll drive you. I don't want you going anywhere by yourself until we know who the guy is who's been asking about you."

She got up and headed for the door. "Thanks for the offer, but I'm driving...and I'm already late."

He gave another sigh. "Fine, but will you at least call me as soon as you hear back from Wheeler?"

"I will. See you this afternoon."

⁂

ERIN GLANCED UP AT the condo, located in one of Sheridan Springs's most prestigious neighborhoods. She rechecked the address Patsy had given her. She didn't know very many, if any, cops that could afford such luxury.

"It's unlocked, come on in," Logan invited after she rang the doorbell.

Erin entered the condo, stunned by her surroundings. With its large open spaces, natural lighting, and vibrant colors, the place looked like the cover of one of the interior design magazines the women at the hospital were always drooling over.

"What do you think?" Logan asked, coming down the hall carrying two bottles of water in his free hand. The other was secured in his sling.

"Are you sure you're a cop? Because either my husband was holding out on me, or cops have gotten substantial pay raises in the last two years."

He laughed. "I take it you've never heard of Sinclair Shipping?"

"Of course I have." It was one of the area's largest import export companies. "I just didn't realize you were part of it."

He handed her one of the waters. "My grandfather's company. Dad is at the helm now." He led her into the living room. Thick, white carpet filled the huge room.

"You're a trust fund baby?"

"Not exactly. It's my uncle's place. He's been out of the country for the last year."

She dropped her backpack beside the black leather couch and sat down. "Is he in the shipping business, too?"

Logan joined her on the couch, propping his feet up on the glass coffee table. "Equal partners. They recently opened offices in London."

"Congratulations." When she'd met his mother in the hospital, she'd gotten the impression she came from wealth, but hadn't made the connection even then. "You said you're grandfather started the business. Would that be your mom's father?"

"Yeah. He passed away last year."

"I'm sorry."

"Thanks. Hey, I thought you were going to call me after you heard from Wheeler?"

"He hasn't called me back yet." She grabbed her backpack from the floor and unzipped it. "Shall we get started?"

"Ready when you are."

A woman's voice filled the room. Erin quickly recognized the police lingo as that of a car being dispatched to an armed robbery in progress. A smile formed on her lips as she spotted the police scanner on a nearby desk. "Never too far from the action."

"Force of habit."

She took out her notepad and glanced over her notes before turning to him. "You said you had some gym equipment. Can I see what you've got?"

"Sure."

She followed him through the condo to a room set up with an impressive assortment of exercise equipment, complete with a padded table used for massages. "All of this is yours?"

"Just the weight bench and treadmill."

"That's fine. For the first two weeks we'll be sticking with a formal physical therapy program, the exercises you were doing in the hospital. Afterwards, we'll start a progressive strengthening program."

"With weights?"

"Gradually. Physical therapy is a deliberate process of strengthening your shoulder and altering how you use your arm. It may be months before complete mobility is attained, so don't get discouraged.

"Three months seems a long way off."

"I know. As your therapy progresses, I'll periodically re-evaluate your condition, set new goals. Remember, we're a team. We work together. If you have concerns or questions, talk to me."

"Okay."

"Good. Let's get to work."

For the next hour, Erin walked Logan through the series of exercises he'd done in the hospital. She took careful notes of his results and whether or not he experienced any pain. Judging from his progress, he'd kept to the regimen since his release. That kind of discipline would aid a great deal in his recovery.

When he'd finished, Erin handed him a towel from the stack positioned on a cart near the door. "How do you feel?"

"Good."

The bright pink scar was healing nicely. "Any pain?"

"A little tenderness is all." He started to step from the padded table.

"Don't put your shirt on yet. I want to massage your shoulder." She had him lie down on his stomach. "Where's it tender?"

"Just below my shoulder blade."

She massaged the area lightly. "There are two types of pain to contend with, Logan. There's pain that is, in fact, a warning signal that you need to listen to because it alerts you that you are overdoing it and are in danger of forcing things, and there's pain that is just there that you have to ignore. The sooner you recognize the difference, the better off you'll be."

"Okay." He draped his chin over his right forearm. "Why did you choose sports medicine to specialize in?"

"I went to college on a basketball scholarship, so as a former athlete, I have a great respect for those who compete professionally," she told him. She loved how he showed a genuine interest in her work. Most guys, or at least the ones she had met before Ben, only pretended to be interested. "It takes enormous discipline to compete at a professional level. I've worked with athletes as young as fourteen who've been training since they were three, their whole lives centered on one goal."

He glanced over his shoulder at her. "Isn't it difficult? I mean, some of them are pretty cocky and temperamental."

"Sometimes, but you have to understand what they're going through." She thought briefly about some of her tougher cases. "I've seen linebackers reduced to tears at the thought of never playing again. It's hard to watch someone suffer a career-ending injury. To see the fear etched in their faces at the possibility of never competing again. To watch someone's hopes and dreams fade away."

He rolled slightly to his right. "How do you keep them motivated?"

Erin shrugged as she stepped back from the table. "By finding out what drives them. For some, it's the fame and fortune. Others, it's their love of the game. Then I learn their limits, and how far they're willing to go to play again. In the end, it's more their mental stability that determines whether or not they'll play at the level they did before they were injured."

She grabbed two more towels, handed him one, and threw the other over her shoulder. "Is there somewhere I can wash my hands?"

"Across the hall."

LOGAN HAD JUST PUT his t-shirt on when Erin's cell phone started ringing. He saw it clipped to her backpack and debated whether or not to answer. It rang again. He heard the bathroom door open.

"Will you get that for me, please?"

Logan grabbed it and flipped it open. "Hello."

"Who is this?"

"Logan Sinclair. Who is this?"

"Marcus Wheeler. I'm calling for Erin."

Logan stepped into the hallway just as Erin exited the bathroom. "It's Wheeler."

"Thanks." She took the phone. "Marcus. Thanks for calling me back. Can you hang on a minute?" She glanced over at him. "Do you mind?"

Yes, I mind. He wasn't entirely convinced she was being honest about her relationship with the football star. "I'll be in the living room."

Logan flopped down on the couch and picked up a throw pillow, hugging it to his stomach with his good arm. He couldn't remember ever being this worked up over a woman. And he had never been jealous of anyone in his life until now.

He understood her reasons for not wanting to get involved with him. But she could at least give him a chance.

"False alarm," Erin announced her entrance in the room. "The guy was a teammate of Marcus'."

He rose as she stepped forward with his sling. As he leaned toward her, she slipped it over his neck. "Good. Can I get you something else to drink?"

"No, I've gotta be going. Are Mondays, Wednesdays and Fridays okay with you?"

"That's fine. Could we move the sessions to a later time, though?" he asked, hoping to work in a dinner somewhere down the line.

"As long as I'm out of here by five-thirty."

"Okay." He walked her to the door. "I see you're driving the Jag. You must have gotten your license renewed."

"I had to retake the tests. I think it's safe to say I won't let that happen again."

"Does this mean you're giving up bike riding?"

"No. I want my bike back. I miss it."

"Then I'll see that you get it back as soon as possible." He had considered buying her a new one, but he suspected she'd rather have the old one. One thing was for certain, he was getting her a helmet to wear.

Chapter Seven

Logan sat on the hood of the unmarked police car, staring down the length of the alley. It was strange being back here, standing in the very spot where he'd been shot over two weeks ago. He unconsciously lifted a hand to his injured shoulder, the dull pain a vivid reminder of what had gone down that night. He'd come close to dying. A few inches had been the only difference between life and death. It was a reality that still bothered him. Facing death makes a person take stock of his life, their achievements as well as their regrets. He only had one regret. That he didn't have someone special to share his life with. He hoped to change that someday soon. But first, he needed to know who had tried to kill him and his partner that night.

He glanced around at the surrounding buildings. Most were businesses that locked up around five or six. Metal and auto repair shops, a small plastic's plant. The shooter had done his homework in choosing the area, knowing there'd be no one around. How had they known they'd be there, though? He thought of Frankie, the informant they were to meet that night. They usually met at the park, near the volleyball courts. Frankie had chosen the alley that night because it was on the way home from his job at the textile plant six blocks over. A job he hadn't shown up for since the night before the shooting.

Logan's stomach knotted at the thought of Frankie setting them up. He knew drug users often went back to their old habits, especially when they continued to hang around friends who still used. He prayed that wasn't the case here. There had to be another explanation for his disappearance.

The sound of an approaching car drew his attention to the entrance of the alley. A smile formed on his lips in recognition of the blue Jaguar. Much to his surprise, Erin had given little resistance at his invitation to join him in his experiment.

He hoped the recreation would jog one of their memories.

Erin got out of the Jag and joined him. Instead of green or blue scrubs, she wore yellow slacks and a top with miniature Garfield's donning stethoscopes. Her attire fit perfectly with the perky smile she wore. "Sorry I'm late. I had to do some quick juggling of my schedule to work this in."

He slid from the hood of the car. "Don't worry about it. I appreciate your help."

"Glad to do it." Pulling a yellow elastic band from her wrist, she bound her hair in a ponytail. "Just tell me what you want me to do."

"I want to go at this from both angles. Either you can go first, or I will."

"Maybe you should go first, so as to stick with the sequence of events."

"Good idea. You want to get behind the wheel?"

"Sure."

Logan climbed into the passenger seat, glanced over at Erin, and found she was on the verge of laughter. "What?"

"I feel like we're filming a segment of *CSI*."

He grinned. "I never would have pegged you for a *CSI* fan. I thought you were more into old mysteries."

"I am. Ben never missed an episode, though."

Logan offered a sympathetic smile. He could only imagine how hard it'd been for her to move on with her life.

"Okay. We're running late for our meeting with an informant," Logan began. "Addison pulls in, notices the SUV. We know it's not our guy so we run the tag. It comes back to an elderly couple from here in Sheridan Springs. We flipped to see who'd check it out. I lost."

Logan opened the car door and climbed out. "I was about here when I heard the car door open, glanced up, saw the guy standing on the running board. I reached for my gun, heard a shot, felt the impact, and fell back. I heard another shot followed by squealing tires. A few minutes later, I heard footsteps running toward the car, and then you talking to dispatch."

He pictured the shooter in his mind, concentrating on his body. "He was wearing a dark blue sweatshirt." He began to think aloud. "And he was wearing gloves. Only they weren't your ordinary black gloves."

"The driver was wearing them too," she said. "They're non-slip athletic gloves. They're used in weight training."

He knew the type she was talking about. "Yeah, those are the ones. Good, Erin."

She got out and joined him in front of the car. "Do you know who owns this building?"

Sidelining the memories of that night, he followed her gaze to the two-story brick building. It was the only empty building in the block with a courtyard. "No, why?"

"Seems a waste to have it just sitting here empty."

"Scouting property for another shelter?"

She glanced over at him. "Youth center."

"The community could use one. It'd help in getting some of these kids off the street. Give them something productive to do."

She rolled her eyes at him. "That's a typical thing for a cop to say."

He chuckled. She was so adorable. "Sorry. I'm getting cynical in my old age."

She buried her hands in the pockets of her smock and looked at him. "Is this your first time back here since the shooting?"

"Yeah." He scanned the alley briefly. "It's kind of strange."

"I bet." She looked at him with soft, brown eyes that made his heartbeat quicken. "Are you still having nightmares?"

Logan's throat suddenly went dry. The only dreams he'd been having lately were of her. *Get a grip, man! You're here in this alley for a reason.* "Not as often. Your tip is working pretty well."

"I'm glad," she answered with a smile. "Okay, it's my turn."

He followed her to the entrance of the alley.

"I was about a block and a half away when I heard the shots. They sounded close, but I couldn't tell where they'd come from. I slowed down to make a left into the alley. I heard the squeal of tires, glanced up and saw the headlights coming toward me. I hit my brakes to avoid the collision and ended up laying the bike down."

She hesitated as if reliving the moment. "As the SUV exited the alley, he crossed underneath the streetlight, looked at me, and then sped away."

"Wait a minute. You said he looked at you. So he does know what you look like?"

"I doubt he would be able to recognize me."

"What makes you think that?"

"Because he wasn't expecting to see me. He looked surprised, scared even."

"And you weren't?"

Grinning, she shrugged her shoulders. "I was more mad than I was scared. I loved that bike."

He laughed and made a mental note to check on the progress of the repairs. "So he got a brief glance if anything?"

"Right. He was almost past me before he even saw me."

"What about the passenger? Any chance he saw you?"

"I don't think he could recognize me either because of the angle. Let me show you. Step over there about eight feet."

He did as she asked. Turning back, he saw her sitting on the ground. She was right. From that angle, in the dark, the passenger would have had a hard time getting a good look at her face.

"What do you think?"

"I think you'd make a good detective."

She smiled. Before he could reach her to offer her a hand, she was on her feet. "So, is this the type of work you normally do, crime scene reenactment?"

"That, interviewing witnesses, court appearances..."

"Getting shot at."

"Not as often as you think. Most of my work takes place behind the scenes. Putting together the pieces of the puzzle, so to speak."

She shot him a disbelieving look before walking back toward their cars. He followed.

"So, how far along are you in putting this puzzle together?" She crossed her arms in front of her.

He wished he could tell her they were close, but the truth was, they were no closer than they had been two weeks ago. His informant had yet to resurface, Erin was still their only witness, and they still hadn't gotten a hit from the sketch. "We're getting there."

She seemed about to speak when her cell phone rang. She reached into the open window of the Jag and retrieved it.

Logan sat on the hood of his car and met her smile briefly before she glanced away.

"Sure, what time? Make it seven-thirty...no you can pick me up." She laid the cell phone on the dash before turning back to him.

"Girlfriend?" he inquired.

"Friend." She joined him on the hood of his car.

He turned with a grin. "Do you have any female friends, or are they all male?"

"I have a few—mostly doctors and nurses. Would you like me to set you up on a date?"

"I haven't given up on you yet. I think I'm wearing down your defenses."

She smiled at him. "You think so?"

"Yeah, I do."

She shook her head, turned, and looked down the alley. "Why do you think they chose this spot?"

"Lack of potential witnesses, most likely." He was lucky she had happened on the scene. "That night, you weren't scheduled to work, were you?"

"I was out with a friend and was paged; a pile up on the expressway."

"Does that happen often...you getting called, in I mean?"

"Occasionally, when they're shorthanded in the ER. Most people don't know this, but I was half way through medical school when I decided Physical Therapy was where I belonged. Had I stuck to the original plan, I would be making enough money to buy my own Jag."

"Any regrets?"

"Only when I think of what I could be doing with that extra money."

He suspected she was referring to her passion for the homeless and youth in the community.

His cell phone rang. Unhooking it from his belt, he answered it. "Sinclair."

"I heard you been looking for me."

His breath caught at the familiar voice. "Frankie?"

"Yeah. Meet me in the usual place in an hour."

"I don't think so, Frankie. I didn't like the way our last meeting turned out."

"I had nothing to do with that, man. I wasn't even in town. We gonna meet or what?"

"I'll be there."

"Your missing informant?" Erin asked when he hung up.

He nodded. "Looks like we're finally going to get some answers."

"Be careful, Logan."

"I will." He slid from the hood and offered her his hand.

She accepted with a radiant blush. "Sorry I wasn't more help today."

"You did fine, Erin. Thanks for coming."

"You're welcome. I'll see you tomorrow."

He watched as she got in her car and drove off. He was already looking forward to tomorrow.

LOGAN TOSSED THE HALF eaten hotdog in the trashcan and glanced at his watch again. Frankie was late. He debated whether or not to go look for him. He was determined to get some answers.

"You look like crap, man."

Logan looked up and saw Frankie walking across the empty volleyball pit. He didn't look too good himself. Normally clean-shaven, he was now spouting a beard and mustache to match his dirty blonde hair, and his left eye had the remnants of a well-positioned fist. "What happened to you?"

"Bar fight, which brings me to the reason I missed our meeting. I've been sitting in jail for the last two weeks in Clearwater."

"What were you doing in Clearwater?"

"Looking up the ex-boyfriend of a bank teller."

"Any luck?"

He grinned. "Seems our gal has pulled this con before."

"I figured as much. Who is she?"

Frankie took an envelope from his back pocket and handed it to him. "There's a photo of her in there, as well, compliments of her ex. With a little persuasion, he might testify. He's still pretty upset that she split on him with his cut."

Logan smiled. Not only because of the tip, but because his instincts about the man had been right. "Any idea who her accomplice is here?"

"Nope. That's all I've got." Frankie moved to a nearby picnic table.

Logan joined him. He glanced at the contents of the envelope. Not recognizing the photo, he stuck it in his back pocket. "Thanks, Frankie, I appreciate it."

"Don't mention it. I owed you one."

"You still clean?"

Frankie's face lit up with a grin. "Going on six months." He tilted his head slightly as he looked at Logan. "I'll never be able to thank you enough for all you've done for me."

"Hey, all I did was get you into detox. You did the rest." And Logan knew it hadn't been easy for him. The few times he had visited him, he'd looked like death warmed over.

"That invitation to church still good?"

"You know it is. You thinking of taking me up on it?"

He ran his hand back through his hair and nodded. "I think so."

Logan smiled again. At twenty-two, and on the streets since he was fourteen, he'd seemed a lost cause when Logan had first busted him. "I'm glad to hear it, Frankie. You need a ride, give me a call."

"Thanks. I dropped by and saw Addison earlier. He looks good. Said he'd be getting out in a day or two."

"Yeah. We were both very fortunate." He immediately thought of Erin and the phone call she'd received earlier. It really irritated him that she was so bent on not letting him into her life, especially when she had all these other male friends.

"And idea who the shooter was?"

Thankful for the diversion, he shook the thought of her with another man from his mind and concentrated on Frankie's question. "Not a clue. You didn't tell anyone you were meeting us that night, did you?"

His eyes widened. "What, do you think I'm nuts? If any of my old cronies were to find out I've turned snitch, you'd be visiting *me* in the hospital."

"I don't get it then. No one else knew we were going to be in that alley at three."

"So maybe they were there for another reason. I'll keep my ears open; see what I can find out." Frankie rose from the table.

"Thanks." Logan shook his hand, then watched as he disappeared in the direction he'd come from. He hoped the kid would come up with something useful. As it stood now, they were at a dead end.

"THAT HAS TO BE THE dumbest comedy I've ever seen, Miles," Erin said to her friend as they exited the theater. "From now on, I'm picking out the movie."

"Oh come on, it wasn't that bad."

"Yes, it was. The least you could do to make up for it is buy me an ice cream cone." She motioned to the ice cream parlor across from the movie theater.

Smiling, Miles slid his arm around her waist and led her across the street. "You skipped lunch again, didn't you?"

She smiled down at him. At 5'6", he made her feel like a giant. "Guilty. Hey, did you see that redhead checking you out in the lobby?"

"No. Was she cute?" He held the door open for her.

"Very." With his dashing blonde hair and muscular build, he was always gathering looks from the opposite sex.

"Then why are you just now mentioning it?"

"Because her date looked like he could mop up the floor with you."

"Doesn't matter. I think Susan and I are getting back together."

"Again?" Erin glanced at the menu and ordered a single scoop of nutty raspberry. "So how many times does this make that you two have split up and gotten back together?"

"I don't know, I've lost track. I think this time I'll ask her to marry me."

"You said that last time. Face it Miles, you're terrified of commitment."

"Hey, until you come out of your shell and start dating again, don't be giving me any advice in the romance department."

She stuck her tongue out at him and walked off. Choosing a back table, she barely got seated before Miles joined her.

"I heard you got a new client. How's that working out?"

Erin met his mischievous grin. "Who've you been talking to? Candice or Patsy?"

"Sorry, I can't betray a friend's trust." He took a couple of licks of his ice cream and looked around briefly before his gaze fell on her again. "So, I hear he's pretty handsome?"

And kind, and generous, and thoughtful, and... She stopped herself. "He's also a cop."

"Yeah, but do you like him?"

She smiled. He was on a fishing expedition and she had a feeling Patsy was the one who'd supplied the bait. "I think it's time I found new friends."

He reached over and tapped her hand. "Oh lighten up. We love you; we only want you to be happy."

"I am happy. I like my life just the way it is." Busy and uncomplicated.

He grinned as he shook his head. "Keep telling yourself that, you just might be able to convince yourself of it."

"Well, dating a cop isn't going to improve it." No matter how charming and compassionate he was.

"How do you know unless you try? You should at least give the guy a chance. He's a good guy."

Her eyes leveled on him. "How would you know?"

"He interrogated me in X-ray, wanting to know all about you," he answered with a smug smile.

"How'd he know we were friends?"

"I don't know that he did. He asked everyone at the hospital about you."

"You mean after he was first admitted." She licked away drippings of raspberry ice cream from her knuckles.

His smile lingered. "I mean the entire time he was there."

She let out an exasperated sigh. Was this guy ever going to give up?

"You like him, don't you?"

"I'm afraid so," she admitted, against her better judgment.

He reached over and wrapped his hand around hers. "Then why don't you go out with him? It's obvious he likes you."

"Because I don't want to get my heart broken again." And she had a hunch Logan was just the man who could do it.

"You don't have to marry the guy, Erin," he said, giving her hand a gentle squeeze.

She jerked her hand back. "I'm not going out with him, Miles, so lay off."

He tossed up his hands in surrender. "Fine! It's your life."

"Yes, it is." And she didn't need Logan Sinclair complicating it.

Chapter Eight

Logan answered the door after the first ring of the doorbell. He wondered if all Erin's patients looked forward to their therapy as much as he did. He doubted it. He'd thought of little else since their alley meeting. "How'd your date go?"

She set her backpack on the sofa, turned, and met him with a quizzical expression. "Excuse me?"

"The phone call yesterday. You had plans to go out?"

"It wasn't a date. I went to the movies with a friend." She walked past him into the kitchen.

He followed and watched as she took out two bottles of water from the refrigerator. "A male friend?"

She handed him one of the bottles and took a sip of hers before answering, "Yes."

"And remind me again why you won't go to dinner with me as a friend."

"Logan, please."

He grinned. It suddenly dawned on him why she was so cautious. "You like me. That's why you won't go out with me. You're afraid you're going to fall in love."

She laughed. "That ego of yours is really something else."

He followed her to the exercise room. "Admit it, Erin. You like me."

"I think we've already established that, Logan. Remember the day you were released from the hospital, the day you conned my boss into taking you on as a client?"

He remembered the vivid description she'd given of her dead husband in the emergency room. The reason she'd given for not wanting to date him. "So, you're telling me that this guy you went out with last night, the paramedic from the hospital roof, and Marcus Wheeler are just strictly friends?"

"Why is that so hard for you to believe? Don't you have any female friends?"

"I told you, I've been away a long time. I need to make some new friends. So, how about it? We could start with dinner."

She tossed him a brilliant smile. "You're hopeless."

"Is that a yes?"

"That's a no. Now can we get to work? I do have other patients to see today."

"Geez, you're stubborn." Not to mention too focused on her work. It was obvious he was going to have to find another way to spend time with her.

"HOW'S THE COUNTERFEIT case going?"

Logan glanced over at his partner. For the past hour they'd been lounging on the deck out back of Addison's house. "The captain handed it off to Wilson and Stewart. They should be making an arrest by midweek. Frankie really came through for us."

"Is the captain going to let you in on the bust?"

Logan sighed as he shook his head. "The doctor won't release me to go back to work for another four weeks; even then I'm restricted to desk duty."

"They're telling me another six weeks." Addison pulled his sunglasses down over his eyes and stared up at the blue, cloudless sky. "How's therapy going?"

An image of Erin popped into his head. She was taking up permanent residence in his mind lately. "That's the only good thing to come out of this mess."

"So, when are you going to bring her around and introduce me?"

Logan glanced over from his lounge chair. "I thought you knew her?"

"I knew Ben. Erin and I have never met."

"Well, at the rate I'm going, you probably won't." Logan leaned his head back and stared across the yard. He noticed that it needed mowing and made a mental note to call a lawn service to have it done. He figured Addison's wife had enough on her hands taking care of him.

"She still won't go out with you?"

Dejected, Logan shook his head. Somehow, he had to find a way to at least get her to go out with him. After that, he'd leave it in God's hands.

"It's only been a couple of weeks. Give her a chance to get to know you." Addison took a drink of his iced tea. "How'd the reenactment go?"

"I'm afraid the driver may have gotten a look at her." If that was the case, it was only a matter of time before something bad happened to her. Only he wasn't about to let that happen. He'd put a twenty-four hour tail on her if he had to.

Addison rose on one elbow and looked at Logan. "I thought she said he didn't see her."

"She doesn't think he got a good enough look to be able to ID her, but my gut is telling me he knows exactly what she looks like."

"So what's your plan?"

"To keep as close an eye on her as I can." He went over his options in his head. As a former cop's wife, she'd probably spot a tail a mile off. So he had to get someone on the inside, either at the hospital or at the shelter, who would report back to him anything or anyone unusual in her life. Erin's friend, the veteran, came to mind. Or he, himself, could do it.

Addison grinned at him. "How are you gonna manage that when she won't even go out with you?"

"I've got a plan." Suddenly, things were starting to look up.

"This oughta be good."

LOGAN SCANNED THE CROWD of teenage boys milling around outside the shelter. Most looked like street kids with no real home of their own. He thought of his own childhood and how fortunate he'd been in having two loving parents. So many weren't that fortunate. Lack of nurturing and guidance, most street kids ended up serving time in prison, or worse, they ended up dead. That's what made places like this a Godsend.

He thought of Erin's plan for a youth center. Judging from the way her patients at the hospital bonded with her, she'd make a difference in a lot of kid's lives. The fact that she loved children as much as he did was an added incentive to get to know her better, and the inspiration behind his plan.

Gathering his courage, he stepped from his truck and made his way across the street. The tallest in the crowd met him at the steps. "Hi, my name's Joey. What can I do for you?"

Logan offered his hand. "Hi Joey, I'm Logan. Is Emma around? I want to talk to her about a job."

"C'mon, I'll take you to her."

Logan nodded toward the others as he climbed the steps. They nodded back. "You stay here, Joey?"

"Next door. I mostly come here to play pool and listen to the jukebox. What kind of work do you do?"

"A little bit of everything," he answered, following the kid through the large dining room toward the back of the shelter.

"That's cool. They could use a handyman around here. The last one up and quit a few weeks ago. Doesn't look like you're gonna be able to do much with that arm of yours."

"Well, maybe you could give me a hand in any repairs that might need to be done."

"Yeah, maybe. That's the office." He pointed to a closed door.

"Thanks, Joey. I'll see you around."

The kid nodded and started to walk off. He hesitated, glancing over his shoulder. "Did you keep the bullet as a souvenir?"

Logan met the kid's grin with one his own. He'd just gotten here, and already, he'd been made. "The news?" he guessed.

His smile widened. "Don't worry, your secret's safe with me. Just hurry up and catch the guys. We don't want anything happening to Mrs. J."

It took him a second to realize he was referring to Erin. "Not on my watch."

"Good. See you around, Mr. C."

"BOBBY TELLS ME YOU'RE a friend of Erin's?"

Logan leveled his eyes on the woman behind the desk. She was attractive, looked to be a couple of years older than Erin, and wore her blonde hair up in a bun. "Sort of. We met at the hospital. I'm one of the cops that was shot in the alley."

"I see. So, you're basically here to keep an eye out in case they come around?"

"Partly," he admitted. When he'd run the idea across Bobby this morning on the phone, it had seemed like a good plan. He'd be killing two birds with one stone.

"I'm afraid I don't understand."

"Can you keep a secret, Emma? Do you mind if I call you Emma?"

"Please do."

"Well, Emma, the thing is, I've been trying to get your sister-in-law to have dinner with me for over two weeks. But because I'm a cop, she won't give me the time of day, outside of therapy that is, so I thought if I was to volunteer here during my rehabilitation..."

"Say no more," she said with a smile. "I have just the spot for you."

He followed her past the dining room to a large room filled with shelves of books.

"The shelter's flashlight ministry is Erin's contribution to the homeless. Churches from around the city donate the books periodically for the homeless kids to check out because local libraries won't loan out books to anyone without an address. Since most of the kids that hang out at the shelter live on the streets, flashlights are given out with the books and they are allowed to come back for free batteries."

"This was Erin's idea?" He quickly recalled their conversation in the alley after she had spotted the empty building. What he hadn't told her, though, was that he was one of the youth directors at his church. Keeping kids off the street and in school had been a goal of his since returning to his hometown.

"Yes. She's great with the kids, and they all love her."

His admiration for Erin just soared through the roof. He glanced around the room and noticed it could use a thorough cleaning. The shelves that were empty needed dusting, the windows needed to be washed, and the hardwood floor could use a good polishing. Most of it he could do himself, but he would need some help with the floor. The thought of actually doing something useful with his free time was exhilarating. *Yep, this is going to work out just fine.* "So, how does it work?"

"Simple," she answered with a smile. "Each kid is allowed two books per week. Just have them sign the sheet. Most don't use their real names, but that doesn't matter. We basically do it to help keep track of them."

"How long are they allowed to keep the books?"

"They don't have to bring them back, but most do, or one of their friends. The program's gone over very well in the community. Word travels fast and new kids show up each week."

"I noticed there were several kids hanging around outside. Do any of them go to school?" Maybe he could enlist their help with polishing the floor.

She sat down on the edge of the wooden desk. "A few do. Some even work doing odd jobs in the community. They are allowed to use the recreation room before eight, or from five o'clock till bed check. The library they can visit throughout the day. If no one is in here, they just sign the sheet."

It was a wonderful ministry. Not only was it keeping them off the street, they were learning to be responsible, and they were reading. "If you don't mind, I'd rather no one know I'm a cop. I wouldn't want to scare off anyone."

"I think that's a very good idea. Most that come here are decent kids who are victims of the system. Several are runaways from abusive homes, both natural and foster. They aren't very trusting, as you can imagine."

He didn't need to use his imagination. His father had grown up in the system and had told him several horror stories from his childhood. Plus, he'd seen the after effects with kids he'd worked with over the years. "I appreciate you letting me do this. I'd really like to get to know Erin."

Her smile faded. "You do know how she lost her husband?"

"Yeah. I'm sorry for both your losses."

She glanced away, her pain still obvious. "Have you ever lost someone close to you, Logan?"

He nodded slowly. "My grandparents, but I don't think that counts in this instance."

"Ben was the best thing that ever happened to Erin, and when he was killed, along with the shooter, there was nowhere for Erin to vent her anger. So she blames God."

Logan blew out a long breath. Up until that moment, he had assumed Erin was in a close relationship with the Lord. "She's angry with God for allowing her husband to die?"

"I'm afraid so. Both Andy and I have tried to reach her, but have failed. It's a shame, really. Erin used to be very active in the church. Taught Sunday school, worked with the youth. I don't know how we're going to get her back. She's searching for answers that only God can give."

He thought back to their talk on the roof of the hospital and wondered if that was part of the turmoil she had been going through that day. It was a tough place to be in. *Lord, please let this work out. If nothing else, at least let me help to bring peace back into Erin's life.*

ERIN BARELY HEARD THE phone ring over the music coming from her stereo. She grabbed a dishtowel, dried her hands, and hit the mute button on the remote control. "Hello?"

"Were you serious about the youth center?"

"Logan?"

"Yeah. Are you busy? Do you have a minute to talk?"

She looked at the remaining dishes in the sink, wishing she hadn't procrastinated all week. "I was doing dishes."

"I won't keep you long. So, are you serious about the youth center?"

"Yes," she replied, surprised he remembered their brief conversation on the subject. "Why do you ask?"

"I'd like to help."

She smiled. "You would?"

"I think the community could really use a youth center."

"Well, I appreciate the offer, but right now, we're still in the planning stages."

"I wanna help anyway I can. For beginners, I can check with city hall, find out who owns that building, and get in contact with the owners for you," he offered.

He must really be bored. "That'd be great. Thanks."

"No problem. I'll get started on it tomorrow."

Her thoughts drifted back to the reenactment and the phone call he'd received from his informant. "How'd it go yesterday?"

"He wasn't much help. Turns out he was in jail the night of the shooting."

"Did anyone else know about the meeting?"

"No. Best I can figure is they were up to no good and we surprised them in the act. They probably didn't even know we were cops."

She felt relieved by the fact there wasn't someone still out there gunning for him. In all honesty, she really did like the guy. *If only he wasn't a cop.*

"Hey, while I've got you on the phone..."

She cut him off. "The answer is still no, Logan."

He laughed. "I was going to tell you your bike should be ready Saturday."

"Oh. Sorry. Where shall I pick it up?"

"I'm having it delivered. Just pick a time that I can tell the guy to bring it."

She thought about it. She usually took the weekends for herself, but had promised to help at the shelter Saturday morning. "Any time after nine."

"I'll tell him. 'Night, Erin."

"Goodnight, Logan." She smiled as she hung up the phone. She wondered if his offer was just a ploy to win her over, or if he was genuinely interested in helping the youth in the community. Either way, she could use the help. The faster she got things moving, the faster she'd see her dream become a reality.

ERIN HAD BARELY MADE it home from the shelter when her bike was delivered Saturday morning. A smile broke out on her face when the older man in overalls rolled it up to her. Not only had the front wheel been replaced, it had been repainted.

"I'm going to need you to sign for it."

Erin took the clipboard and signed her name. "Thank you."

"You're welcome. Oh, I almost forgot. I have a package for you, too." He returned to his truck, retrieved a gift-wrapped box, and handed it to her. "Enjoy."

She sat down on the porch and opened the box. Inside, she found a purple helmet to match the bike. She opened the enclosed card.

Try not to break your pretty little neck. Your friend, Logan

She laughed.

After putting her things inside, she locked the house, and took it for a test ride.

She rode around the neighborhood first before venturing out further. Before she knew it, she was at the park. Taking the trail, other bikers greeted her in passing. It felt good to be riding again. She didn't even mind the helmet. It was a perfect fit. Making the loop, she headed back in the direction she'd come, then decided to swing by the office. She spotted Wade's car in the parking lot. Pulling in beside it, she was about to climb off when she saw him exiting the building.

"New bike?"

She took off her the helmet and rested it on her leg. "Feels like it. Logan had it fixed and repainted."

"How's that working out?"

"Okay. What are you doing working on a Saturday?"

"Catching up on my paperwork. Which reminds me; I got a call from Rydell's coach. He wants to know if the kid's going to be ready to start the season."

"Tell him I'll let him know in three weeks."

"Summer practice starts in two. He isn't going to like that."

"I'm increasing his strengthening program next week. I'll know more after that."

"I thought you said he'd be ready start the season."

"He will, providing everyone but me keeps off his back."

He laughed. "I'll tell him you'll give him a call at the end of next week."

"Gee, thanks."

"Hey, you were always better with coaches than me."

WHEN ERIN RETURNED home, she found Logan perched on her front steps. "How's it ride?"

She smiled at him as she removed her helmet. "Great. And I love the color. Purple's my favorite."

"I thought so."

"How?"

"The wheel chair race. You'd mentioned you were on the planning committee."

He was quite the detective. "You want to come in for some iced tea?"

"Thanks, but I can't stay." He stood. "I just dropped by to let you know I found the owner of that building you were interested in for your youth center."

"That was fast."

"That's why I get paid the big bucks. His name's Eric Dixon, he lives in Orlando." He handed her a slip of paper with his name and number. "He's expecting your call."

"Thank you, Logan."

"You're welcome. Enjoy the rest of your weekend, Erin."

Erin looked at the name and address he'd given her. Marcus's donation would make a nice down payment and help with the renovation if the guy was willing to sell at a fair price. She prayed he would. So many kids stood to gain from the center. Not just the street kids, but all the children in the community.

She thought of the outing planned for tomorrow. She was looking forward to seeing the kids from church again. Bobby's invitation to accompany him to church lingered in her mind. The children weren't the only ones she missed. She missed her church family. She had become good friends with many of them. Candice, Tom, Wade, Patsy, Miles. Regardless of her drifting away from the church, they had stayed loyal to her. Their devotion, just like the stories in the Bible, confirmed God's love for his children.

A vision of Ben's lifeless body flashed in her mind, and suddenly the longing to mend her relationship with God vanished. The anger and resentment were as sharp as the day she'd walked into that examining room and saw his blood drenched body. She had believed in God since she was a teenager. She knew He could have prevented Ben's death. Why hadn't He?

Ben was one of your most faithful children, and you abandoned him. How do you expect me to get past that? He was my life, Lord. All my hopes and dreams for the future rested with him, and now they're gone.

Chapter Nine

Erin looked around the nearly deserted restaurant. She was early. Church didn't let out for another ten minutes. She motioned to the young brunette behind the counter.

"Can I help you?"

"I've got a large group coming in, maybe twelve. Is it okay if we push a couple of these tables together?"

"Of course. I'll give you a hand."

Together, they managed to make a table for twelve near the front entrance.

"Can I get you something to drink while you wait?"

Erin glanced at the young woman's nametag. "Thanks, Amanda. An iced tea would be great."

The restaurant door opened. Erin glanced up, meeting the eyes of a tall, muscular man in his early twenties with black hair. There was something familiar about him. With barely a glance, he continued on to the counter. Erin watched as he paid for his call-in order. As he left, he glanced her way again. A Florida Cougars player she'd seen on campus, maybe?

A few minutes later, the door opened again, and a rowdy group of teenagers entered. A smile sprang to her lips in recognition of her former youth group.

"Erin," one of the teenage girls hollered, running toward her.

Erin stood to greet her with a hug. "Hi, Jessica."

"Bobby said he had a surprise for us. We never imagined it'd be you. It's so good to see you."

Jessica was one of only four girls in the group. "It's good to see you, too. How have you been?"

"Good. I've missed you. We all have."

One by one the teenagers hugged her. By the time Joey got to her she was a teary mess. "You're mascara's running, Mrs. J."

She ruffled the top of his chestnut head. "Take a seat and behave yourself."

The next half hour was spent filling up on pizza and catching up on the latest events in their young lives. "How about you, Johnny? Are you still on the honor roll?"

"I'm having a little trouble in history, but I'm getting by."

"Listen to Mr. Harvard over here," Joey teased his friend. "The guy hasn't gotten below an A- since the first grade."

"Hey, I can't play basketball or football. An academic scholarship is my only hope of getting into college."

Erin smiled at the boys. These, and other kids like them, were the reason the youth center was so important to her.

"We're planning a trip to Disney World this summer. Will you come with us?" Jessica asked.

"That sounds like fun, count me in."

"Have you ever been?" one of the children asked.

"No. I've driven by it plenty of times."

They all laughed.

"Jessica, why don't you tell Erin your good news," Bobby spoke from the other end of the table.

Erin turned to the young teenager sitting on her left. A brilliant smile lit up her face.

"I went forward today. I accepted Christ as my Lord and Savior."

"Oh Jessica, that is wonderful." She leaned over and hugged the young blonde.

"You see, I told you I was paying attention in Sunday school."

Erin laughed. "I'm so happy for you, Jess."

A woman's scream shattered their joy. Erin glanced over her shoulder and saw two masked men standing near the cash register. Both were armed with handguns. Her heart leaped in her chest.

"Everyone down on the floor...now!"

Erin felt her heart slamming against her chest as she grabbed Jessica and pushed her to the floor. The teenager began to sob. "It'll be okay, Jess. As long as we do as they say, they won't hurt us."

She heard a few of the children begin to pray the Lord's Prayer. She wondered if God would listen.

"Erin," Joey whispered, "Bobby said to use your cell phone to call 9-1-1."

She shook her head. "Just be quiet and keep your head down. It'll be over with soon." Had she been alone, she may have risked calling the police, but as it was, she had a table full of children to worry about.

"Come on, sweetheart, hurry it up."

"Anyone with cell phones, you best not be using them."

She blinked, thankful she had gone with her instinct.

"Grab a hostage."

Erin looked up. One of the robbers was heading toward their table. *Oh no, not one of the children.*

He looked directly at her. "You, get up."

Erin forced herself to swallow. "Okay. Just don't harm the children," she pleaded, rising slowly to her feet.

"Erin, don't," Bobby screamed as he rushed around the table.

Erin turned. A loud explosion caused her to jump. Her ears began to ring.

Jessica screamed.

Erin's eyes widened at the sight of Bobby falling to the floor, clutching his stomach. She started toward him, but the man beside her grabbed her arm. "You're coming with us."

Joey stepped forward, grabbing Erin's other arm. "You're not taking our friend."

Oh dear Lord, do something.

"Great. I knew this was a bad idea."

"Let's go!" The man who shot Bobby was now at the door.

She turned to the man beside her. "Please, I have medical training. He could die before an ambulance gets here. I can help him."

"I'm serious, man, you're not taking her," Joey said, refusing to turn loose of her arm.

"Joey," Erin pleaded.

The man beside her turned to his partner. "We're running out of time. What do you want me to do?"

Erin looked into the shooter's cold eyes. "Please, you don't want to do this. You have what you came for. Please go."

"Let her go. It's not worth it."

The robber turned loose of her arm and turned to Joey. "You're either very brave, or very stupid, kid."

Erin watched as the two men ran from the restaurant.

Johnny stood and joined his friend. "Very blessed is more like it."

Erin took out her cell phone and handed it to Johnny. "Call 9-1-1. Joey, get me as many clean towels as you can find. Jessica, you okay?"

She barely managed a nod.

Erin stepped past her and knelt beside Bobby. She searched for a pulse. It was weak, but at least he had one. She leaned over him. "Don't you die on me, Bobby, do you hear me?" she whispered in his ear.

"I hear you," he answered in a weak voice.

A sob caught in her throat. "You're going to be okay. Just hang in there."

He wrapped a bloody hand around hers and gave it a gentle squeeze.

Joey returned with a hand full of towels. "Here you go. What do want me to do with them?"

She turned loose of Bobby's hand and grabbed the towels. Placing them over Bobby's stomach wound, she applied pressure. "Come and hold his hand. Talk to him."

"What do you want me to say to him?"

She glanced up through teary eyes. "It doesn't matter, Joey, just talk to him."

"Listen you big goof, the ambulance is on its way…it'll be here any minute. I hope they're big boys, it's going to take some muscle to get you up off this floor."

"HEY, YOU AWAKE?"

Erin glanced up at Logan's voice and fought off the temptation to run into his arms. "Thanks for coming." She had debated about calling him, but he seemed the natural choice.

His gaze settled on her as he joined her on the waiting room couch. "You okay? You looked pretty out of it when I came in."

She drew her legs up to her chest and wrapped her arms around them in a lame attempt to still the anxiety that continued to linger. "I was just thinking."

"About the robbery?"

She swallowed hard and met his sympathetic eyes. "I was married to a cop for three years, yet I never really realized just how much evil is out there."

"You seem to be seeing more than your share of it lately." He picked up a magazine and began to thumb through it. He seemed agitated, even mad. Ben had been the same way. It was tough to see bad things happening to good people, and even harder to accept when they happened to someone they knew.

She thought back to robbery again. She'd never been so scared in her life. Not so much for her, but for the kids. They could have all been killed. "Don't you ever get tired of it?"

"That's what vacations are for." He put that magazine down and picked up another. "So, how's Bobby?"

"Still in surgery; I can't believe he was so foolish."

"Sounds to me like you wouldn't be here if it wasn't for him and Joey," he said as he continued to flip through the pages.

"You already know the details?"

"Just the highlights." He tossed the magazine aside and finally looked at her. "I ran into one of the responding officers downstairs. I took a look at your statement."

She could sense that he wanted to say more. Then, it dawned on her that maybe he was upset on a more personal level—that his feelings for her were deeper than she had imagined. She pushed that thought right out of her mind. It didn't matter how much he cared for her, or on what level. Becoming his friend was more of a risk than she was willing to take.

"I'm afraid it won't do much good," she finally answered. She ran a hand through her hair and leaned back against the couch in an attempt to ease the throbbing muscles in her back. All of this standing and sitting around was killing her.

"You ID'd the type of guns, that's something. Did Ben carry a 9mm?"

The casual use of her dead husband's name was unnerving. But even more disturbing was the compassion she saw in his gorgeous green eyes. "Yeah. I used to nag him into letting me go to the range with him. I was actually a pretty good shot. Now I hate guns."

The waiting room door opened. Erin glanced up and saw Andy. "Don't get up," he said. He leaned over and gave her a much-needed hug. "You okay?"

"I'm fine. How are the kids?" She shifted her position again, hoping to bring relief. Her spill on the basketball court the other day had played havoc with her body.

"All are home safe and sound. Joey is spending the night at Johnny's. The two can't stop talking about the robbery."

She shook her head at the memory of Joey standing up to the robber. "My little hero...I'm going to wring his neck the next time I see him."

"That's funny, to hear him tell it, you were the hero," Andy said.

"Me...I didn't do anything." Other than being scared out of her mind.

"He said you talked the guy into letting you stay and treat Bobby."

"A modest hero."

A nurse entered the waiting room. "Mrs. Jacobs. I need you to come with me please," she said in urgent tone.

A kaleidoscope of fears soared through her mind.

Logan took her hand and gave it gentle squeeze. She smiled her appreciation before joining the nurse.

LOGAN WAS ON HIS THIRD cup of coffee by the time Erin returned to the waiting room. He and Andy both stood as she entered. She looked on the verge of tears. Logan stepped forward, fearing the worst.

She smiled. "He's going to be okay. The bullet missed any vital organs. They had to remove his spleen, and he looks horrible, but they said he's going to make it."

"They let you see him?"

She gave a dry chuckle. "Like they could stop me."

Both men laughed.

Though she was putting up a brave front, she still looked like she was on the verge of tears. Logan closed the distance between them, taking her into his arms. Surprisingly, she laid her head against his shoulder. "I was so afraid I was going to lose him," she said softly.

"I know." He ran his hand down the length of her hair, surprised at how natural it felt to hold her in his arms. "You were all very fortunate."

"Was anyone able to get a tag number or direction of travel…anything?" Andy asked.

"Nothing yet. The police are still canvassing the area."

"I need to sit down." Erin stepped out of his arms and walked to the couch. He watched as she gently lowered herself onto the cushion, her twisted expression reminding him of their talk about her ongoing battle with chronic pain.

Logan moved to the coffee pot and poured two more cups before joining her on the couch. He handed her one of them, set his on the table, then took one of the throw cushions and placed it behind her.

She tossed him a lovely smile. "Thanks." She leaned back, crossing her legs. "This is not the way I like spending my Sunday afternoons."

He smiled at her resilience. "How do you like to spend your Sunday afternoons?"

"She used to enjoy spending it with the youth," Andy said.

She looked up at her brother-in-law with a scowl. "Now I bike or go to the beach with friends."

"So, today was a special occasion for you?" Logan asked.

Her expression softened. "Bobby suggested it, and I have to admit, I was truly enjoying it. I miss the kids."

"Good, then you'll consider taking over for him until he's able to return to church?" Andy asked.

"No, I won't consider it."

"Please, Erin, there's no one else that has the same rapport with them that you do."

"I'm sorry, Andy, I can't."

"Fine, I'll try and find someone else to do it."

Logan watched as Andy sunk down in a chair. He looked at Erin, and she turned away. It was obvious from the tension this had been an ongoing discussion between them. "Would you two like to be alone?"

"No," she was quick to reply. She folded her arms in front of her.

Andy leaned forward in his chair. "After today, how can you not believe in God?"

She looked over at him. "I'm not denying there's a God, Andy. I know there's a God. I just don't like him very much right now."

"Be careful, Erin."

She gave a dry laugh. "Do you know what we were talking about in the restaurant just before those two men came in brandishing guns? We were talking about Jessica going forward this morning, accepting Christ as her Lord and Savior. Don't you think that's a bit ironic?"

Andy stood abruptly. "I'm not going to sit here and listen to this."

"C'mon Andy, you're supposed to be one of His shepherds. Don't you have some wise words of wisdom for me?"

Andy shifted his gaze to Logan. "Will you make sure she gets home safely?"

He nodded, feeling somewhat sorry for the guy. Two years of anger and resentment toward God had come to a head, and she was lashing out at the next best thing. *Lord, draw near to Erin; help her through this spiritual crisis. Somehow, remind her of the love you have for all your children.*

Several minutes passed before he looked at her. He was surprised to see tears trickling down her cheeks. "Are you okay?"

"I'm sorry. I don't know what came over me."

"Don't worry about it. You've had a very traumatic day, it's understandable," Logan surmised, somewhat relieved that she wasn't the pillar of strength she portrayed herself to be.

Logan offered her a box of Kleenex.

"Thanks. I'm gonna go wash up. Then, if you don't mind, will you take me home?"

"Sure."

LOGAN WAITED OUTSIDE the restroom for Erin. When she finally emerged several minutes later, any evidence of tears had been wiped away and covered with makeup. Her gloomy expression warned him there was still plenty of turmoil lying just below the surface, though. The story of Jacob wrestling with God in the book of Genesis immediately came to mind.

"Would you mind if I stopped by my farm first?" Logan asked. "I need to check on the animals."

"I don't mind. I could use the fresh air."

"Fresh air I've got plenty of, the rest needs work."

His remark barely got a reaction. "Was that a smile? That surely wasn't a smile?"

She grinned.

"Now that's a smile." He grabbed her hand. "Come on, I'll buy you a soda along the way."

Half an hour later, they arrived at his farm.

"You were very generous in your description."

He laughed at her observation. The place *was* a mess. The previous owners hadn't been able to take care of it properly. The house and barn needed painting. The maze of shoots leading out into the large opened arena was rusty, many of the gates missing hinges. And the shrubs and weeds had practically over taken the place.

"I've got to go inside the house a minute. You're welcome to come along, or you can hang around out here. I won't be long."

"I'll stay out here, have a look around."

"In my defense, I got the place for practically nothing."

"That's good because it'll probably cost you a fortune to fix it up."

He smiled; somewhat disappointed that she didn't see the same potential that he did.

Logan was met at the door by his only indoor pet, a large, orange tomcat he'd named Boris. Boris followed him into the kitchen and waited patiently next to the refrigerator while he poured a bowl of milk. "You better be earning your keep here. I don't want to find any mice when I move in."

Boris meowed.

Logan smiled, set the bowl of milk down next to his bowl of dry food, then ran his hand along his silky coat. "Sorry I can't stay and visit longer, I've got a friend waiting. Keep an eye on the place, and remember, no mice or you're back in the barn."

Logan found Erin leaning against the gate, large enough to drive a truck through, resting her chin on folded arms. He followed her gaze out across the pasture to the surrounding green hills where a dozen or so head of cattle grazed near the pond.

"What are you thinking about?"

"If you're interested, the kids and I could help you clean up this place. Repair the shoots, and corral. Maybe paint the barn, cut the grass and stuff."

"Really? That's awfully generous of you."

"Don't get too excited. There are strings attached."

"There usually are. Go on, I'm listening."

"I'd like to start an afternoon work program when the youth center is opened. Get some of the area farmers to donate newborn animals for the kids to raise and care for. It'd teach them responsibility, self-esteem, give them a goal. The animals would be kept here and in the afternoons, and on weekends, either I or someone else from the center would drive them out to help with the chores and caring of the animals."

"That's a good idea, Erin. And here I thought you were a city gal."

"I had a foster family that lived on a farm. I loved it. I remember the feeling of accomplishment I felt helping with the animals, seeing them grow. Knowing I took part in their nurturing."

Stunned by the news she'd been raised in foster care, he stood silent for several seconds. Though he was tempted to ask questions, he sensed this was something she didn't normally talk about. There'd be another time, a better time, to talk about her childhood. Right now, he was more interested in her dreams for the future. "Tell me more about this youth center."

"It would offer youth counseling, job training, some sport programs, and eventually a mentoring program. You see, the kids that hang out at the shelter do so because they don't feel comfortable anywhere else. Some are street kids that have been moved around so much in the system they've been forgotten, or are runaways. Others are latchkey kids whose parents work and can't afford day care so they let them run wild in the streets. The youth center would give them a place where they could be themselves, a place where they feel they fit in."

"Sounds like you've been planning this for a long time."

"For three years. Due to a recent donation, and the promise of future funding, it's finally going to become a reality."

"Tell me, Erin; is it because of Ben's death that you stopped working with the youth at the church?"

She turned and looked at him. "What makes you think that?"

"Just a hunch."

She turned back around, gazing out across the open field. Several seconds passed before she answered his question. "I couldn't bring myself to go back. I knew it'd never be the same, and I just couldn't face the memories."

"That surprises me. You don't seem like the type of person that runs away from their fears."

"Sorry to disappoint you," she said, and started to walk off.

He grabbed her hand, preventing her escape. "You know, this youth center isn't going to fill the void left by your leaving the church."

She met his gaze straight on. "The only void in my life is the one God put there when he allowed my husband to be gunned down."

"Do you blame God for every rotten thing that has happened in your life?"

"Who else am I supposed to blame?"

"Why do you have to blame anyone? Things happen, Erin, that aren't always in our control, but that doesn't mean God is at fault. That He did it, or allowed it to happen to somehow punish you or make you miserable."

"I'm really not in the mood to talk theology with you, Logan."

God help him, she was the most obstinate person he'd ever met. "All right, how about a tour then?"

"A tour would be nice. Thank you."

He started with the barn. Sliding back the large, metal door, every color of cat imaginable sprinted in opposite directions.

Erin laughed at the sight. "It's probably safe to say you don't have any mice around here."

"You would think. But I still see one every now and then, so I hope you're not skittish."

At his warning, she moved closer to him, prompting him to smile.

"You like working with your hands," she commented, looking toward his workbench.

"My brother's a contractor. I worked my way through college on one of his crews." He watched as she stepped toward a cedar chest that was almost completed. "A Christmas gift for my sister," he informed.

"It's beautiful, Logan."

He smiled at her compliment, watching as she ran her fingers along the lid. "Thank you. I just hope I get it done in time." Getting shot had really put a crimp on things.

They left the barn and walked toward the two-story farmhouse. "Now keep in mind, it's a work in progress."

They were met at the door by his tomcat. "This is Boris, top guard cat and main mouser."

She knelt to pet the orange tabby. "Hi Boris, it's a pleasure to meet you."

"Are you sure I can't talk you into taking a cat home with you?"

"No, thank you." She stood and looked around at her surroundings.

"Can I offer you something to drink?" He stepped into the kitchen and opened the refrigerator. "I've got apple juice, grape soda, or bottled water."

"Grape soda."

He took two out and rejoined her in the empty living room.

She took the soda he offered. "Thank you. When are you planning on moving in?"

"Hopefully in a few weeks. I'm still deciding on furniture. I'm thinking a Santa Fe theme."

"It'll fit well with the rock fireplace and wood beams. Are you going to keep the wood floors?"

"You think I should?"

She shrugged her shoulder. "It'd be a shame to cover them. They look like they're in great shape."

"That's what I thought. You did a great job decorating your place."

"I'd like to take credit for it, but it was all Candice."

"Candice?"

"Morning charge nurse at the hospital. You mean, she wasn't one of those you interrogated during your stay?"

He grinned. Someone had been telling on him. "A lot of good it would have done. Your friends are very protective of you."

"Sometimes a little overly protective, I'm afraid."

After a quick tour of the rest of the house, they headed back to the city. Erin was silent most of the drive. It wasn't until he pulled up in front of her house that she spoke. "You never gave me an answer about using your farm for the youth project."

"I'll have my attorney check into it, see what type of insurance coverage such a venture would require, and get back with you."

"Thanks, Logan, and I really appreciate your support today."

He smiled. The fact that she'd called him instead of one of her friends was encouraging. "Don't mention it. I'm glad Bobby's going to be okay."

ERIN WENT INTO THE house long enough to retrieve her messages. As expected, none were from Andy. She felt terrible for lashing out at him at the hospital, and knew the more time she let pass; the harder it would be to apologize.

On that thought, she grabbed her bike helmet from the counter, locked the house, and retrieved her bike from the garage.

"Going somewhere?"

She turned at the familiar voice of her brother-in-law. "As a matter of fact, I was coming to see you."

"Then I saved you a trip. Can we talk?"

He followed her into the house and sat at the counter while she put on a pot of coffee. "The reason ..."

She cut him off. "I'm sorry, Andy." She went over and hugged him.

He smiled. "So am I. I shouldn't have put you on the spot like that, especially after the day you had."

She stepped back and crossed her arms in front of her. "That doesn't excuse my behavior. I honestly don't know what came over me, Andy. I feel terrible."

"Two years filled with anger and bitterness probably had a lot to do with it," he said as he tilted his head slightly.

"Yeah." She sat down across from him. "I guess I thought by lashing out at you, it would somehow make the pain go away."

"What pain is that, Erin?"

She hesitated. She really didn't want to get into this, but knew he deserved an explanation. "The pain of God ignoring my pleas for answers."

"He's not ignoring your pleas. You're just not listening. When you shut yourself off, it's hard to hear Him when He's speaking to you."

Deep down, she knew he was right, but she didn't know what to do about it. She had been angry for so long. It wasn't like she could just push a button to make it stop. "I can't come back to your church, Andy. There are just too many memories there."

He reached across the counter and wrapped his hand around hers. "Then find another church. You don't even have to find a church, just open up the communication lines. You know that God isn't confined to a building. You can seek him out wherever you are."

"I know. It just hasn't been that easy." She stood, poured two cups of coffee, and set one down in front of him. "You see, Andy, I've been struggling with God a long time. Ben's death was the tip of the iceberg."

"You mean because of your childhood, and other things that have happened in your life."

She nodded. "I know I'm no exception, that others have had lives just as difficult. The Bible is full of them. But when it happens to you personally, it's sometimes difficult to accept gracefully."

"Then that's what you need to pray for. You need to ask God for the grace to accept the things you can not change." He took a quick sip of his coffee and then met her gaze.

"The prayer of serenity?"

"Next to the Lord's Prayer, I can think of none better."

She smiled. "Maybe you're right."

"What have you got to lose?"

Chapter Ten

Erin took off her apron and hung it on the hook near the kitchen sink. She usually helped serve, but with Bobby out for the last two weeks, the job had fallen to her. She didn't mind, though. The new industrial dishwasher that'd been donated last year made the task a lot less tedious. And she loved volunteering at the shelter, no matter what she was asked to do.

She looked at her watch; she had time to kill. She thought of the library. She needed to do some straightening up to make room for some donations that were coming in this weekend. She headed in that direction.

Joey and a couple of his friends met her in the hallway. "Morning, Mrs. J."

"Good morning, Joey. What are you fellas up to?"

"Not much. Fixin' to go to school."

She was pleased by the excitement she heard in his voice and knew, since their talk, he'd been improving on his people skills. She turned the lights on in the library and stood stunned. Someone had done her work for her. The room had never looked better.

"What do you think?" one of the boys asked.

Erin turned to the three boys. "Did you guys do this?"

"Mr. C did," another informed. "We helped, though."

She had yet to meet the new volunteer the kids had been raving about for the last two weeks since they never worked the same shift. He'd turned out to be a big help in Bobby's absence, though. Joey especially seemed quite taken with the guy, making her wonder if it was he who'd brought about the change in the teenager instead of her.

"Mr. C lets us help him with all his work. He's a pretty cool guy," Joey said.

She smiled at Joey. His refusal to use people's first names was just another way of detaching himself from personal relationships. "Well, you tell Mr. C that I appreciate all his hard work, as I do yours."

"I'll tell him. Are you gonna be able to come watch us play Thursday?"

"I wouldn't miss it." For the past few months, Erin had reserved Thursday afternoons for the weekly basketball game in the park. Sometimes they'd ask for pointers, but most of the time, she just enjoyed watching. It brought her closer to the street kids, and it helped to relieve some of the stress in her life.

"See ya later, Mrs. J."

"Bye, guys."

"Erin. I'm glad I caught you."

She turned at Emma's voice.

"Mr. Dixon called about the property up the street. He wants to meet with you tomorrow afternoon. Can you make it, or shall I call him back and reschedule?"

"No. We need to get the ball rolling on this. Our first fundraiser is in two weeks. I'll see if I can shift a couple of my appointments around."

"That reminds me, Marcus called. He's got six players and three cheerleaders on board."

"Awesome." She made a mental note to call and touch base with him. "And Andy is still going to be the MC?"

"Yep. And the printers called this morning; everything should be ready in plenty of time."

"I can't thank you and Andy enough for all your help on this."

"Are you kidding? Marcus has done most of the work. This auction is a great idea."

"Yeah. It should bring in more than enough for the renovations."

"Ben would be so proud of what you're doing."

Erin smiled and glanced at her watch. She was late for her shift at the hospital. "I've got to run. See you later."

ERIN WAS SURPRISED when Logan's mother answered his door that afternoon. Dressed in an elegant dress and blazer, she looked like she'd just stepped off the cover of a fashion magazine.

"Erin. What a pleasant surprise."

"Hi, Mrs. Sinclair."

"Marilynn," she reminded.

"Of course. How have you been?"

"Wonderful. I didn't realize Logan had an appointment with you today."

"I have to cancel tomorrow. I thought we could make it up today."

"I see. Well I'm sure he won't mind. I must say, you're doing a tremendous job. He has improved so much since his release from the hospital."

"He deserves the credit, not me."

"Don't be so modest. Logan has told us what an inspiration you've been to him."

Erin merely smiled. The past two weeks had proved to be an enlightening experience. Though she'd never admit it, she'd enjoyed the time she spent with him. And at times, found herself wondering if maybe having him as a friend wouldn't be all that terrible. After all, they had a lot in common and enjoyed each other's company.

"I hate to rush off, but I've tons of errands to run. Logan's in the exercise room."

"It was nice seeing you again, Marilynn."

She leaned in and hugged Erin. "You too, dear."

Stunned speechless, Erin barely managed a wave as the woman stepped out the door.

Gaining her composure, she walked back to the exercise room where she found Logan lying on the weight bench lifting a barbell high above his head. Sweat beaded his forehead and the front of his shirt was soaked. She tried her best to stay calm. They were weeks away from the weights he was lifting now.

She went to stand beside the bench. A familiar Christian rock tune played in the background. "What are doing?"

"What?" he hollered above the music.

She stepped to the boom box and shut it off. Crossing her arms in front of her, she peered down at him. "I asked what you're doing? You're not sticking to the assigned strengthening program."

He grinned. "Busted."

She had suspected he'd been boosting his strengthening exercises in the last two weeks, having been disappointed that she made him start out with a bare minimum of what he had been lifting prior to his injury. "This isn't funny, Logan. If you don't slow down you're going to hurt yourself."

"I'm fine."

"No, you're not." Erin grabbed the barbell, forcing him to lower it onto the stand. Moving to the other end, she straddled the bench facing him. "I didn't study for six years so I could watch athletes pump iron, or to give massages. I know what I'm talking about when I say you're pushing yourself too hard."

"I said I was fine, Erin."

"Great, then I guess you won't be needing my services any longer."

She started to stand, but he grabbed her hand. "Wait a minute. Just hold on."

She sat back down, her eyes level with his. "Please listen to me, Logan. You have the personality of an athlete, which means you have a pretty deep well as far as the pain threshold goes, but you're pushing too hard and are going to end up setting back your progress for weeks."

"But I feel fine."

"That's good. But I set goals and limits for a reason. So you won't hurt yourself. You keep pushing past those limits, eventually you're going to pay the price."

"All right, you win."

"This isn't a competition, Logan. This is about getting you in the best physical shape your body will allow."

"You're right, I'm sorry." He stood, grabbed a towel from the cart, and began to dry off. "You know, I think I have a sense of what you must have gone through during your recovery. Not being able to work is driving me nuts."

Her heart went out to him. "You're going to be released to desk duty soon."

"It isn't the same thing."

"I know." She admired his dedication. Ben had had that same passion.

"What was it like, Erin, having to relearn to walk?"

"Very humbling."

He pulled up a chair and sat down across from her. "How so?"

"In the beginning, I couldn't do anything but lie there in the hospital bed. The pain was horrible, and I was totally dependent on other people." She gave a nervous laugh. "That was perhaps the worst part for me, having to depend on others. After I was moved to the rehabilitation center, it was even more frustrating because I couldn't work on anything right away."

"Why not?"

"Because of the extent of my injuries." She crossed her arms in front her. Talking about her rehabilitation had never been easy, but she had often shared it with patients to help boost their morale. It usually worked, especially with males. Very few men liked being showed up by a woman. "My left collarbone was fractured. I couldn't carry any weight on my left leg because of the broken pelvis and hip. My right leg was broken, my ankle shattered, and I had a brace around my body because of the fractured disc in my back. You see I was literally crushed underneath the truck that hit me."

"And when you finally could start therapy?"

"I was delighted and miserable at the same time. Learning to walk and enhancing the distance that I could cover was difficult. At first, I learned using parallel bars. Later I progressed to a walker, and then to quad canes. In the beginning, I had no balance so I had to hold on to something or I'd fall. And I did that a lot. It was like watching a baby taking its first steps."

"How often did you have to go to therapy?"

"I practically lived at the rehab center for almost a year, working therapeutically at least six hours a day."

"Seems excessive."

"The doctors said I'd never walk again. I was determined to prove them wrong."

He tossed her a gorgeous smile. "Through your experience, what was your most important milestone?"

"Going to the bathroom by myself." She grinned sheepishly. "I can't believe I just said that."

He grinned. "What was your most difficult milestone?"

"Accepting my limitations, and adjusting to the fact that there are some things I'll never be able to do."

"Like what?"

She hesitated. She'd already shared more than she should have. The fact she was unable to have children wasn't any of his business. "It doesn't matter."

"What about the pain? How is it now?"

"The mornings are hard sometimes, or when I've been sitting for a long period of time."

"And the nights?"

"If I've overdone it that day, I usually pay for it with a sleepless night." She thought of the sleepless night she'd had last night. It wasn't pain that had kept her from sleep, but disturbing dreams—dreams that he kept appearing in. And it wasn't the first time he had managed to sneak into her subconscious. He'd been appearing in it a lot lately. She shook the memories right out of her mind, reminding herself again that Logan was all wrong for her.

He leaned back in his chair and propped his feet on the bench beside her. "That's why you like to ride your bike, isn't it?"

She nodded, only mildly surprised by his perception. "It seems the more active I am, the less it hurts."

"There's nothing more they can do to ease the pain?"

"After seven surgeries, I'm fortunate to be as active as I am."

"And here I was feeling sorry for myself." He glanced away as if embarrassed.

"We all have our weak moments, Logan."

He looked at her. "Even you?"

She chuckled as she shoved her hands into back pockets of her jeans. "Especially me. I've thrown more than my share of self-pity parties. Just ask Wade or Andy."

"So what brings you by for an unscheduled visit?"

Reminded of the reason she'd come, she couldn't help the huge grin that formed. Finally, something good was happening in her life. "I have to cancel tomorrow. I'm meeting with Mr. Dixon to finalize the purchase of the building for the youth center."

"That's great, Erin. I'm really happy for you."

"Thanks." She glanced at her watch; it was getting late. "Have you done the other exercises?"

"Not yet."

"I'll go grab us some water and we can get started."

"Do you work at the shelter throughout the week?" he asked before she reached the door.

She turned, "Except for Thursdays."

"What happens on Thursdays?"

"I spend the afternoon with the kids; basketball in the park, dinner out afterwards."

"They're lucky to have you, Erin."

She tossed him a smile. "No, I'm the lucky one. They're great kids."

LOGAN'S SMILE LINGERED. Erin had the special gift of encouragement. Not only did it benefit her career, but the children, as well. If there was one thing he'd learned about her in the last two weeks volunteering at the shelter, it was that they all adored her. Joey especially.

He'd also learned that the children were their greatest commonality. And since her visit to his farm, she had inspired ideas of his own. He had known the place offered many possibilities, but it wasn't until she'd shared her dream, that he began to see its full potential.

Despite his efforts to spend more time with her, she had managed to evade him at the shelter. At first, he thought she had somehow found out about his scheme, but according to Emma, she was clueless. That was about to change. Finally pinpointing her schedule, he had managed to talk one of the other volunteers into switching hours with him. So, beginning tomorrow morning, there was going to be a new face on the morning crew.

"You were out of bottled water. I got us juice instead."

He accepted the bottle of apple juice she offered. "Can I ask you something?"

A smile crept to her lips as she peered down at him. "Okay."

"This youth center of yours, was it Ben's idea?"

"No. Though Ben loved the kids, he was never very supportive of the idea of building a youth center. He felt the money would be better spent on feeding the hungry and housing the homeless."

"How do Andy and Emma feel about it?"

"They weren't very supportive either till Joey came into their lives."

"Well, I think it's a wonderful idea, and I want you to know if there is anything more that I can help with, I'm there."

She smiled. "Thank you, Logan. I'm going to hold you to that."

"I hope so."

Chapter Eleven

Erin grabbed the cart and headed to the dining room to get another load of dirty dishes. It was an unusually busy morning. With the evening temperatures hovering around one hundred degrees, the shelter had been full to capacity, and more than usual had stayed for breakfast. Exiting the kitchen, a familiar face stopped her in her tracks. Logan was standing not ten feet from her, helping some of the youth clear tables.

"Something wrong?" Emma asked, pushing past the cart blocking the entrance.

"That's Logan Sinclair, the detective that was shot."

"I know. I hired him."

Erin whirled around, banging her knee into the cart. "You what?" she asked, rubbing her knee at the same time.

"I hired him as a volunteer just over two weeks ago." She moved further into the kitchen.

Erin followed. "Wait a second...is he the one the kids have been calling Mr. C?"

"Yeah. Though I don't know why. He's really great with the kids. They like him almost as much as they like you and Bobby."

She recalled the conversation she'd had with Joey and his friends yesterday. She never would have guessed that the man they spoke of was Logan.

"Is there a problem? Because you know we can use all the volunteers we can get."

"No problem. You could have mentioned it before now, though."

"Is there a reason this cart is blocking the doorway...oh...good morning, Erin."

She glanced over her shoulder at the familiar voice. "Logan. Or is it Mr. C?"

He grinned, glanced at Emma, then back to her. "I take it I've been busted...again?"

"What are you doing here, Logan?"

Before he could answer, Emma stepped between them. "I hate to break up whatever is going on here, but we still have half a dining room to clear away. So, if you don't mind..."

"We'll talk later," he said with a wink.

"Oh you can count on it," she replied, shielding her grin.

He smiled, grabbed the cart, and disappeared back into the dining room.

For the next half hour, Erin busied herself with the mass accumulation of dishes. Her thoughts still centered on Logan. *What is he up to?* He didn't strike her as the type to volunteer his time to community service. Coming from a wealthy family, he seemed more the type to cut a check instead.

Still baffled, she put away the last of the dishes, dried off her hands, and took off her apron.

"Hey, Erin." She jumped at the sound of Logan's voice. "Sorry, didn't mean to startle you. I've got someone out here that refuses to leave until you come speak with him."

She shot him a puzzled look and followed him into the dining room. Everyone had cleared out, the tables empty, except for one. Sitting in a chair near the exit was a large, white teddy bear with something hanging around its neck. A smile formed on her lips as she moved closer.

HI, I'M ROSCOE, was printed on the envelope hanging around his neck. She shook her head, grinning.

"He came with a letter." Logan motioned to the envelope.

Her hand trembled as she took the envelope and opened it. *I would like to introduce a good friend of mine. His name is Logan. He's a little rough around the edges, but once you get to know him, he's a pretty decent guy. He's been away for a while, doesn't know too many people outside of work, and could really use a friend. He heard you liked hanging out in the park on Thursday afternoons watching the kids play basketball, and would be honored if you'd allow him to accompany you this afternoon. I will chaperone, of course. You're friend, Roscoe.*

She turned to Logan. "You play very dirty."

He smiled. "I think there's room in your life for one more friend, Erin."

"I think you're right."

"Really?"

She laughed. "I'll meet you there after three." She picked up the bear and hugged the furry animal to her chest. "Him, I'm taking with me. Thank you, Logan."

"You're welcome."

ERIN WAS STILL SMILING when she pulled into her reserved parking place at the hospital. Taking out her keys, she glanced over at the white teddy bear. She had to admire his tenacity. Most of the men that had pursued her over the last two years had given up after only a couple of rejections. Not Logan. He was determined to melt her resistance. He had proven that this morning. The thought that he had spent two weeks volunteering at the shelter, drawing close to the people she loved, just to get her attention was both flattering and unnerving. She suddenly found herself re-thinking the situation, wanting to get to know the man who had captivated her thoughts, and often, her dreams.

She got out of her car. With her thoughts still centered on Logan, she was barely aware of the dark blue van that parked two spots over.

LATER THAT AFTERNOON, Erin joined Logan in the park. Not usually a clock watcher, she had found herself checking her watch periodically during the day, looking forward to their meeting. So, it wasn't surprising that she showed up fifteen minutes early.

"Did I miss much?" Erin joined Logan on the blanket he'd spread out underneath a large palm tree.

"Joey just scored for the second time. He's pretty good."

"I keep telling him if he keeps at it he could land a scholarship someday." She took her shoes off and folded her feet underneath her.

"He told me." Logan reached over and opened up his picnic basket. "I know it's a little late for lunch, but I brought along some chicken from the deli and some cold drinks."

"Really? I love fried chicken."

"I know, Emma told me."

"What else did Emma tell you?"

"Don't worry, most of my recon work was done with the kids. They're under the impression you walk on water."

"They seem to think a lot of you, too."

He held out the container of fried chicken. "So I can't be all that bad, can I?"

She smiled, chose a leg, and leaned back against the tree. She watched Joey guarding a boy twice his size and smiled when he tried to snatch the ball away and knocked it out of bounds.

"I'm surprised you don't play with them."

"I do sometimes. Mostly I just watch." Erin accepted the soda he offered, then watched as he leaned back on his good arm and gazed toward the court. She was seeing a new side to him that she hadn't known existed and, she had to admit, she liked it. "I get the impression you've worked with kids before?"

"I'm one of the youth leaders at my church."

"So, your volunteering at the shelter wasn't just a ploy to get my attention?"

"Only partly. What else was I going to do with my time? Captain won't let me on desk duty for another two weeks."

"That's probably for the best." She took a drink of her soda and met his lazy gaze. "So, why do the kids call you Mr. C?"

"Joey pegged me for a cop my first day. It stuck."

"Do all the kids know you're a cop?"

"Just Joey, as far as I know. I came up with the idea after your buddy Wheeler's friend came to the shelter…thought it might be a good idea to have someone hanging around just in case our boys show up."

"It's been almost five weeks. If they were worried about my being able to identify them, wouldn't they have tried something before now?"

"Not necessarily. They're probably still shaken by the fact they shot two cops."

"Sounds like you're pretty certain that you weren't set up that night."

"Makes more sense that they were casing one of the buildings."

From what she knew of the circumstances, she had to agree. But she didn't think there were any businesses in the area that would net enough money or goods to constitute such a risk. "How are the nightmares?"

"Getting better. I think I'm finally coming to terms with it."

"You mean the realization that you're not invincible?"

He flashed a curious look.

"Pro athletes are just as bad sometimes. They walk around thinking they have this invisible shield surrounding them. So, when they do suffer a serious injury, it can be a rude awakening."

"Before you came"—he looked down briefly as if gathering courage—"there were a few seconds where I thought I might die. And I started thinking about the things I wish I'd done in life."

She smiled. She admired his candor. "Now you have that chance. Just don't go skydiving out of a plane until your shoulder is healed."

He laughed.

Joey scored again. They both cheered. Joey glanced over with a smile and waved.

"So, how much longer am I gonna have to volunteer at the shelter before you'll accept a dinner invitation?"

She thought about it, but only briefly. The teddy bear had been a brilliant move on his part. Plus, the more time she spent with him, the more she liked him. "It's not a date, right?"

"Right. Just a casual dinner with a friend."

"Okay. I'll have lunch with you on one condition," she said with a smile.

"Name it."

His enthusiasm made her chuckle. "You help me Saturday. All you have to do is drive."

He arched an eyebrow at her. "Are we robbing a bank?"

She laughed again. "No, we're picking up books and flashlights at some of the area churches."

"For the flashlight ministry?"

"Let me guess, Emma?"

"Yeah. It's a very good idea." He grabbed another piece of chicken, started to take a bite, but then paused. "Which reminds me, I discussed the farming project with my attorney and have decided it's a go."

"Great, thanks." With all that had been going on lately, she had almost forgotten about her proposal. "And thanks for the work you've been doing in the library. It looks real nice."

"Glad to do it." He took a bite of his chicken and glanced out at the court briefly. "So, what time shall I pick you up on Saturday?"

The butterflies in her stomach took flight just thinking about their morning together. "You can pick me up at my place at nine. Afterwards, we'll have lunch."

He tossed her another gorgeous smile. "Perfect. I know just the place."

She smiled. "I'm sure you do." She wondered how many other women had been taken in by his charm.

Erin's cell phone rang. She glanced at the screen. It was Derrick. "This better be important."

"Can you come to the practice field?" He sounded upset.

"I'll be right there." She hung up and turned to Logan. "I'm sorry. I have to go."

"Do you mind if I take the boys out for pizza afterwards?"

She grinned. He seemed to genuinely care for the kids at the shelter and it was obvious they thought the world of him. "No. I'm sure they'd love it. Thanks for lunch. I enjoyed it."

ERIN WHISTLED AT THE young quarterback as he made his way to the sideline. Derrick removed his helmet, looked at her, and waved. His performance had improved remarkably over the last few weeks. He wasn't quite at a hundred percent yet, but she had no doubt he'd make the start of the season. She met him half way. "You're looking good, kid."

"I think increasing the weight training is helping," he said as he rotated his right arm. "Thanks for coming, Erin."

"No problem. What's up? You sounded pretty down on the phone."

"Look around you. What's wrong with this picture?"

She didn't have to look to know what he was talking about. This time last year the sidelines had been littered with scouts from across the nation getting a look at the NFL hopeful.

He looked toward the empty stands and shook his head. "Before I got hurt, I had teams from all over the country looking at me, but now…"

She reached out and took his hand. "Listen to me, Derrick. You've got to forget about all that."

"I'm trying, Erin." He stared down at the helmet in his left hand. "Have you ever wanted something so bad that it was all you ever thought of? That nothing else mattered?"

"Yes." She thought briefly of her accident.

He glanced at her curiously. "What?"

"To walk again." Letting go of his hand, she slipped her hands into her pockets, and met his gaze. "I don't know if you know this, but when I was in college I was in car accident that put me in a wheel chair for almost two years."

He nodded slowly. "Marcus mentioned it."

"When the doctors said I'd never walk again, in that instant, all my hopes and dreams of being a doctor, a wife, and a mother were crushed. But I was determined not to let go of them. There were days when I was relearning to walk that I was in so much pain that I thought I would die. I imagine your fear of not coming back at a hundred percent is much like my fear of never walking again."

He sighed as he kicked at the ground with his right cleat. "I'm afraid with, as long as it's taking, no one will want me."

Erin knew that was a possibility. Very few teams were willing to offer a multi-million dollar contract to the average player after they'd been hurt. No matter how good they were at playing college ball before they'd been injured. Somehow, she had to convince him that wasn't going to be the case with him. "Derrick. I've been doing this for eight years, working mostly with football players like yourself. I know natural talent when I see it, and if I can see it, so will others. I promise you, if you continue to give me your best, push yourself the way you have been, you will be noticed."

"Will I ever be as good as I was, though?" He looked at her with pitiful eyes that made her heart ache.

"Between you and me, I think you'll be better," she answered honestly. "I know it may not seem like it, but being injured was like a blessing. You've recaptured that hunger you had as a kid. You're playing now because you love the game. And when you're doing something you love, you're naturally better at it. A lot of professional athletes forget that hunger once they make it big. Success blinds them, making them forget their roots. The sport becomes just a habit, a paycheck."

"I see what you mean, and you're right," he admitted. "I'm not the same guy I was before I got hurt."

"I know, and it's made you a better man."

Smiling, he leaned over and hugged her. "Come on, I'll walk you to the parking lot."

Making their way from the Cougars Practice Field to the parking lot, they were greeted by a half dozen players along the way.

A lone security guard stood near the entrance. The man was every bit of six-four, and would probably weigh in at two-ninety. "See you later, Cal."

"Take care, Erin."

Derrick followed her out the gate. "Where's your bike?" Derrick asked, shifting his gaze to where she usually left it.

"It's a long story, one I really don't care to go into right now."

"Well, how'd you get here?"

She pointed to the parking lot where twenty or so vehicles were parked, two of which were Jaguars. "The blue Jag is mine."

"I was wondering what you did with all the money my folks pay you."

She laughed. "I'll see you tomorrow."

He gave a quick wave before being joined by two other players.

Erin walked between her car and a dark blue van while reaching into the pocket of her scrubs for her keys. Behind her, the side door of the van slid open, startling her. Keys in hand, she started to turn.

A masked man grabbed her around the waist and pulled her to toward the van.

Erin screamed, slammed the heel of her foot into the shin of her abductor, turned awkwardly, and shoved the key into his eye.

He yelped, grabbing his face.

Erin stumbled backwards on wobbly legs, lost her footing, and fell against the hood of her car.

She heard shouts, followed by the sound of footsteps. The masked man grabbed her arm and pulled her backwards. Panicked, she whirled around, shoved the man with all her might and caused him to fall backward into the open door of the van as it leaped forward, squealing its wheels.

Chapter Twelve

Logan pulled up in front of the athletic center and got out of his truck. Captain Connelly followed. He'd been in the captain's office pleading to come back to desk duty early when the call had come in about Erin's attempted abduction.

They were met at the entrance by a security guard who was bigger than the both of them put together. Logan flashed his badge at the security guard and asked where Erin was.

"She's in Mr. Wineheart's office. I'll show you."

"Were you on duty when Mrs. Jacobs was assaulted?" Logan asked as the guard led them through the building.

"Yeah. Beat anything I'd ever seen. In broad daylight, I mean. There we were, had just said goodbye to her, and out of nowhere, the guy tried to grab her."

"Were you able to get a tag number?" the captain asked.

"No. We were more concerned about Erin."

Logan's breath caught in his lungs. "Was she hurt?"

"Pretty shaken is all. I hate to think what might have happened if we hadn't started hollering and running toward them."

"Have you given a statement?" Captain Connelly asked.

"Yes, sir. So did Derrick and the others."

"Derrick Rydell is here?" Logan asked. He wondered if he was the one who had called Erin at the park.

"Was. He and the others just left. They all gave their statements, though. Here we are."

Logan glanced up and saw a middle-aged gentleman walking toward them dressed in a tailor-made suit. He quickly recognized him as Richard Wineheart, the head coach of the Florida Cougars.

"Mr. Wineheart, Detective Sinclair and Captain Connelly, we're looking for Erin Jacobs."

"She's in my office. Go on in. Sorry I can't stay; I've a meeting I'm already late for."

"No problem. Thank you."

"If there's anything else I can do, please let me know."

Erin was standing behind the desk looking out at the Cougars practice field. She glanced over her shoulder as they approached the desk. "They said I couldn't leave until you got here. I've already given my statement. I wanna go home."

The captain offered her his hand. "Hi, Erin. It's good to see you again. I wish it were under better circumstances."

"Are you okay?" Logan asked, trying to sound as calm as possible.

She nodded as she sat down in one of the leather chairs.

She looked more than just shaken. She looked terrified. He wanted to take her into his arms so bad he could hardly stand it. "What happened, Erin?"

"I don't know...I mean, I was about to get into my car, and all of a sudden, this guy leaps out at me and is trying to drag me into the van parked next to my car. It all happened so fast, it's almost like a blur."

Logan moved to stand in front of her and leaned against the desk for support. A mixture of emotions had soared through him from the time they'd received the call till now, ranging from raw fury to angst, much like the day of the robbery. "Did he say anything?"

She shook her head. "The only sound he made was when I jammed my key into his eye."

"Good girl," the captain said with a chuckle.

"It was the only thing I could think of doing. He was so strong...and big."

"Athletic?" Logan asked as a memory flashed in his mind of his shooting.

She nodded slowly.

"The driver of the SUV?" he wondered aloud.

"I don't know, he was wearing a black ski mask." She glanced up at him, but seemed to be looking right past him, as if she were searching her memory. "He had dark eyes, but I don't think this was related to your shooting."

"What makes you think that?"

"They tried to grab me in broad daylight, for one thing," she said in a sharper tone. "And why try and abduct me at all? Why not just shoot me like they did you and your partner?"

"You can tell she used to be married to a cop...sorry...that was a stupid thing to say."

She shook her head at his apology. "It's okay. You're right. Ben's work did rub off on me sometimes."

"If this isn't related to the shooting, then who'd want to abduct you?" Logan asked.

Erin shrugged her shoulder. Her hands shook as she raised a can of soda to her lips. Logan fought off the urge to move to the chair beside her and take her hand.

"What about an angry ex-boyfriend?" Captain Connelly suggested.

"I haven't been in a serious relationship since Ben," she answered, but looked at Logan as she spoke. "What men I have gone out with have all been friends or co-workers."

Logan thought back to the reenactment they'd done in the alley. The shelter was only a block and half from where he'd been shot. Then there had been the robbery at the restaurant, and now this. Things were beginning to add up in a way that made him very uncomfortable. "That leaves work."

"She's a physical therapist, Sinclair."

"Exactly." He looked over at the captain. "We've been looking at this thing all wrong. That SUV in the alley was waiting for Erin. And I wouldn't be surprised if the robbery two weeks ago is also somehow connected."

Erin glanced up and her eyes widened. "Wha...what are you talking about?"

Logan moved from the desk and stood between them. "Think about it. That SUV was parked so that the back entrance of the shelter was in plain view."

"But I usually don't go to the shelter till five or five-thirty in the mornings and evenings. The only reason I was there at that time of the morning is because of the rain."

He considered her answer and didn't like what it meant. "They'd been watching you, knew your habits, the route you took home. The shelter is on the way to your house. They were waiting till you passed the alley to follow and grab you."

"But why?" she asked softly.

He could only think of one reason. "There are a lot of people who are interested in Derrick Rydell's long term prognosis, some who are betting he'll never play again," Logan suggested.

"Good point." Captain Connelly looked at Erin. "So, what is his long-term prognosis? Will he be ready to play?"

Her gaze went from Logan to the captain then back to Logan. "I've no intention of answering that question, or any others you have concerning one of my patients."

"Then how are we supposed to figure out who did this?" the captain asked.

"That's your problem." She stood, deposited the empty can in the trash, and left the room.

Logan sighed. She was infuriating, but he had to admire her loyalty. He recalled the conversation they'd had about her car accident and how Wade had pushed her to limits she never thought she'd be able to go. "I have a feeling the answer to whether or not Derrick Rydell has a future in the pros rests solely on her ability to inspire and encourage the kid to play again. And speaking from experience, I know how stubborn and persuasive she can be."

"Well, if you're right, she's in more danger than either of us anticipated. Go after her. Don't let her leave this building without protection. I'll get a ride back to the station."

Logan caught up to Erin at the stairs. "We need to talk. Let me take you home. I'll have one of the officers drop your car off."

"Look Logan, I know you have a job to do, but so do I. My livelihood is based on discretion as much as anything else. My clients need to know they can trust me."

"I realize that, Erin, and I give you my word that anything you say about your clients will be kept off the record. I just need some idea of what we're dealing with. Who wants you out of the way so badly?"

"I don't know who it could be. It's all so absurd."

"There's got to be someone or we wouldn't be having this conversation."

LOGAN SUCCEEDED IN persuading her to let him drive her home. After a quick sweep of the house, he joined her in the kitchen. "The captain ordered a patrol car to watch the house. I'll hang around until they get here."

Erin started a pot of coffee, then went and changed out of her work clothes.

The coffee had just finished brewing when she returned wearing blue jeans and a sleeveless sweatshirt. She brushed passed him, took two cups from the cabinet, then glanced over her shoulder. "Black, no sugar?"

"Right," he answered, pleased she remembered. He sat down at the table. She joined him moments later with the coffee. Her expression void, her shoulders slumped, she seemed to be carrying the weight of the world on her back. He hated seeing her like this. "You okay?"

"I'm fine."

She didn't sound very convincing. "Who would gain the most if Derrick Rydell doesn't make a full recovery?"

"You can't be serious about this?"

He crossed his arms in front of him, awaiting an answer.

She sighed, rubbing her left temple. "I don't know. I guess maybe someone who's in the running with him in next year's draft."

"I need names, Erin. Who is Rydell's biggest threat?"

"Tennessee, Dallas and Oakland were all looking at him before he got hurt. If Tennessee stays interested, he'll go number one, which means he'll be in the running with Maddox from Southern Cal, Burlap with Nebraska, and there's a new guy from Texas A&M. I don't remember his name. They're all quarterbacks."

He leaned back and took a drink of his coffee. "Do you know any of them personally?"

"No."

There had to be a connection here somewhere. "Their agents or managers...personal trainers?"

"The kid from Texas. I know his agent, Gage Washington."

"How well?"

She looked at him as she nibbled at her lower lip. Several seconds passed before she asked, "This is just between you and me?"

"You have my word."

She sipped her coffee. Several more seconds passed, as if she was debating whether or not to trust him. "I first met Washington, personally, three years ago when he was Marcus Wheeler's agent. After Marcus got hurt, he pawned him off to another agent in the firm. It devastated Marcus. That was when I lost all respect for the man. He doesn't care about the sport or the kids he represents."

"These agents make good money, don't they?"

"It depends on the deal they cut with the drafting team, but yeah. The draft is like being on the trading floor of the New York Stock Exchange. Hearts are broken and millionaires are made."

"And at the center of it all are the sports agents?" he guessed.

She nodded. "They're the middle man. They make a basic percentage of the contract with the signing team, plus endorsements and appearance fees."

He wondered if the agent would risk losing that. "How greedy is Washington?"

Her face took on an expression he'd never seen on her before—one of disgust. "Let's just say his bank account is where his heart used to be."

"Okay, he's heartless, but is he ruthless?"

Her eyes narrowed. "What do you mean?"

"How far would he go to assure his boy goes number one in the draft?"

She reared her head back, looking at him. "Are you suggesting he's behind all this?"

"It'd make sense. Derrick needs you. With you out of the way, his boy has a clear shot."

She shook her head. "Washington is a successful sports agent; he wouldn't risk his entire career over one client. Besides, you're giving me much more credit than I deserve."

"I don't think so, Erin. And I'm sure if I were to ask Marcus Wheeler and Stuart Granger, both would agree that their miraculous comebacks were due largely to your influence." He briefly recalled the first time he'd seen her special gift—the day of the cookout at the hospital—the day he'd realized just how amazing she really was.

She stood, poured a refill, and offered him some.

"Thanks." He shook the memory from his mind so he could concentrate on the present. "Any chance either of those men in the restaurant fit Washington's build?"

"No. He's a good two inches shorter than I am."

"How long has Derrick been practicing at the Cougars practice field?"

"He only recently started suiting up again, and only for a couple of hours a day. He's not one hundred percent yet, but he will be within the next four weeks."

The fact that she told him that convinced him she was beginning to trust him. At least he had that much going for him. "Who else knows that he'll be starting the season?"

"Besides Wade...only his coaches. Norm Peters, his offense coach, cornered me last week. I told him, barring any setbacks, he'd be ready."

He considered Wade briefly. He was in the position to know her whereabouts most of the time. But judging from their talk at the cookout, he'd never do anything to hurt her. "Is the field open to the public during practice?"

She sat back down. "Pretty much. It's part of the campus."

"Have you seen Washington hanging around there?"

She shook her head. "I haven't seen him for months. Not since he was sniffing around Derrick."

His almost leaped forward at the news. "Wait a minute. He was interested in representing Derrick?"

"He was until I warned Derrick not to get involved with him."

The fact she had that kind of influence on the quarterback didn't really surprise him much. He suspected they had a close bond similar to the one she had with Wade. "You mean because of what happened with Wheeler?"

She nodded.

"Does Washington know you warned Derrick to stay away from him?"

"I don't know."

He needed to talk to Derrick Rydell. If Washington did know, that made him a very good suspect. If there was a better motive than greed, it was revenge. "Can you arrange some time off, a week maybe?"

"I have people depending on me, Logan. I can't just go into hiding for a week," she said before taking a drink of her coffee.

"Then consider me as your official shadow. I don't want you going anywhere by yourself." He wasn't about to risk anything else happening to her.

She smiled for the first time since they'd left the stadium. "If I didn't know better, I'd think you were behind all this."

"I want to get to know you better, but not like this."

She let out a heavy sigh. "This really sucks, you know it? Just when things were starting to come together with the youth center, this has to happen."

He'd meant to inquire about her progress today in the park, before Derrick Rydell's call. "You got the building?"

"We closed on the sale yesterday afternoon. Our first major fundraiser is in two weeks. If it doesn't go well, I'll be living at the youth center because I'll have to sell my house to make the mortgage payments."

Not as long as he was around. "What kind of fundraiser do you have planned?"

She smiled again, and this time, it reached her beautiful eyes. "An auction and dance. The winning bidders get to spend an evening dancing with their favorite sports celebrity."

"Let me guess, former patients?"

"A few," she answered proudly. "The rest are gracious teammates and cheerleaders."

"Cheerleaders?" he teased.

She laughed. "I thought that might get your attention. Would you like a ticket?"

"What's it going to cost me?"

"One hundred and fifty a ticket."

He pretended to think it over, when in fact; nothing short of World War III could keep him away. "Are you included on the list to be auctioned off?"

"Afraid not."

"Too bad, it would have been interesting to find out who my competition is."

Her blush drew a chuckle.

LOGAN TOSSED AND TURNED that night, haunted by the image of Erin sitting in the coach's office. She'd looked so frightened and vulnerable. He hated seeing her that way. He wanted back that carefree woman who'd breezed into his hospital room almost six weeks ago, the same woman who now possessed a very large portion of his heart.

He'd been over the possibilities more than a dozen times, and had come to the same conclusion each time. Whoever wanted Erin out of the way saw her as a threat. The only logical answer was Derrick Rydell and whether or not he would be starting the season. And Gage Washington seemed the most likely suspect.

Before going to the captain with his theory, Logan decided to run it past his partner. After ordering a large pepperoni pizza for lunch, he called Addison and warned him that he was on his way over.

"How's Erin?" Addison led Logan into the kitchen. "The captain said she was pretty shaken."

Logan watched as his partner grabbed some paper plates from the cabinet. "Wouldn't you be? I tell you, Addison, I don't know how she keeps it together."

"Leaning heavily on family and friends, I would imagine."

He gave up a dry laugh. "Not Erin. She's as independent as they come."

"That may be, but the woman was a witness to a shooting, an armed robbery, and was almost abducted all within a few weeks. Either she has nerves of steel, or there's someone special she's confiding in."

He immediately thought of Marcus Wheeler. According to the kids, he'd been hanging out with Erin a lot lately, working on the upcoming fundraiser for the youth center.

He stifled his jealousy; Erin had assured him there was nothing more than friendship between them. He had to believe that.

"Okay, let's hear this theory of yours."

Logan glanced over at his partner just as he grabbed a large slice of pizza. It was almost like old times. "Ever hear the name Gage Washington?"

"The sports agent?"

Logan nodded. "Gage Washington is a man who makes his living off the dreams of others. I imagine most of these college kids are pretty naïve when it comes to the real world of sports...so suppose you have a backup quarterback that's suddenly thrust into the limelight. Washington is feeding him full of talk about how he could go number one in next year's draft. There's a problem, though. Derrick Rydell's recovering a lot faster than expected. There's only one thing he can do to ensure his boy stays in the running, and that is to take away Rydell's momentum. He knows Erin's track record and can't afford to chance another miraculous recovery. So, he and the kid come up with a plan to take her out of the equation. What do you think?"

"Seems an awfully big risk for someone with a bright future ahead of him," his partner argued.

"Not if he's obsessed with going number one in the draft. You know as well as I do if someone wants something bad enough they'll do whatever is necessary to attain it."

"Why her? Why not go for the kid directly? Taking her out of the picture doesn't ensure he won't continue his rehabilitation."

"True, but it's doubtful he could find someone as hardheaded and inspirational. Plus, her turning up missing wouldn't draw as much attention as the kid's disappearance."

"Is she warming up to you yet?"

"She has a wall around her that makes breaking into a maximum security prison seem easier. I'm making progress, though. We're spending the day together Saturday."

Chapter Thirteen

Erin loaded the last box into the back of Logan's truck; glad they were almost done.

"I hope this was the last stop. I'm getting awfully hungry."

She glanced through the open window at his smiling face. It was three in the afternoon and neither had eaten since Emma had feed them donuts and coffee at nine-thirty. "I'm sorry it's taken so long. I wasn't expecting this well of a response."

"Are you going to have room for them all?"

She glanced at the truck bed full of boxes of books and flashlights. "I'll make room. You want to eat first, or drop these off?"

"Shelter first, then we'll eat. At least you'll have help unloading them."

"I will?" With the use of only one arm for lifting, she'd done most of the work. He'd done his share, though, by getting the door for her and climbing in and out of the back of the truck after securing each load.

"I phoned ahead. Joey and his pals promised to be waiting to help unload."

"Bless your heart. I'm so sore now I don't know if I'll be able to get out of bed in the morning."

"Hey, I offered to help. You wouldn't let me," he reminded

With his shoulder still on the mend, she knew he had no business lifting or carrying anything. "You did help, Logan. I couldn't have done it without you."

"You should've let me swing by and pick up Joey."

"I thought I could handle it. I was figuring on ten boxes at the most, not thirty-five."

"Well, you're not to lift another box, understood?"

"You'll get no argument from me."

As promised, Joey and his friends were waiting on the steps of the shelter when they got back, and quickly got to work unloading the materials. "Just stack them in the library. I'll unpack them tomorrow."

"You sure? We can help you put them away."

"Thanks, Joey, but not today." She'd put up with the back pain as long as she could.

While her helpers were busy in the Library, she snuck off to the office she shared with Emma and Andy. Unlocking the bottom desk drawer, she took out the prescription pain medicine she seldom took, shook out two of the pills, and swallowed them dry.

The pain had been constant since Thursday night. Not the occasional nagging pain she'd learned to deal with, but much worse. In the scuffle she'd had with her abductor, she had wrenched her back, and the workout she'd had today hadn't helped matters.

Erin heard footsteps approaching. As she went to get up, a sharp, searing pain shot up her spine, causing her to cry out.

"Erin."

She quickly recognized Patsy's voice. Shoving the pill bottle into the pocket of her jeans, she glanced up and met the worried expression of her friend. "Hi."

"What's wrong?"

Erin moved out from behind the desk. "Nothing's wrong. What are you doing here?"

"Looking for you. Wade and I are on our way to dinner and a movie. Thought you might like to join us?"

"Sorry, I already have plans." She moved passed her friend into the hallway. She waited for Patsy to step out, and locked the door.

"Are you sure you're okay?"

Erin forced a smile. "Of course, I'm fine."

Wade joined them in the dining room. "There you are. Logan said to get a move on. He's hungry."

"You and Logan have a date?" Patsy asked with a smile.

"It's not a date. Just dinner."

"Dinner and a movie, actually. You're coming with us."

Erin looked at Wade. "I can't." All she wanted to do was get something to eat and go home and go to bed.

"You can, and will."

"I'm serious, Wade; I can't sit through a movie. Not tonight."

"Logan said you'd over done it today on the lifting. Why didn't you call me? I would have helped."

"What's taking so long?" Logan asked, joining them.

"Erin doesn't feel up to a movie. How about dinner, and then picking up a video and going back to her place?"

Erin tossed him a disgruntled look. "How about dinner, period?"

"You're hurting pretty bad, aren't you?" Wade asked.

"I'm just tired." She didn't want him to fret over her any more than he already was.

"Yeah, right." Wade slipped his arm around her shoulder. "Okay, dinner it is."

ERIN BARELY MADE IT through the meal. The medication had managed to ease the pain, but had also drained her of all her energy. She could barely keep her eyes open as they left the restaurant.

She leaned back against the headrest and gazed out the windshield at the traffic in front of them. "I'm sorry I was such lousy company."

"Even half asleep, you're the best date I've had in a long time."

"This wasn't a date," she reminded.

"Oh yeah, I forgot."

She turned and looked at him. He was smiling. "Don't, Logan."

"Don't what?"

"Don't make me fall in love with you."

"Would that be such a bad thing, Erin?"

She didn't know anymore. What she did know was that she enjoyed being with him, and thought about him whenever they were apart. "It seems every time I get close to someone, God takes them away from me. I'm tired of losing people that I care about, Logan."

"I understand your anger at God. It's only natural. But sooner or later, you have to realize he didn't pull that trigger. Could he have prevented Ben's death that day? I'm sure he could have. But not without taking away the free will of those involved.

"That isn't to say He just sits back and let's evil rule. Throughout the Bible we see God using the evil of others to bring about his purpose. He takes a bad situation and turns it around for the good for those who love Him."

"I want to believe that...really, I do."

He turned briefly, reached across the seat, and took her hand. "I know it's hard for you, Erin. You've suffered a tremendous loss. But all this anger and resentment isn't doing anyone any good. It's only keeping you from using the gifts that God gave you to carry out his work. If you don't, He'll find someone else who will. So, in the long run, you're only cheating yourself."

She leaned back and closed her eyes. She thought about the Bible story of the Exodus of the Israelites from Egypt. Despite their obstinate behavior, God never abandoned them. He continued to provide for them, but they never got to see Canaan. All the original generation, except for Joshua and Caleb, died off before they were allowed to enter the Promised Land. They had cheated themselves out of their reward.

Erin felt the truck come to a stop. She opened her eyes, glad to be home.

After a quick search of the house, Logan bid her goodnight at the door. "I hope you get to feeling better."

"I'll be fine. Thank you for your help today, and for dinner."

"You're welcome. And I did have a nice time with you."

She smiled. "I had a good time, too."

AFTER ANOTHER SLEEPLESS night, Erin called Wade Monday morning and told him he'd better get someone else to cover her appointments for a couple of days. Usually able to work through her pain, the uncharacteristic behavior caused some alarm.

"This is more than sore muscles, Erin." His concern was evident in his voice. "Promise me you'll go in for an MRI."

"I have an appointment to get one done this afternoon. With the auction and dance coming up, I can't afford to be laid up in bed." She thought of all the things that still needed to be done in preparation. Then there was the work at the youth center that needed to be done before the contractor could get started.

"Good. Will you call me if you need anything?"

She gave a dry laugh. "I've got a cop practically perched on my door step. I'll be okay."

"What about Rydell? You're the only one he listens to."

"I've already talked to him; I changed his appointment to Friday."

"And Logan?"

She hated to miss their sessions, but she had no choice. "I left a message on his voice mail telling him that you'd be covering for me for a few days. I don't see any other patients till the end of the week."

"All right. Let me know if there's anything I can do."

"I will. Thanks, Wade."

"Take care of yourself, Erin."

ERIN SIGHED IN ANNOYANCE at the ringing telephone. She debated whether or not to endure the pain of answering it. Finally, she gritted her teeth, rose gingerly from the recliner, and slowly moved toward the counter.

"Erin. It's Logan, are you okay?"

She smiled. It was good to hear his voice. "I'm fine. What's up?"

"Wade said you were taking a few days off. Is your back still bothering you?"

"A little. Nothing that a couple of days rest won't cure."

"Is there anything I can do to help?"

"No, I'm fine, really." She took the cordless phone with her back to the recliner that had served as her bed for the last two nights. "How'd your session go this afternoon?"

"You were right. He's not nearly as compassionate as you are. One day, and I'm ready to fire him."

She chuckled. "You're tough, I'm sure you can handle it. How are things at the shelter?"

"Fine. Everyone missed you this morning. Emma appointed me the new dish washer."

"Sorry."

"Don't be. You just worry about getting back on your feet."

"This couldn't have happened at a worse time. There's so much I need to get done at the center. The contractor is coming next week, and I haven't even begun to get ready for him."

"It's not so bad. Nothing that a couple of afternoons of young labor can't take care of."

"Now how would you know that?" She shifted uncomfortably in the recliner, hoping to bring relief.

"Andy took me on a tour of the building this morning. He didn't think you'd feel up to doing anything with it for awhile so I told him I'd help out."

She smiled at his offer. "You're doing so much already. Besides that, you shouldn't even be using your arm yet outside of therapy."

"Don't worry, Doc. I promise I won't over do it. It's not like I'll actually be doing any of the work. I plan on using young, healthy volunteers for that."

She smiled. "You're a good man, Logan."

"I've got to do something to win you over."

"Thanks for calling."

"Get some rest. I'll call you tomorrow."

She hung up. As she shifted in the chair, tears formed in her eyes. She hadn't hurt this bad in a long time. Leaning back, she closed her eyes. She had to get her mind off the pain.

She thought of the center, wondering if she'd bit off more than she could chew. Her schedule was already full between working at the hospital, private duty, and volunteering at the shelter. Something was going to have to give.

Okay Lord, you've got my undivided attention. What do you want me to do? I love my job at the hospital and at Home Health. Even if I were to give up volunteering at the shelter, I'd still have to give up one of them so I can run the youth center.

She gave a heavy sigh and wiped the tears from her eyes. *It seems like I've been batting my head against the wall most of my life, trying to figure out your will. Wondering why my life has been filled with so much heartache and loss. I'm tired of struggling with you, Lord. Questioning you at every turn. I've always followed your lead, even when I didn't understand your will. But it's getting harder, and that scares me. You are my Shepherd. You've always provided for me, watched over me, and protected me. I'm afraid all this anger and bitterness is driving me further away from you, and I don't want that. Help me to find my way back.*

Forgive me, Lord, for the anger that has burned inside me since Ben's death. Grant me the grace to accept the things I can't change and don't understand. Make me like a child again, Father. This I ask in Jesus' name. Amen.

ERIN BATTED HER EYES open at the sound of the phone ringing. She grabbed it from the table next to the chair and answered it.

"Did I catch you napping?"

She smiled. It was Logan, making his nightly phone call. "Yes, but that's okay. How'd your session with Wade go today?"

"He makes me appreciate you all the more. Are you doing all right?"

"I'm fine. How's the cleanup coming?"

"We should finish up by Thursday."

"I'm really grateful for all you're doing."

"It's my pleasure. So, what have you been up to? Have you watched any good movies?"

"A couple, before I lost the remote." She searched the vicinity of her chair again. It was nowhere in sight. "I've looked everywhere and can't find it."

"You sound desperate. You want me to come look for it?"

Her heart fluttered at his offer. She'd love to see him, but no way did she want him seeing her like this. "No, it'll turn up sooner or later. In the meantime, I'm catching up on my reading."

"What are you reading?"

She looked at the open Bible lying on the arm of the chair and smiled. "If you don't think God has a sense of humor, you ought to try spending a few days alone with Him."

"You're reading the Bible?"

"The book of Judges."

"Why the book of Judges?"

"I've been thinking about what you said the other day, and about how God uses the evil of others to accomplish His purpose. I know that Ben saved a lot of lives that day, but it's still hard to swallow that God could have prevented it, but didn't. Free will or not."

"As hard as it is to accept or understand the events of that day, you have to have faith the ripples of that day will far outweigh the losses. And that God does, if we allow Him, bring some good out of everything bad that happens. For instance, remember the stoning of Stephen. Who was one of the official witnesses to his death?"

"Saul, later called Paul," she answered.

"Who, just a short time after the stoning of Stephen, was met by Jesus on the road to Damascus, and later became the greatest missionary of all time. Who knows what impact Stephen's murder had on Paul subconsciously. How Stephen's final words may have gnawed at him. And Paul himself could serve as a poster child for adversity. Look at how many times he was thrown into prison, and how God used Him even then."

She thought of the letters that Paul wrote from behind bars, the impact they'd had on the lives of others. She then thought of the accident that nearly paralyzed her, how she drew on the experience to encourage others. "You know the verse in the Bible, 'Be still and know that I am God'. Well I think these past couple of days has been God's wake up call to me. A crude reminder of how very fortunate I am."

"Have you gotten the answers you've been searching for?"

"No, but He's got my attention. It's time I stop screaming at Him and start listening."

"Does this mean you're no longer mad at Him?"

"Let's just say I'm working on it. Sort of like anger management classes. It's a gradual process, but eventually, I'll graduate."

"Hang in there, Erin."

"Thanks, Logan." As she hung up, she looked down at her left hand and the wedding ring she still wore. Without hesitation, she took it off and placed it in the drawer of the table. It was time to move on.

LOGAN WAITED TILL LATE Thursday morning to drop by Erin's. He'd wanted to go by sooner, but sensed from their phone conversations it'd be better to give her a few days of much needed rest. She answered the door dressed in gray sweats, a white sweatshirt, and fuzzy booties. One glance at the living room and it was obvious she wasn't any better.

"Your housekeeper on vacation?" he teased, hoping to draw out a smile. It didn't work. He followed her into the kitchen. She was moving very slowly. It was obvious she was in a lot of pain.

"How much longer am I gonna have to put up with that brute of a man you call a friend?"

She eased herself down in a chair. "Hopefully just tomorrow. I have an appointment after a while for an epidural."

Wade had confided in him yesterday about the severe pain she sometimes experienced, which usually brought her life to a complete standstill. But until he saw her open the door a while ago, he hadn't realized just how miserable she was. The vacant look in her eyes told him everything he needed to know. He should have ignored her repeated *I'm fine* replies the last three days, and persisted she go to the doctor sooner. Well, she had managed to fool him once. It wouldn't happen again.

He sat down across from her. "Is this flare up because of Saturday, or that day in the parking lot?"

"Insult to injury on both accounts. Remember the basketball game at the fire station? I took a hard fall. I hate to admit it, but I'm not as agile as I used to be." She was putting up a brave front, but he wasn't buying it.

"I know what you mean. It's tough to accept we're getting old."

She shifted in her chair and her discomfort immediately registered on her face. She covered it up brilliantly with a breathtaking smile. "How's everyone at the shelter?"

"Fine. They all miss you." He got up and helped himself to two cartons of juice from the refrigerator.

"And Bobby?"

"Tough as nails. Doctors released him to go back to work next week." After handing her one of the juices, he sat back down.

"Thanks for taking over for me in the mornings."

It hadn't been the same without her. The place seemed almost lifeless in her absence. "Glad to do it. Listen, Erin. If it's okay with you, I'd like to take you to your doctor's appointment. Afterwards, if you feel up to it, I'll treat you to dinner."

"Anything but soup."

"How about a steak?" he offered.

She smiled. This time, it was genuine. "I would hug you if it didn't hurt so bad to get up."

Her words were a painful reminder of just how miserable she was. He wished he could do something, anything to ease her pain. "You know asking for help isn't a sign of weakness."

"I know. Bad habits are hard to break, though."

He suspected she was referring to her childhood. "How long were you in the system, Erin?"

She crossed her arms in front of her. "From the time I was almost nine till I was fourteen and legally adopted."

"What happened to your parents?"

"I'd rather not talk about this, Logan." She shifted in her chair, her eyes fastened on the opened newspaper.

It was maddening how she always kept him at a safe distance, as if she was terrified to reveal too much of herself. Well, he wasn't giving up. He was just as stubborn as she was. "Please. I'd like to know."

She glanced up. "Why, so you can feel sorry for me? I don't want your sympathy."

"I don't feel sorry for your circumstances. They've made you who you are today...someone who has affected the lives of probably hundreds of kids."

She returned her attention to the newspaper, without answering him.

Whatever happened to her parents had left scars that still hadn't healed. Although she didn't seem like the type who dwelled on the past to the point it prevented her from moving on with her life, he did suspect that a lot of her inner turmoil with the Lord derived from it. "You know the ones God uses most often go through more fire than the rest of us."

She seemed about to say something, but then stopped.

"Do you know anything about pottery?" he asked as an illustration quickly came to mind.

"No, but I have a feeling you're fixing to give me a lesson in it," she snapped.

He smiled. He'd hit a nerve and, as usual, her first defense was sarcasm and anger. "Well, the potter begins with a lump of clay that is hard and unyielding. He kneads and pounds it to make it pliable. He then places the clay on his wheel and begins to turn it. As it's going around, he pours water over it. He then carefully places his hands on both sides of the clay, applying just the right pressure to force the clay to rise up and take shape.

"It is the potter, not the clay, who determines the outcome. The potter then cuts away the excess clay and begins to mold it into a vessel that makes it unique from all his other pieces. When finished, he places it in a kiln. The fire is what strengthens the vessel, and the potter knows just how much heat the vessel can endure."

Erin choked back a sob. He leaned over and wrapped his hand around hers, quick to notice she was no longer wearing her wedding ring. "God uses our fiery trials to make us strong so we can help others. But in the middle of the fire, the Lord is with us, reaching out through those around us."

"Well, I'm ready to be taken out of the kiln. I don't know how much more fire I can withstand," she said softly.

He fought the urge to take her into his arms. He'd never seen her look so vulnerable. "Tell me about your parents, Erin."

She looked up; he saw tears forming. "My parents and a brother and sister were killed in a house fire when I was eight." She raised her hand to wipe away a stray tear. "I don't have any memory of it, though. I can barely remember my family. I remember having a brother a year or two older, and I remember a little sister, but I don't remember much about them. I don't even know what their names were. The only memory I do have is waking up in the hospital with a broken arm and concussion and being told I no longer had a family."

He swallowed hard. He understood now her bitterness toward God. He doubted there were many Christians who could go through what she'd been through with their faith still intact. "You had no other family?"

She took a drink from her carton of juice before answering him. "I had an uncle. I don't really remember him either. He was single and didn't really want to take on the responsibility of raising someone else's kid. So I became a ward of the courts. At least that's what I was told by my first foster family."

"The photograph in the living room isn't of your parents?"

"My adopted parents—Walter and Julia Brannon—they were wonderful people." She hesitated briefly as she looked at him. "I wish you could have met them."

Her comment gave him hope that she cared more for him than she was willing to admit. He squeezed her hand gently. "I suspect I will someday."

She grinned. "What makes you think they were Christians?"

"Just a hunch." After a childhood like hers, it was a wonder she even believed in God. It would have taken some special people in a close walk with the Lord to convince someone of such.

"You remind me of them sometimes. They had a strong faith, too," she said, confirming his suspicions.

"I credit my parents for that. They insisted upon daily devotions and being active in the church."

"Tell me more about your family, Logan. I've met your mom, of course. She's a wonderful woman."

"She said the same thing about you." He gave her hand another squeeze. "I have two siblings. A brother, Robby, who owns a construction business in Dallas, and a sister, Stephanie, who lives in Germany with her husband, Danny, that's in the Army. You'll love Steph. You and she have a lot in common. She's a fitness nut, and avid biker."

"I like her already." She took another drink of her juice, then glanced down at their intertwined hands. "Does she visit often?"

"Not often enough. We talk on the phone at least once a week, though."

"So, are you the middle child?" She began to move her thumb back and forth over his knuckle.

"Yeah." He tried hard not to smile. Deep down, he sensed she was finally giving into her feelings for him. Why else would she have asked about his family? "Steph is three years younger, about your age. Tom is six years older."

"Do either have children?" she asked softly.

"Steph has three kids. Robby isn't married."

She glanced up at him. "So, why aren't you married?"

He hesitated at the unexpected question and searched his mind for a clever answer. "Mom says I'm too picky," was the best he could come up with.

Erin grinned. "Are you?"

"I don't think so. I just want someone who gets me." *Someone like you.*

"You know, you were right about my childhood. I mean, that it's made me who I am." She hesitated briefly as if reconsidering what she'd just said. "Don't get me wrong, I wish I hadn't lost my parents and siblings in that fire, but I feel fortunate because of the way things turned out. A lot of kids aren't as lucky as I was in being adopted by good people."

"You're referring to Joey and the other kids at the shelter?" he guessed.

"Joey's had a rough go of it, that's for sure. When he first showed up at the shelter, he wouldn't talk to anyone, not even me. It took me weeks just to get a smile out of him. Andy and Emma have been good for him."

"Not to mention the effect you've had on him." From the beginning, he'd sensed a close bond between them—almost as close as a mother and child.

"I should go shower. Make yourself at home. I'll try not to be too long."

He helped her out of her chair and watched as she slowly walked from the kitchen. He prayed the procedure she was having done would help ease her pain.

While Erin showered and dressed, Logan did up the sink full of dishes and picked up the living room. His thoughts lingered on their talk, and how open and at ease she'd been toward the end. He was slowly making progress in getting her to trust him. He thought of Joey. The two were so much alike. Their tough exterior hid their vulnerability well.

"You're hired."

He turned and found her smiling. God, he'd missed that smile. "Are you sure? I'm expensive."

"On second thought."

She started to move past him, but he caught her hand. "I'd settle for that hug you mentioned earlier."

Without hesitation, she stepped into his open arms, wrapping hers around his waist. "Thank you for stopping by, and for the phone calls."

"You're welcome." He gazed down at her. The vacant look was still present, but her color had returned.

"We better get going. Tom is slipping me in between surgeries."

"Tom?"

"Dr. Thomas Duncan. You remember him; he's the guy that dug the bullet out of your shoulder. He's also Candice's boyfriend, and my latest in a long line of orthopedic surgeons."

Lord, please be with the doctor today. Use him to bring relief from the pain.

Chapter Fourteen

Logan eased Erin down in a chair in the waiting room. "Can I get you anything?"

"No, thank you. You don't have to wait around Logan. It usually takes a couple of hours. I'll give you a call on your cell phone when I'm ready to go."

"I've got nowhere else to be." He sat down across from her

"Suit yourself." She picked up a sports magazine and thumbed through it, keenly aware that his eyes were still fixed on her. She thought back over the last three days. His daily phone calls had been like a lifeline to her, bringing joy to an otherwise dismal time. He was proving to be a very dear friend.

"This must have been pretty tough on Ben."

She looked at him. "Excuse me?"

"I'm guessing this isn't the first time you've dealt with chronic pain to this extent. It must have been hard for Ben to see you suffer so much."

She lowered her eyes back to the magazine, avoiding his searching eyes. "I suppose." The truth was, at times it had been an awful strain on their marriage. Pain had a way of bringing out the worst in people, and she was no exception.

"I imagine he felt pretty helpless. Probably similar to how you felt dealing with the dangers associated with his being a cop."

Was he ever going to give up in his pursuit? She decided to play along. "Are you just making conversation, or do you have a point to make?"

He grinned. "My point is, how was his worrying about you any different than your worrying about him getting hurt on the job?"

"The difference is, I'm sitting here and he isn't."

"Death can just as easily happen to you, Erin. You were almost killed in that car accident in college," he reminded. "That night in the alley, if you hadn't been paying attention, you could have been run over and killed. And then there's the robbery and attempted abduction. If someone hadn't intervened, what do you think your chances would've been of staying alive?"

He made a valid point. One she had no argument for. "You're getting better at this."

"Erin. You ready?"

Erin glanced up at her friend, Candice, quick to notice the surprised look on her face at seeing she wasn't alone. "As ready as I'll ever be."

Logan stood, offering his hand. He gently pulled her to her feet.

"In case I'm not my usual charming self when I come out, thanks for bringing me."

He smiled. "That's what friends are for."

"HOW BAD IS IT, ERIN?" Tom stood over the gurney in his surgical scrubs and mask.

"Much worse than it was six months ago." The last time she'd had the procedure done.

"The MRI shows a lot of swelling. What brought it on?"

"I took a hard fall about three weeks ago while playing basketball, and some heavy lifting last weekend."

He stepped back as a nurse inserted a local anesthetic into the shunt of the IV. "You know you're not twenty-one anymore?"

"Save the commentary and just give me the shot."

He laughed. "Candice tells me you have a new friend."

"Candice has a big mouth."

"I heard that." Her friend came toward the gurney. A green surgical mask was covering the lower portion of her face and she was wearing a matching cap. "You look terrible, girlfriend."

"Thanks. Promise me you won't let Logan into recovery."

"Logan, is it?" Tom teased.

"Logan. Isn't he the cop?" Candice asked.

"Yes. And before you go jumping to conclusions, we're just friends. Anything further than that, I'm not interested."

"You looked pretty interested sitting in the waiting room."

"Promise me, Candice."

She smiled. "If you aren't interested in the guy, why would his presence in recovery matter one way or the other? If you ask me..."

Her words were lost to Erin as she gave into the darkness.

LOGAN SHIFTED HIS GAZE from the sleeping woman to the nurse standing beside the bed. "How much longer will she be out?"

"She should be coming around soon," Candice advised. "She's going to kill me for letting you back here."

He was tempted to ask why she'd think that, wondering if Erin had been talking about him, but right now none of that was important. "Will this help her pain?"

"She was given an epidural steroid injection. It'll decrease the inflammation and irritation to the nerves that are causing the back pain. Some patients notice improvement within hours of the injection; others improve over a number of days."

He had a feeling this wasn't the first time for Erin. "How often does she have to do this?"

"It varies. Usually about every six months."

That often? He shifted his gaze back to Erin. *Lord, hasn't she been through enough already?* "She said there was nothing else that can be done. Is that true?"

"I'm afraid so. She's had some of the best doctors review her case. Most are amazed she gets along as well as she does. You know she wasn't even expected to walk again?"

"That's what I hear." He recalled their rooftop discussion about the accident. She was lucky to even be alive. *Sorry Lord, it's just that...well, you know.*

"Forgive me for prying, but I get the feeling you're interested in Erin on a much deeper level than friendship."

He glanced over at her. She now stood with a hand on one hip in a very protective manner. "I suppose I am. I'm afraid it's one sided, though."

"It's because you're a cop."

"I know." He looked back at Erin. She looked so peaceful, so beautiful. "I just wish I knew some way of changing her mind."

"Well, your being here is a start," she said in a softer tone. "Whether she says it or not, I'm sure it will make an impression. In case you haven't noticed, she's real big on loyalty. As a matter of fact, you couldn't ask for a better friend."

"I'm starting to learn that. Thanks, Candice."

"You're welcome. I hope to see you around."

"I hope so, too."

It was another half hour before Erin started to awaken. He watched as she batted her eyes open, stared at the ceiling as if trying to discern where she was, then moved her head in his direction. Her eyes widened the second she saw him. "Don't be mad at your friend. I insisted."

She ran a hand back through her hair. "I didn't say anything embarrassing in my sleep, did I?"

"You mean besides the fact that you think I'm handsome and charming?" She closed her eyes and her cheeks took on a red tint. He chuckled. "I'm kidding, Erin."

"That was mean."

"It was. I'm sorry." He grinned. She looked much better than she had earlier. "Any pain?"

She shook her head. "Have you been here the whole time?"

"I didn't mind. Emma called on your cell phone; she said she'd be dropping by later this evening with the kids. Oh, and Wade wants you to call him."

She rose on one elbow. "You didn't tell him I was here, did you?"

"I just said you were asleep."

"Thank you. I love him dearly, but he's worse than a mother hen."

"Are you still up for that steak I promised you once they release you?"

She tossed him a brilliant smile. "You bet I am."

***

LOGAN WATCHED IN AMUSEMENT as Erin took the last bite of a three course meal. "How long has it been since you ate?"

She tossed him a sheepish grin. "I've been eating soup all week."

"That explains it." He pushed his piece of apple pie towards her. "Knock yourself out."

She smiled, pushing it back. "I couldn't. I'm so stuffed now I can barely breathe."

The waitress dropped off the check and asked if they wanted refills on their coffee. "No thanks, just a container for the pie. She'll be taking it with her."

"I'm not going to take your piece of pie," she argued.

"Yes, you are. You might get hungry in the middle of the night."

His generosity won him another beautiful smile. "Thank you."

"You're welcome. Listen, Erin, if you feel up to it tomorrow, I'd like you to look at some pictures I downloaded off the Internet of Texas A & M players."

"Unless they're wearing black ski masks, I'm afraid I won't be of much help."

"You saw their eyes, didn't you?"

"Yeah, but..."

"It won't hurt to look. If you feel up to it."

"All right."

THEY WERE BOTH QUIET on the drive home. It wasn't an awkward silence, but a comfortable one. Like the kind experienced between longtime friends. Erin took the time to think back over the day's events. How he'd just showed up out of the blue to check on her. His offer to take her to her appointment had come as a pleasant surprise. So much, in fact, she'd called Emma and canceled the ride she'd promised. An act that surprised her more than it had Emma, it seemed.

She thought back to their conversation in the waiting room. He'd made a good point. Her fears seemed almost ludicrous when viewed from his perspective. The one thing she was sure of was the thought of him not being a part of her life was more frightening than falling in love with a cop. She was tired of not having someone special to share her life with.

"I'll walk you in?" Logan offered, announcing their arrival at her house.

"Thank you."

When they arrived at her front door, he held out his hand for her keys. She smiled and handed them to him. Once inside, he did a quick sweep of the house while she waited just inside the doorway. "All clear. I'll call the station and have 'em dispatch a car."

"Wait." She tossed her backpack on the counter. "If you want...I mean if you haven't any plans, you're welcome to stay for a while. We could watch a movie."

He grinned. "Alfred Hitchcock?"

"Sure, why not. Popcorn?"

"You put in the movie. I'll make the popcorn."

"Deal."

She went to her DVD cabinet and began to search the titles for one she hadn't seen in a while.

"Do you have any soda?"

"There's a twelve pack of grape soda chilling in the bottom of the fridge."

She found a movie and was about to put it in when her doorbell rang.

"I've got it." He peered through the window before turning back with a smile. "It's Emma and the kids."

"Sorry."

"No problem. We'll watch the movie later." He opened the door and stepped back so they could enter.

"Hope we're not intruding." Emma moved past him into the living room. Ryan and Sammy Jo ran to Erin.

She greeted each with a hug. "You're just in time for popcorn."

"And a grape soda," Logan added.

"No soda's unless you want to baby-sit all night."

"Aw mom, you're no fun," Erin teased. She sat down on the couch. Ryan and Sammy Jo joined her.

"Bad timing?" Emma whispered, motioning toward the kitchen.

"You're fine. We were just going to watch a movie."

"We won't stay long. The kids had to see you. They've been pestering me all week to bring them over."

"We've missed you," Ryan said, snuggling up next to Erin.

Erin wrapped an arm around each of them. "I've missed you too."

"Are you feeling better?" Emma asked.

"Much. I think I'm going to take a few more days off, though, if you don't mind."

"Of course not. Everything is all set for next weekend, and with Logan and the kids pitching in, we've plenty of help. Take as much time as you need."

"Thanks. How's Bobby?"

"He's doing great. He said to say, 'hi.'"

Logan came into the living room carrying a tray of bowls filled with popcorn and bottled waters. "Hope everyone likes lots of butter."

"Yeah," the kids spoke in unison.

He handed Erin a bowl. "Soda or water?"

"Water for now. Thanks."

"Where's your popcorn?" Ryan asked.

"In the microwave," Logan said. "The second batch is always the best."

"Where did you get the bear?" Sammy Jo asked.

Erin followed the girl's gaze to the large, white bear sitting in a rocking chair next to the TV. "That's Roscoe. Logan gave him to me." She shifted her eyes to Logan. They exchanged smiles.

"Can I hold him?"

"I think he'd probably like that."

"After you eat your popcorn and wash your hands," Emma added.

Erin watched Logan reenter the kitchen.

"Has he been with you all day?" Emma asked with a grin.

"Most of it."

"Interesting. How do you feel about that?"

Erin met her sister-in-law's smirk. "He makes me laugh. He inspires me. He makes me want to love him—and that scares me."

"Don't be scared, Erin. God wouldn't have had your paths cross if there wasn't a reason. And having worked closely with him for the last three weeks, I can tell you he's a good man, and that he genuinely cares for you."

Knowing that her sister-in-law was in his corner didn't surprise her. That had been his intention when he'd gone to work at the shelter, to gain the trust of those closest to her. He'd gone to extraordinary lengths in an attempt to win her heart. "How about a game of Clue?" she finally asked of the kids, hoping to get her mind on something other than the man in her kitchen.

"Clue...do they even make that game anymore?" Logan poked his head around the corner.

Erin met his smile. "Hey, for someone who still worships Roadrunner, you shouldn't knock a classic. Besides it's gone DVD."

"I want to play," Ryan said.

"So do I," Sammy Jo sided with her brother.

"We don't want to impose," Emma argued.

"I don't mind," Logan said.

"You're out-voted, Mom," Ryan said.

Erin smiled as she watched Logan and Ryan set up the game. After a brief argument over the rules, the game got underway. Ryan turned out to be the better detective of them all, his skills prompting a good dose of teasing toward Logan.

"Hey, give me a break. I haven't played this game since I was in the second grade."

"And here I thought crime scene reenactment was your specialty." Erin joined the teasing.

He flicked a kernel of popcorn at her, bouncing it off her right cheek. The kids laughed.

Another half hour passed before Emma insisted that they needed to be getting home. Ryan was the first to grumble.

"You have school tomorrow, and I'm sure Aunt Erin is getting tired."

"Aunt Erin never gets tired. We've stayed up lots of times past midnight when we've stayed over."

"Excuse me?"

Ryan grinned sheepishly.

Erin elbowed the young boy. "There you go, getting me into trouble." She looked over at Emma, smiling. "I've no idea what he's talking about."

"Yeah, right. Come on, kids. Thank Erin and Logan for a fun evening and let's go before your dad comes looking for us."

Ryan hugged her. "Thanks, Aunt Erin, we had fun."

"You're welcome, sweetheart."

ONCE THEY'D GONE, LOGAN looked over at Erin. She was getting that look in her eyes again. "You do look pretty wiped out."

"A little. Is it okay if we watch the movie another time?"

"Sure. I'll call the station. Have them send out a car."

While he made his call, Erin gathered the dirty dishes and took them into the kitchen. He noticed she was more agile than she had been. It appeared the procedure had been successful in relieving at least some of her pain. Either that, or she was putting up a brave front again.

Logan joined her in the kitchen and helped clean up his mess. "I couldn't help overhearing you telling Emma you were going to take some more time off. Didn't the shot help?"

"It helped."

"But you're still taking off work?"

"With the fundraiser coming up and all the preparations that have to be made, something had to give, so I arranged for an emergency leave of absence from the hospital. That leaves my private duty patients in the afternoons, which I'll be able to handle with ease."

He didn't think she should be driving yet, not until she was off the pain medication. "How do you plan on getting to these afternoon appointments?"

"A police escort, I would imagine," she said with a smile. She went to the fridge, took out two sodas and handed him one of them.

"I could take you," he offered. "I've plenty of free time on my hands."

"You just want to interview Derrick."

He grinned at her perception. "It wouldn't hurt to see if he remembers anything else."

"After you get your answers, will you stay out of the way?"

"You won't even know I'm there. Afterwards, you can have a look at those photos I mentioned."

"I don't see how looking at those photos are going to help."

"Out of twenty-one witnesses, you were the only one that described the type of guns they carried. You're the best shot I've got."

"There's no pressure, though."

He sighed at her sarcasm. "All I ask is that you do the best you can. And as a reward, I'll fix you dinner."

"Dinner huh? What are we having?"

"Do you like spaghetti?"

"Spaghetti just happens to be my second favorite food."

"There, something else we have common. You see, we're destined to be together."

Instead of the usual rejection or crude response, she smiled at him. He smiled back. He was definitely wearing her down.

Chapter Fifteen

Friday afternoon, Logan took Erin to her only appointment of the day. A young Spanish woman met them at the door of the two-story colonial mansion. "Come in, Ms. Jacobs. Derrick's on the phone. He'll be with you shortly. You're welcome to wait in the family room, or you can head on to the gym."

"Thank you, Ester."

"Wow!" Logan followed Erin down the hallway. Oak floors and a mahogany staircase off the entryway almost gleamed. It reminded him of his parents' home. "Do all your patients live in mansions like this?"

"A lot of the athletes do...and then there are your trust fund babies."

He met her smile. "I'm not a trust fund baby."

"Your parents are loaded. It's the same thing."

"You don't know my parents very well. Besides, you've seen my farm."

She chuckled. "You call that a farm?"

"It has a lot of potential. Where is your imagination?"

"I'm kidding, Logan. I like your place. I think it's charming."

He stopped in his tracks and looked at her. "You do?"

"Yeah, it reminds me of *Green Acres*. You know the old sitcom."

He laughed. "I should have seen that coming."

"Yeah, you should have."

His smiled lingered. There was something different about her today. She seemed more relaxed than he had ever seen her.

"Erin. I was afraid you weren't going to make it."

Logan quickly recognized the young quarterback from television. He was dressed in shorts and a sleeveless Florida Cougars sweatshirt.

"I ran into Patsy yesterday and she said you were still out sick."

"I'm all right. Derrick, I'd like you to meet Detective Logan Sinclair. He's looking into the incident that took place last week."

"I was wondering if they'd caught the guys yet."

"We're working on it. That's one of the reasons I'm here. I need to ask you a few questions," Logan said.

"Sure. Come on back to the gym."

The room they were led to was the equivalent of a public gym that most people would pay a small fortune to utilize. It was equipped with every exercise tool imaginable, plus an assortment of weights and bar bells. "You have a nice set up here."

"Thanks. So, how can I help you, Detective?"

Logan's first impression of the young quarterback was that he was self-centered and used to having people cater to his every need. But that was just from the interviews he'd seen the kid do on TV. Now he needed to see what he was really like. "We're looking at the attempted abduction from several angles, one of them being that it's somehow connected to Erin's work. So, we're talking to everyone she works or associates with."

"Okay. I'll help in any way I can." He folded his muscular arms across his broad chest, his attention fixed on Logan.

"What can you tell me about Gage Washington?"

"According to Erin, he's a heartless scoundrel that preys on young, naïve athletes." He shrugged his shoulders. "Other than that, I can't really say much about him."

"Was he ever interested in signing you on as a client?" He already knew the answer, but wanted to hear his side of the story.

"Yeah, but Erin advised me against it." He glanced briefly at her. "She's been around, knows the ropes, so I took her advice and told him to shove off."

"Did you ever mention to him that it was Erin who'd advised you against signing?"

Derrick took a seat on the weight bench. "I don't recall giving him a reason. He was only one of about a dozen agents who've contacted me about representation."

Logan doubted he was exaggerating. The kid was the hottest quarterback in college football right now, which made him think all the more that this whole thing with Erin was connected to him somehow. "When was the last time you talked to Washington? Have you seen him around campus lately?"

"It's been a few months since I've seen or talked to him." He turned to Erin, who stood only a few feet away with her hands shoved into her back pockets. "Is he somehow involved with what happened to you?"

"We don't know, Derrick. Like Logan said, there are several possibilities."

The kid stood, hands on his hips. He seemed agitated, almost angry.

"What about any unfamiliar faces hanging around the practice field? Guys big enough to be ball players."

"No. I don't get it, why would someone want to hurt *you*?"

Logan was about to answer for Erin when she stepped forward and placed her hand on his arm. "That's enough questions. We need to get started with his therapy."

"I just have a couple more questions."

She glanced over her shoulder, "Derrick, could I get some juice please?"

He looked at her, shifted his gaze to Logan, then back to her. "Sure. How about you, Detective? Would you like something to drink?"

"No thanks."

Erin waited until Derrick had left the room before turning back to him. "I realize you're only doing your job, but I'm asking you to back off."

"Erin. I need..."

"Derrick is under a lot of pressure. He doesn't need any more on his plate right now."

"But..."

"Please, Logan."

He met her soft brown eyes. It finally dawned on him what she was doing. She was protecting him. She didn't want him knowing that her association with him had inadvertently placed her life in danger. "All right. No more questions."

"Thank you."

⁂

"ANY LUCK?"

Erin glanced up at Logan. She smiled at the sight of him standing at the stove wearing her apron. "No." So far, she'd managed to make her way through half of Texas A & M's line up from last year. "Who taught you how to cook?"

"My college roommate. He said it'd impress the girls."

"Did it?"

"Not in my case."

She laughed. "Is that a warning?"

"I've gotten better over the years, and spaghetti is my specialty."

"Well, it sure smells good." She returned her attention to the stack of photos in front of her. It was hard to imagine that a kid with a bright future would risk losing it by participating in criminal activities. But she knew it happened. Kids often got talked into doing things they normally wouldn't do when under the wrong influence.

"So, when are you going to let me take you out on a real date?"

Erin smothered a grin, pretending she hadn't heard the question. She was still getting used to having him as a friend. Flipping to the next photo, her breath caught in her lungs. She stared at the black-haired athlete with dark eyes. She'd seen him before.

She thought back to the day of the robbery, recalled the young man that had come into the restaurant a short time before the kids arrived. He was tall, muscular, early twenties, black hair with very dark eyes. "Logan, I've seen this guy."

He moved to the counter and looked at the photograph. "Where?"

"He came in about a half hour before the robbery, picked up a call-in order. There was something familiar about him. At the time, I thought maybe he was a Cougars player I'd seen on campus."

He picked up the photo and looked at the name he'd printed on the back. "Lincoln Phelps."

"He's one of the quarterbacks in the running with Derrick. I didn't remember his name until just now. The day I was playing basketball at the fire station, some of the guys were talking about him."

"Is he the one who has Gage Washington as his agent?"

She nodded slowly. Was Logan right? Was the robbery staged to get at her? Was she the one they had been after in the alley that night?

"You said there was something familiar about him. What was it?"

"I don't know. His size, the way he looked right at me when he first came in."

"Could this guy be the driver of the SUV?"

Her mind drifted back to the night Logan had been shot. The guy had black hair, but he'd also had a mustache. She thought back to her attempted abduction, and the man that had grabbed her at the restaurant. All three had dark eyes, but she couldn't be sure. "I don't know," she said softly. Her hands began to tremble.

"Come on, Erin, think. Could it be him?"

Tears formed in her eyes. "Maybe. I don't know. I mean, I can't be sure."

He stepped around the counter, pulled her up into his arms, and held her tightly against his chest. "It's okay, don't worry about it."

The solid beat of his heart reassured her, easing the fear tonight's revelation had brought. "I want to help you, really I do, but so much has happened since the night you were shot."

"Hey, look at me."

She glanced up through her tears and met his light green eyes. Her heart melted at the compassion she saw within.

"You gave us a possible suspect. I couldn't ask for more."

"You think he was one of the robbers?"

"Seems more than a coincidence that he just happened to be in that restaurant a short time before it was robbed."

As she stepped out of his arms, a sudden loneliness swept over her. She quickly shook it off and sat back down on the stool.

"You said before that the night of the shooting you were out to dinner when the hospital paged you. Right?"

"Yeah, with Marcus."

He seemed about to speak, then moved to the stove to stir the sauce.

She continued to watch him. "So, what happens now?"

"I fly to Texas and have a chat with the young Mr. Phelps, find out why he was in Florida and who his friends are."

That's what she was afraid of. Either this guy or his partner had already put a bullet in him once. "You can't do that, Logan. You haven't been released to go back to work yet."

LETHAL DREAMS

He grinned. "Is that concern I hear in your voice?"

He was gloating. He knew he'd managed to win her heart. "You're enjoying watching me crumble, aren't you?"

"It's refreshing to know we're finally on the same page." He wrapped his hand around hers. "Yesterday, watching you before you went to the doctor, I've never felt so helpless. That's when I realized that I'm in love with you, Erin."

Erin swallowed hard. She never thought she'd hear those words again, nor had she ever expected to find a man who made her so happy and frightened at the same time. With his admission, the ball was now in her court, and she wanted to be completely honest with him. "Listen, Logan. There's a part of me that wants to let you in; that wants to love you. But then I feel myself put up this wall. I'm just so afraid of getting my heart broken again."

"I understand your being scared, Erin. But I don't think it was an accident we met that night in the alley, and I don't think you do either. All I ask is that you give us a chance. Leave the rest up to God."

He was right. God had placed them together that night for a reason. "All right." She gave his hand a gentle squeeze, and thought about her next words carefully. "But I don't want you going to Texas unless Tom releases you to go back to work at full capacity."

He smiled. "I feel a conspiracy coming on."

"No. I just want the assurance that you'll be able to protect yourself if the need arises."

He lifted her hand and kissed her knuckles. "Okay."

"Great. Can we eat now? I'm starved."

MUCH TO LOGAN'S SURPRISE, the spaghetti had turned out great despite nearly scalding the sauce. He couldn't remember spending a more pleasant evening with anyone. His declaration of love surprised him. He hadn't intended to confess his feelings, fearing a rejection, but was glad he had. He had a feeling if he hadn't, he never would have known that the feelings were mutual. Though she hadn't verbally expressed her love for him, he knew without a doubt they were there. Had been for days. Her anger at God wasn't the only thing she'd been struggling with.

He glanced over at her and watched as she dried the last of the dishes he'd just washed. He knew her struggle with God presented a problem in their relationship. Being a Christian himself, it was important to him that the woman he loved be as active in the church as he was. But knowing her character and the other obstacles she'd overcome in her life, he had faith that this, too, would be conquered.

"Where would you like to go on our first official date?" Logan asked later as Erin walked him to the door.

She smiled. "I don't know. I haven't been out on a date since I met Ben...over six years ago."

"Well, what do you like to do when you aren't working?"

"I like going to the movies."

"The movies, huh?"

"But, would you mind if we waited until after the fundraiser? There are still some last minute preparations I need to tend to."

"I've waited this long, another week or so won't kill me."

She laughed. "You are coming, aren't you?"

He thought of all the ideas she'd inspired in him since first mentioning the youth center. He wanted so much to be a part of her dreams for the future. "I wouldn't miss it for the world." He leaned over and kissed her cheek. "See you Monday?"

"Thanks for dinner. It was delicious."

"You're welcome."

As soon as Logan got to his car, he pulled out his cell phone and punched in the captain's home phone number. "Good evening, Sir. It's Logan Sinclair."

"Do you know what time it is, Sinclair?"

He glanced at his dashboard clock. "Almost midnight, Sir. Mind if I drop by for a visit? We need to talk."

"Does this have to do with Erin Jacobs?"

"Yeah. I think you're right. We're going to need a lot more help."

"HOW MANY PLAYERS DO we know for sure are involved?" Captain Connelly asked Logan. For the past half hour they'd been sitting on the steps of his front porch, discussing their next move.

"One...maybe two. I also think we need to take a closer look at Marcus Wheeler." It bothered him that Erin had been with him when the hospital had paged her that night, and the fact that they'd been spending so much time together lately.

"Aren't they friends?"

"Yeah, that's why I pray to God I'm wrong."

"What's his connection?"

"I'm not sure there is a connection. I just think we ought to have a look at him, especially since, up until three years ago, Gage Washington was his agent."

"I'll have Wilson check into it. I hear you've been saving the tax payers some money by doing private security at her place. Do you know what you're getting yourself into?"

"I think so. Is there a problem?"

"The last I heard, you were still on medical leave."

"I've been meaning to talk to you about that."

"Save your breath, you aren't coming back for a good while. You need to stay as close to Erin as you can. We don't want these guys getting another shot at her."

He couldn't think of a better assignment. "What about the Texas connection?"

"I'll get someone on it in the morning. Go home and get some rest. I'll let you know as soon as I hear something."

Chapter Sixteen

"You're all in knots, what's wrong?" Erin asked of Logan as she kneaded the tense muscles of his shoulder.

"Nothing, everything's fine."

She knew better. He'd said less than a dozen words to her since their session began, which wasn't at all like him. "Don't lie to me, Logan. It's the case, isn't it? Something's happened."

He rolled over onto his side and glanced up at her. "We're bringing in more help on the case. Maybe even the feds."

"Why? I mean, why the feds?"

"Given our main suspect is an NFL hopeful, it's likely the press will get wind of it and we don't want this turning into a media circus."

She prayed that wouldn't be the case. "Is that the only thing bothering you?"

He sat up and took her hand. "Would you quit worrying? Everything is fine."

She had a feeling it wasn't. She sensed he was keeping something from her. "All right. So, how are you feeling? Have you had any pain since increasing the weight limit?"

"Nope."

"Would you tell me if you were?"

"Probably not." He grinned. "But it feels great, really."

"You're coming along better than I expected."

"Does that mean you're going to recommend an early release?"

"Whoa, slow down. You still have at least two months of therapy to get through."

"It'll be a breeze." He stood and put on his shirt. "Do you have dinner plans tomorrow night?"

She smiled. Butterflies began to flutter in her stomach. "I thought we agreed to wait until after the fundraiser to go out on a date."

"It's not really a date. My parents are having a dinner party and they asked me to invite you."

Her eyes widened at the thought of meeting his family. "Why? What have you been telling them, Logan?"

He laughed. "It's not what you're thinking. I mentioned your plans to open a youth center and they are very interested in helping. The friends they've invited are...well...very influential in the community, and they're also members of our church. They want you to discuss your ideas, some of the projects you hope to implement at the center."

"You're kidding?" It was a wonderful opportunity to rally support of the center, but no way could she be the one to do it. The butterflies in her stomach felt like hornets now.

"No." He smiled. "Why are you turning green?"

"Because I'm terrified of speaking in front of large groups," she admitted reluctantly.

"There will only be twelve, maybe fourteen, guests."

"Influential guests." She'd known there would have to be fundraisers, but had planned to get Andy to do the begging for her. He was a much better speaker than she was.

"I should have mentioned it sooner, huh?"

She gave dry laugh. "That might have been nice. Logan, not only do I not have anything to wear, I'm in no way prepared to do a sales pitch to raise support for the center."

"You're speaking Saturday night, aren't you?"

"No, Andy is." The fact that he didn't think this was a big deal made her think that he had no problem with talking in front of a bunch of people, which wasn't really a big surprise. She doubted there was little he wasn't good at—including sweeping women off their feet.

"But you wrote his speech, what you want him to say?"

"I gave him notes, and we've discussed the various projects I'd like to put into operation." She put her hands on her hips. "I'm serious, Logan; I'm no good at public speaking. The last time I spoke to a crowd of strangers was at a conference a couple of years ago and I barfed afterwards."

He grinned. "You'll do fine. Just borrow his speech or use your notes, and I'm sure you can find something to wear. With as much money as my insurance company is paying you, you can afford to go shopping for an evening dress."

She stepped away, moving her hands to her stomach. "Oh Logan, I'm already starting to feel nauseous."

"Come on, Erin, I've seen you in stressful situations. You'll get through this," he said in a gentler voice.

She smiled at his confidence in her. She could use all the support she could get for the center. But this..."I don't know. I'm nervous enough about meeting your parents."

"They're great people. You're going to love them." He closed the distance between them and took her hand. "You're nervous about meeting my parents, huh?" he asked with a mischievous grin.

"Shut up," she said, shoving him playfully.

He laughed. "There's nothing to be nervous about. Besides, you've already met my mother, and she's the tough one. My dad's a pussy cat compared to her."

"Really?"

He held up three fingers. "Scout's honor." He slipped his arm around her shoulders. "So is okay if I pick you up at six?"

She sighed. "I suppose."

"Good. You're going to have a wonderful time, I promise."

"HOW DOES THIS ONE LOOK?" After an hour of searching her friend's closet, Erin was running out of options.

"It makes you look too skinny. I'm telling you, the purple chiffon halter is perfect."

"Candice, his parents are going to be there." She should have taken the time and just went shopping, or just worn the one she'd bought for the auction.

"The neck line isn't that bad, trust me. And it has a matching shawl."

Erin grabbed the dress she suggested from the bed and held it up in front of her, glancing into the floor length mirror. She did like the fit, and the length was perfect. What was she going to do with her hair, though? "Remind me again why I'm doing this?"

"Because you've dreamed of opening a youth center for over three years, and because you want to impress your future in-laws."

"That isn't funny."

"It wasn't meant to be." Candice slipped her arm around her. "Face it, honey; you're head over heels for this guy. I've never seen you this nervous about a date before."

"I'm not nervous, and this isn't a date."

"Deny it all you want. I've known you since college and I've never seen you this freaked out about anything."

"You do know who his parents are?"

"So they're rich. You pal around with celebrities all the time. Probably could've even married a couple. Besides, his mother is a real sweet woman."

"You've met Marilynn?"

"A few years ago. She was on a fundraising committee that was raising support for *Doctors Beyond Borders*. Of course, I didn't know who she was at the time. I never would have guessed she was one of the richest women in the state of Florida."

"You're not helping."

"Would you relax? They're people just like you and me."

Erin turned back to the mirror. "What am I going to do with my hair?"

"You let me worry about your hair and makeup. You just concentrate on your speech."

LOGAN SUGGESTED DRIVING Erin's Jaguar to his parents, insisting she looked much too beautiful to be arriving in a truck. Pleased with his compliment, she made a mental note to thank Candice again for her makeover.

They drove through a gated entrance, continued on the paved road lined with palm trees, to the end of the circular drive where a beautiful Spanish style mansion stood next to an open courtyard with a fountain centered on gorgeous green grass.

"It's not as nice as the Rydells', but it's roomy."

"It's beautiful."

"It belonged to my grandfather. He bought the estate after my mom was born."

"It's quite a contrast next to your Green Acres."

He laughed as he pulled the car to a stop behind a black Lincoln. "You ready?"

"I suppose it's too late to change my mind."

"You'll do fine. Just flash one of your gorgeous smiles and you'll have them all eating out of your hands."

As they entered the foyer with gray marbled flooring, Erin stood in awe of the huge crystal chandelier that hung from the vaulted ceiling. To her left was a cream-colored, suspended spiral staircase. Next to it were three marbled steps leading up into what she guessed was the family room. To the right was a large living room with light blue carpet and modern furniture made from mostly oak and covered in a light-colored floral design.

Marilynn greeted her with a hug. "Erin, I'm so pleased you could come."

"Thank you for having me."

"Darling," she greeted her son, following up with a hug and a kiss to his cheek.

"I hope you two are hungry. Gladys outdid herself." She took Erin's hand. "Come on, I'll introduce you to everyone."

Marilynn led Erin up the marble steps, through the family room and out onto the veranda where more than a dozen men and women dressed in evening gowns and suits were either seated or standing. "Everyone, I'm pleased to introduce Logan's girlfriend, Erin Jacobs."

Erin glanced over her shoulder to see Logan standing behind her with a smile planted firmly on his face.

Before she could comment on the introduction, she was bombarded with handshakes and hugs. Along with names, she received job titles or a family connection. Among the guests were two city commissioners, an assistant to the mayor, the pastor of their church, seven business acquaintances, and several spouses. Her butterflies were quickly turning into bumblebees.

Moments later, Erin looked out from the veranda. A large garden with a variety of flowers was growing next to an 18X30 swimming pool. Its crystal blue water was enticing as the receding sun beat down on her.

"Tempting, isn't it?"

She turned and quickly recognized the man introduced as Frank Sinclair, Logan's father. "Very much so."

"It's a pleasure to finally meet you. Logan has told us so much about you we feel we already know you."

Erin smiled. She wondered just how much Logan had said about her.

"I admire your passion and vision; you're going to make a wonderful director at your youth center."

"Thank you, and thank you for this opportunity."

"You're welcome. Hopefully, with the support you gain tonight, and with the proceeds of your auction, you'll be well on your way."

"Erin, Dad, dinner is ready."

"Hope you like lamb; it's Gladys's specialty," Frank announced before stepping inside.

Logan took her hand and started to follow. She pulled him back. "I've never eaten lamb before. What if I don't like it?"

He smiled. "Then don't eat it. Afterwards, we'll stop for a burger or steak."

"NOT ONLY WILL IT BE a safe environment where the youth can interact, I hope to have a mentoring program available, as well. Most of these kids have never had any real structure in their lives. Being shuffled from one foster home to another, it's hard for them to form relationships. They're afraid to get too close to anyone because they know, sooner or later, they're going to be uprooted. A community center of their own will allow normalcy in their lives with kids who are going through the same situations they are."

Erin scanned their faces, pleased she still had their attention. Her nausea had yet to dissipate, but at least her hands had stopped shaking. She reminded herself again why she was doing this. *Lord, please get me through this without barfing.* She took a drink of water and continued.

"The work program I mentioned earlier will allow the youth to take part in something productive. It'll teach them responsibility, self-esteem, give them a goal. We hope to offer classes two or three evenings a week, taught by volunteer teachers from the college who would rotate their time, each teacher serving one or two nights a month. Anything from art to auto mechanics will be offered, depending upon the volunteers.

"This, of course, is just a rough draft of the initial programs the center would offer. What I want to express the most is the great need in this community. These children, caught in situations beyond their control, have the potential to be our future civic leaders. It is our responsibility to see that they are not forgotten, and are given the chance to develop their individual God-given gifts. It is my hope that you will consider supporting this youth center, not only financially, but also through prayer. Thank you."

Erin sat down to the sound of applause. Logan took her hand and leaned toward her. "Absolutely perfect."

"Thanks. Can I go throw up now?" she whispered in his ear.

He laughed, giving her hand a gentle squeeze.

A SHORT TIME LATER, Erin stepped out on the veranda for some fresh air. A brisk north breeze helped to settle the lingering anxiety.

"You did a beautiful job."

She glanced over her shoulder and was surprised to see Frank Sinclair sitting behind her. "Thank you. Mind if I join you?"

He motioned to the empty chair next to him. "Please do." An older version of Logan, with a full head of silver hair and a tranquil personality, Erin had taken an instant liking to the man.

She leaned back in the chaise lounge, staring back at the mansion. Though huge, and located on some of the richest land in Sheridan Springs, it was modest compared to what she had expected. They lived comfortably without flaunting their wealth. She was impressed.

"You're taking on a lot of responsibility."

"Yes, sir, I realize that. But I'm willing to do whatever is necessary to make it happen."

"What about your career? Isn't it just as important to you?"

"Yes."

"And your work at the homeless shelter?"

"I know I have a lot on my plate, and I've got some tough decisions ahead of me, but the youth center is my main priority above all else."

He crossed his legs and shifted his gaze toward the well-lit grounds beyond the veranda. "You're going to need a board of directors. Men and women who will help share the responsibilities that such an undertaking will incur."

Erin grinned, sensing the Lord's hand at work...or Logan's. "You wouldn't, by chance, know of some individuals who might be interested?"

His gaze fell on her. "I could probably come up with a few prospects for you to consider."

"That's good. I could use all the help I can get, because I have no idea what I'm doing."

"On the contrary. Taking into account your speech, I'd say you know exactly what you're doing. That's why Marilynn and I would be honored to serve on your board of directors, as well as help financially."

"I don't know what to say...except maybe thank you."

"Then you'll accept our help?"

"That is why I'm here, to beg for support. I am curious, though...did Logan put you up to this?"

He laughed. "He said you would suspect as much. No, my dear, Logan didn't even know about this dinner party till yesterday morning."

"But he did mention the youth center to you?"

"Yes, but I was already aware of your plans. You see, my secretary is a member of your brother-in-law's church. She mentioned the project a few weeks ago. Having been raised in foster care myself, I was immediately interested. I wish I'd had something like this growing up. I might not have gotten into so much trouble."

Surprised by his admission, she was temporarily at a loss for words. She never would have guessed they came from the same background. "How long were you in the system?"

"Seven years before adoption. You?"

"Five years. Did Logan tell you?"

"No. It was obvious from your speech tonight. That sort of passion and commitment comes from experience."

"There you are." Erin turned to see Logan approaching. "I've been looking all over for you. I was afraid you'd bailed on me."

"No. Your father and I have just been discussing our future partnership in the youth center."

"*Dad.*"

"What? I merely offered our help."

"Just remember this is her project. She doesn't need…"

"Logan. I don't want this to be my project," Erin said. "I want it to be a community project. I have a career that I love. If more people like your father were to get involved, I won't have to give it up."

"I was wondering how you were going to juggle all your activities," Logan said.

"So was I, but it seems the Lord already had that figured out."

Logan smiled. "So He did. Are you about ready to go?"

She stood. "Thank you for a wonderful evening, and for your generosity."

Frank got to his feet. When she offered her hand, he took it, but instead of shaking it, he pulled her in for a hug. "Thank you, my dear. You've given this old man a purpose other than making money."

She stepped out of his arms, smiling. "Don't worry, that money will come in real handy in the future."

He laughed, glancing over at his son. "You were right, she is quite a gal."

LOGAN PULLED INTO ERIN'S driveway, shut off the engine, and handed her the keys. "So, was it as bad as you thought it'd be?"

"No. I even liked the lamb."

He got out, walked around, and opened her door. "You know, you really were very persuasive tonight. I'd be surprised if you don't hear back from most of them."

She smiled. "I appreciate your parents' offer to join the board of directors. They're going to be a great asset, and I don't just mean financially."

He took her hands, gazing into her soft eyes. "I know what you mean, and you're right, their influence and experience will be very beneficial to the center."

"You know, it might come in handy to have a cop on the board of directors."

He smiled at her offer. "Thanks, but I'm more of the behind-the-scenes type a guy. Besides, I've got some ideas of my own I'm working on."

"For the center?"

"In a roundabout way."

"Care to share them?"

He thought about it. Now wasn't the time. She had enough on her mind as it was. "Not yet. But soon."

The patrol car he had called ahead for pulled up in front of the house. "Guess that's my cue."

"Thank you for this evening, Logan; I had a wonderful time."

"I'm glad." He leaned in and kissed her forehead. "I'll see you tomorrow."

Chapter Eighteen

"Erin, I think we should postpone the auction?"

"What?" She bolted upright in the bed, fully awake now. Marcus's early morning phone call had surprised her. Had it been anyone else calling her at four o'clock in the morning, she would have hung up on them. As it was, she could barely remember the first three minutes of their conversation. "Why would you want to postpone?"

"You've had three attempts made on your life. It isn't safe for you to be out in public till these guys are caught."

She couldn't postpone. There were too many kids counting on her. "The civic center will be swarming with cops; they would need an army to get at me. Besides, it's less than forty-eight hours away. We couldn't cancel now even if we wanted to."

"You say the cops will be there?"

"Yes, and knowing Logan, he'll have the National Guard on standby."

"You're getting awfully chummy with this guy. Is there something you're not telling me?"

Though their relationship had always been a platonic one, there had been a brief interest on his part after Ben had been killed. She knew his interest now was strictly out of concern, though. "I'm in love with him, Marcus."

"I thought so." She could almost hear him grinning. "So when do I get to meet this Mr. Wonderful?"

"Tomorrow night." It felt good to admit the feelings she'd been struggling with for weeks. "Oh Marcus, I never thought I'd feel this way again. I never thought I'd be able to love someone like I loved Ben. To have what we had together. Not only do Logan and I have a lot in common, he loves kids, and has really been supportive of the youth center."

"I'm really happy for you, Erin."

"Really? I was afraid you'd be...I mean I thought after Ben died..."

He laughed. "You're an attractive woman, Erin. A man would be nuts not to hit on you."

"Don't you think it's kind of odd that we didn't click? I mean, we have a lot in common too, our backgrounds, our interests. I never thought of you in that way, though."

The line went quiet.

"Are you still there?" she asked.

"I'm here," he answered.

The tone of his voice had changed; it seemed heavier now. "I'm sorry, Marcus, that was callous of me."

"No, you're right. What we have goes much deeper than physical attraction." There was another brief lull before he spoke again. "Listen, Erin, no matter what happens, I want you to know that you're very special to me, and I would do anything in the world for you."

His words prompted tears. "Likewise. Now I'm hanging up before I start bawling. I'll see you tomorrow night. Remember, you're picking me up at the shelter."

"All right... Hey Erin, be careful, okay?"

"I will."

LOGAN GLANCED UP AT Erin as she wrote in her notepad. For some reason, she wasn't as cheery today. Lowering the barbell onto the stand, he sat up on the bench, still looking at her. He never grew tired of watching her. He especially enjoyed the amusing expressions she made. The way she would nibble at the inside of her lower lip when she was deep in thought...like she was doing now.

"So how am I doing, Doc?"

"Remarkably well. Still no pain?"

"The only pain I have is trying to figure out your moods."

She glanced over the top of her notepad, smiling. "You're supposed to be concentrating on your workout, not on me."

"Can I help it if you're so distracting?"

She grinned. Stepping toward him, she laid her pad on the bench beside him. "Let's test your resistance."

He held out his arms. "You seem a little anxious today. Anything wrong?"

She pushed against the outside of his hands. "It's nothing."

"It's something or you wouldn't be gnawing at your lip. Keep it up and you're going to look like a sucker fish tomorrow night."

She sighed. "It's just that I got the strangest phone call from Marcus this morning wanting to postpone the auction."

"Postpone...why?"

"He's worried that something will happen."

"There's no need to be frightened, Erin. Someone makes a move on you and they'll have half the department on top of them in a second."

"I know. I'm not worried about that."

"Well, what are you worried about?"

"I don't know."

"What exactly did you two talk about?"

Her crimson cheeks made him grin. They'd talked about him. He would have liked to have heard that conversation. "Does he not approve of us seeing one another?"

"It wasn't that either. I don't know, Logan, there was just something unsettling about it, is all. It's not that big of deal. Forget I mentioned it."

Her sharp tone made him think it was a big deal. He thought back over what she'd said so far. Why would Marcus want to postpone the auction on such short notice when it had been his idea to have it in the first place? He made a mental note to call Captain Connelly and see if Wilson had found out anything on the pro wide receiver.

"I'm sorry I snapped at you, Logan. I'm just nervous about tomorrow night."

"That's all right, don't worry about it. So, are we done here?"

"We're done." She leaned over and picked up her notepad. "What do say we move it up a notch next week? Do you feel comfortable with that?"

"We are talking about my rehab?" he teased.

She laughed. "You're incorrigible."

He walked Erin to the door. "Guess I'll see you tomorrow night."

"Is it okay if I meet you there? I promised Marcus I'd ride with him. We want to be sure and get there early enough to make sure everything is set up and that the sound system is working okay."

"As long as you save a dance for me."

"You're at the top of my dance card, just as a boyfriend should be."

He grinned sheepishly. "Sorry about that. I had no idea my mother was going to introduce you like that."

She shrugged her shoulder. "It did have a nice ring to it." Before he could reply, she was out the door. "See ya," she yelled over her shoulder.

He watched her skip down the steps toward the blue Jaguar. Tomorrow night couldn't get here fast enough.

He went into the living room and picked up the cordless phone. After punching in the captain's cell phone number, he took a seat on the sofa.

"I was wondering if you were ever going to get back to me," Captain Connelly said.

"Did Wilson find out anything on Wheeler?"

"Only that he's a standup citizen. No drugs or alcohol in his past. No assaults. Other than a speeding ticket last year, the guys squeaky clean."

He was glad of that, but for some reason, Marcus had spooked Erin. He wanted to know why. "Do me a favor and have him dig deeper. I've got a bad feeling about this guy."

"It's called jealousy, and it doesn't suit you, Sinclair."

"It's more than that, Captain. He phoned Erin this morning wanting to postpone the charity auction that he, himself, instigated. I don't know, there's just something about him that isn't kosher."

"All right, we'll see what we can find."

Chapter Nineteen

"Looking good, Mrs. J," Joey complimented as he came into the recreation room.

"Why thank you, Joey." She smoothed her hand over the light blue evening gown she'd purchased for the occasion. It had cost her a small fortune, but it was worth it. Tonight was going to be a very special night.

After glancing briefly at her watch, she looked toward the door. Marcus was due any minute. Andy and Emma had gone on ahead to the Civic Center, leaving her in charge of giving last minute instructions. She turned back to Bobby. "I wish you were coming, too."

"Sorry, I seemed to have misplaced my tux," he said with a smile. "Besides, someone's gotta hold down the fort."

"Don't worry, Mrs. J. I'll make sure he stays out of trouble," Joey said.

"Who's going to make sure you stay out of trouble?" she teased.

"Probably the cop standing guard outside."

"No, I'm pretty sure he'll be coming with me, although you're welcome to keep him here."

"I think he better come with us," Marcus spoke from the doorway.

Erin greeted him with a smile.

"Hey, beautiful." He leaned over and kissed her cheek.

She stepped back and looked him over. "I'd forgotten how handsome you look in a tux."

"Let's hope you aren't the only lady there tonight thinking that."

"Oh, I think you can put your worries to rest. You'll be beating them off with a stick."

182

LETHAL DREAMS

ERIN PEERED OUT AT the gathering crowd. The turnout was better than she'd hoped for. She saw Candice talking to Marcus. Her friend looked up and Erin waved at her. She then spotted Logan near the end of the stage and smiled. He looked great in his tuxedo, just as she had imagined he would. Stepping back from the curtain, she went over the last minute preparations in her head. There was just one more detail to check.

She waved down one of the stagehands and asked for a printed list of the celebrities. Having gotten sidetracked with the specifics, she had over looked the minor details.

He reached into his inside pocket and handed her one.

Emma joined her. "It's a wonderful turnout."

"Yes, much better than I expected." She scanned the list of celebrities to be auctioned off. Her eyes widened at the sight of her own name. She turned to Emma. "Did you see this?"

"What?"

"My name has been added to the list."

"You're kidding, really?"

She looked at the list again. Marcus's name had been omitted and hers added. She immediately thought of the conversation she'd had with Logan a few weeks ago. "You knew about this didn't you? He put you up to it?"

"I have no idea what you're talking about." Emma snatched the list from her hand. "You're the one who dropped off the list at the printers."

"Yes, but my name wasn't on the list I dropped off."

"Well, I had nothing to do with it. Bobby's the one who picked them up."

"Did you see this list?" Andy asked, joining them.

"Yes, I saw the list." Erin poked her head through the curtain. "Where's Logan. I saw him just a minute ago."

Andy laughed. "You've got to give the guy credit for his imagination. This is going to be a memorable first date."

※

"ONE THOUSAND," A FAMILIAR male voice bid from the side of the stage where Erin stood on the runway. She glanced over through teary eyes to find Marcus smiling at her. She continued to laugh, awaiting Logan's next bid. The whole room was in laughter at the two caught in a bidding war.

"I have a thousand; the bid is a thousand. Do I hear eleven hundred?" Andy asked, his own amusement heavy in his voice.

"Eleven hundred," Logan hollered from left stage.

"Fifteen hundred," Marcus counter offered.

"We have fifteen hundred; do I hear sixteen?"

"Twenty–five hundred," Logan bid.

Hushed whispers went up throughout the room.

"The gentleman bids twenty-five. Do I hear twenty-six? Twenty-five...do I hear twenty-six. Going once, going twice...sold to the gentleman at left stage for twenty-five hundred."

"Who did you say you were?" one of the cheerleaders asked Erin as she exited the stage.

Erin was laughing so hard she couldn't answer.

Emma quickly rescued her. "That's one way of guaranteeing that you won't change your mind."

"He's just lucky I didn't bring my platinum card," Marcus commented, joining them backstage. He slipped his arm around Erin's shoulder. "Either he's got a mean jealous streak or he's nuts about you."

"I think it's a little of both," Emma said with a wink.

LOGAN SCANNED THE CROWD again for Erin. The auction was over, the band was beginning to play, and there was still no sign of her. Then, he saw them. Up until that moment, Marcus Wheeler had been one of his favorite NFL players, but seeing him with his arm draped across Erin's shoulder had a sobering effect on him. What bothered him more was the smile planted on Erin's face.

They looked so natural together, like they'd been friends for life instead of only a few years. He could tell just by watching that there was a strong bond between them.

"Sizing up the competition?"

Logan turned and found Andy approaching. "Is it that obvious?"

The pastor chuckled. "Don't worry, they're strictly friends."

"You sure about that? They seem much closer."

"If you'd gone through what those two have been through together you'd know the bond they share goes much deeper than the usual friendship."

"His football injury?"

"And Ben's death. I hate to think what may have happened had he not been there for her. As you probably know by now, Erin doesn't give up much of herself without a fight."

"I know. It's like chipping away at a concrete wall with a butter knife."

Andy laughed. "I couldn't have said it better myself. Erin has a handful of close friends, but I think Marcus is the only one she really confides in."

"Sort of like Joey and Erin's friendship?"

"Exactly. They all share the same bond, that feeling of abandonment, the sense of not belonging anywhere."

"Marcus was an orphan?"

He nodded. "I don't know his whole story, but I know he was in foster care growing up."

"So was my dad. He and Erin clicked right away. I guess that's why."

"I would imagine. It's like when I go to a pastor's retreat. I never have a problem making new friends. We all share the same stories."

"Hey, are you going to stand around here talking all night or are you going to ask me to dance?"

Logan turned at the familiar voice and smiled at his date. "Believe me, I have every intention of getting my money's worth out of you. You've cost me a small fortune."

"Money well spent, I assure you," Marcus said.

"Marcus...Logan Sinclair."

Marcus offered his hand. He was much bigger in person. "It's nice to meet you, Logan. Erin has said a lot of good things about you."

"Likewise. Thanks for letting me off easy."

Marcus laughed. "You two enjoy your evening." He turned and kissed Erin on the cheek. "I'll catch up with you later."

Logan watched as he made his way through the crowd. He couldn't shake the feeling that the man was hiding something.

"Any idea how much we brought in?" Andy asked.

"I haven't heard the total yet, but it's better than we'd hoped for."

"Did you really have any doubts?" Logan challenged.

"Maybe a few, but I shouldn't have."

He took her hand. "Come on, let's dance."

MUCH TO ERIN'S SURPRISE and pleasure, Logan proved to be a skillful dancer. The modern steps she managed to keep up with him, but when the band switched to classical, she ended up stepping on his toes a few times.

After the fourth time, she giggled with embarrassment. "Sorry, I'm a little out of practice." Plus, she was a nervous wreck.

"Don't worry about it. Next time I'll just have to remember to wear steel-toed shoes."

The hint of many more dates made her heart flutter. "Are you sure you'll be able to afford them after tonight?"

"You are definitely the most expensive date I've ever had." His hand slid further down her back, drawing her even closer.

She grinned. "Serves you right for having me placed on the list."

He leaned back, his eyes narrowing. "What are you talking about?"

For a second, she thought he was fibbing, but his puzzled expression said otherwise. "You didn't have my name added to the list?"

"How could I have done that?"

She looked into his eyes and knew he was telling the truth. "Well, if it wasn't you, who did?"

"My guess would be the guy who thought of the idea in the first place," he answered, seemingly amused that the plan had backfired.

"Why would he do that?"

"Revenge probably, for taking his girl."

She laughed. His jealous streak was endearing.

"Oh, you think that's funny, do you?" He pulled her closer, wrapping his arms around her.

Her smile lingering, she slipped her arms around his neck and met his gaze. "And here I thought you planned all this out as our official first date."

"Sorry to disappoint you, I was thinking more along the line of a candle lit dinner followed by a good mystery."

"I could go for that."

"Tell me, is there some sort of rule that you have to be officially dating before a guy can expect a kiss?"

"I certainly hope not," she replied boldly.

"Well, in that case." He lowered his lips to hers.

Butterflies fluttered in her stomach at the gentleness of his touch. Her heart raced as she eagerly kissed him back. Being in his arms, feeling his arms around her, the taste of his breath, it felt more natural than she ever would have imagined. And she knew in that instant she was where she belonged.

Erin ended the embrace just in time to see Candice pushing her way through the crowded dance floor. "Erin, sorry for the interruption—hi, Logan—Erin, you need to come quick. Marcus has been hurt."

Erin stopped dancing. "What?"

"Someone's beat him to a pulp. One of the officers found him outside in the parking lot. He's refusing treatment until he sees you."

"Oh, no."

Logan slipped his arm around her. "Take us to him."

Chapter Twenty

Erin exited the building and ran to the awaiting ambulance. She climbed in after Candice, Logan right behind her with his hand resting gently at the small of her back.

"Erin, you're all right," Marcus managed in between labored breaths. He looked like someone had taken a bat to him. Both of his eyelids were swollen, his right cheek bruised, his lip busted, and from the sound of his breathing, a broken rib had punctured a lung.

Erin took his hand, careful of the IV. "I'm fine. Who did this to you?"

"No time...to explain." He squeezed her hand. "I'm so sorry." He looked at Logan. "Get her out of here...she's..."

"We're losing him, people," one of the paramedic's advised.

Candice practically shoved them from the ambulance. "I'll call you as soon as I can," she promised, closing the door.

"Where'd you park?" Erin asked Logan. She searched the parking lot for his truck, but didn't see it.

"I'm sorry, Erin, but I'm not letting you go to the hospital. It's not safe."

"I have to go, Logan. He's got no one else."

"Listen to me, Erin." He took her hands into his. "Whoever did this to him will anticipate you going to the hospital. So, until we can secure it, you're coming with me."

"Where?"

"Somewhere you'll be safe."

"YOUR PARENTS' HOUSE! You've got to be kidding me."

Logan glanced over at her. She didn't look too pleased. He punched in the entry code and the large, steel gate swung open. "They have a state of the art security system, the estate is surrounded by a 10 foot rock wall, and a private security company patrols the neighborhood regularly. You'll be safe here." He drove on through, looking in the rearview mirror to make sure the gate closed behind him.

"Why are they doing this, Logan? Why don't they just shoot me and get it over with? Why do they keep hurting my friends?"

"I don't know, Erin, but we'll get them. One of the officers was able to get a partial plate; we should be able to get a match." He pulled his truck to a stop in front of the courtyard. "Do you know where Marcus was going?"

"I assume he just stepped out for some fresh air. He gets claustrophobic in enclosed places where there are a lot of people."

She looked as if she could start crying any minute. He scooted over and slipped his arm around her. She snuggled against him for several minutes, but the tears never came. "You ready to go in? I'll make you some hot chocolate."

"I'd rather go to the hospital."

"I know. Tomorrow, I promise."

"What if he doesn't make it?"

He took her trembling hand and gave it a gentle squeeze. "He'll make it. You have to believe that, Erin."

She leaned back and met his gaze. "I wish I had your faith, Logan."

"Don't worry. I have faith enough for the both of us." He leaned over and kissed her forehead.

"I love you, Logan," she said softly.

He smiled. Oh, how he had longed to hear those words. "I love you too, Erin. More than I ever dreamed possible." He pulled her into his arms. Several seconds passed before he was able to turn her loose. "Come on. Let's go get that hot chocolate."

THROUGHOUT BREAKFAST, Erin barely spoke a word, and her plate looked almost untouched.

"I'm sure Gladys would be happy to fix you anything you'd like to eat," Marilynn said from one end of the table.

"No. This is fine," Erin replied quickly. "It's really delicious. I'm just not very hungry."

Logan had chosen the spare bedroom right across from the room she'd been given, and had heard her off and on throughout the night talking on her cell phone to the hospital. Though Marcus made it through the surgery that repaired his damaged lung, he was still listed as critical.

He knew she wasn't pleased with the idea of staying with his parents, but he didn't know where else to take her. His parents, of course, had welcomed the idea, hoping to get to know her better. They'd known for weeks now his growing attraction toward Erin, and were pleased that he had finally found someone to share his life with. His sister, of course, had been the first to learn that he was in love, their weekly phone calls becoming even lengthier than usual. It was at her prodding that he'd been more patient in his pursuit of Erin, and more honest about his feelings. He wished she were here now.

Of his two siblings, Stephanie had always been the one he could confide in, the one he always turned to when he had a problem. Although younger, her faith was much stronger, and no matter what the obstacle, she had the ability to make him believe it wasn't as bad as it appeared.

Logan's cell phone rang and he reached for it under the scrutiny of his mother's eyes. No cell phones at the table was a cardinal rule he seldom broke. "Sorry, Mom," he murmured before excusing himself from the room.

He stepped into the hall. "Sinclair," he answered.

"It's Connelly. How's Erin?"

"Still insistent on going to the hospital."

"I've posted three guys. One at the main entrance, one on the floor he's been moved to, and one at his door."

"Okay. Did you get a match on the plates?"

"They came back stolen. And no one's heard from Washington or Phelps in over a week."

"That it?"

"No. Are you someplace where you can talk?"

He moved further down the hall and stepped into the library. "I am now. What's up?"

"Wilson's been doing some more digging. Seems Wheeler had a gambling problem a few years back, was mixed up with some pretty rough guys.

The commission was even looking at him for a while, suspected he may have bet on some games. Nothing was ever proven, though."

Was Marcus back to his old habits? It was no secret he and Erin were good friends. Was he taking part in Washington's scheme to pay off a gambling debt? "I don't like this, Captain."

"I know. Why don't you talk to Erin? See what you can find out, and get back to me."

"All right." He closed his cell phone, turned, and looked out the window. He thought about what the captain had said. If it turned out Marcus was involved, Erin was going to be devastated.

"Logan." He glanced over his shoulder to find Erin standing in the entryway. "Was that the hospital?"

"No, it was Captain Connelly."

"Any luck on the plates?"

"They came back stolen."

"Same as the SUV in the alley."

"Yeah. We'll get them, though, Erin. It's just a matter of time."

"I know you will." She folded her arms across her chest, her gaze still holding his. "Your mom said I could borrow some more of your sister's clothes. After I shower, I'm going to the hospital whether you like it or not. I'll call a cab if I have to."

He smiled at her ultimatum. "You won't have to call a cab. I'll take you."

ERIN LOOKED AT MARCUS through teary eyes. The respirator made a hideous sound at the steady rise and fall of his chest. There wasn't a part of his body that didn't appear bruised or battered. *Dear Lord, please let him pull through this. He's been my rock for so long. I don't know what I'd do without him.*

She wrapped her hand around the tips of his swollen fingers. Judging from his bruised knuckles, he had put up a tremendous fight. Leaning across his body, she drew near to his ear. "Marcus, I know it hurts, I know that the temptation to give up is strong. But you can beat this. I know you can. You have the strength in you, I've seen it. Now grab hold of it and don't let go.

You told me once the Lord has big plans for me...well he's got big plans for you, too. Don't you dare let us down."

"Erin, can I come in?"

She glanced over her shoulder and saw Logan standing in the doorway with two Styrofoam cups. "As long as one of those coffees is for me."

He smiled. "I thought you could use some about now."

She rose, wiping away a stray tear. She'd been here most of the day, leaving Marcus just long enough to grab a sandwich from the cafeteria. She hadn't wanted to leave him then, but Logan had persisted, threatening to have the doctor bar her from the room if she didn't.

It was the little things he did that warmed her heart the most. "Thank you," she said, accepting his love offering. She moved to the couch that two orderlies had brought into the room earlier. She smiled as Logan joined her. "Were you responsible for this, as well?"

"Candice or Tom, I suspect. Probably to save you from another epidural shot."

"They worry too much about me."

"They love you. They can't help but worry."

She smiled again. Through all the loss and heartache in her life, God had never failed to put people on the path with her that ministered to her needs.

"When I was in the cafeteria a few minutes ago, I noticed they have spaghetti on the menu. What do you say we go check it out? See if it's as good as mine."

"I'm sure it couldn't hold a candle to yours, but I'm not hungry."

"You have to eat, Erin. You barely touched your sandwich earlier."

"I don't want to leave, Logan. I'm afraid if I do...God will take him from me."

Logan slid over and put his arm around her. The tears she had been struggling to suppress finally broke free.

He took the cup from her hand, placed it with his on the floor, and then pulled her into his arms.

The steady beat of his heart soothed the fear that gripped her. *Lord, I'm doing my best to trust you, not to question your will. Give me strength; renew my faith in you. Give me back my friend.*

"ERIN."

She opened her eyes and saw Candice hovering over her. The room was darker now, the sound of the machines giving off an eerie melody. "What's wrong? Is Marcus okay?"

"Marcus is fine, Erin. You, on the other hand, look like death warmed over."

Erin threw back the light blanket and swung her legs over the side of the couch. "Did Logan go home?"

"He's not leaving this hospital without you. His words, not mine. He's in the cafeteria with his captain. I had the cook put you back a plate of spaghetti. You should go join him."

Her suggestion was tempting. She glanced over at Marcus, relieved to see the rise and fall of his chest.

"Go on, Erin. I'll stay with him."

"Okay. You'll page me if there's any change?"

"I'll page you," she promised.

Erin was almost to the door when she hollered at her. Glancing over her shoulder, she met her friend's horrid expression. "What?"

"You go down there looking like that and you're liable to scare the living daylights out of him." She reached into the pocket of her scrubs, pulled out a comb, and tossed it to her.

"Thanks." She ran the comb thru her hair, using the mirror above the sink to inspect the results. Her friend was right; she looked terrible. Her crying jag had left her eyes puffy, and dark circles had formed underneath. "I think maybe I better stop off at my locker on the way."

"Good idea."

"YOU SEE, THERE HE IS. Now back off or you're liable to find yourself in the emergency room."

Both Logan and Captain Connelly looked up at Erin's entrance. The young, plain-clothed officer beside her looked on the verge of bolting. Logan moved to the entryway before she could draw any more attention to herself.

"I'll take over from here, Rick. Relieve Douglass at the elevator. He's due for a break."

"Yes, sir."

He turned, his eyes narrowing on her. "He's just doing his job, Erin."

"Sorry. But the guy practically came into the restroom with me."

"Well, if you're going to insist on staying here in the hospital, you'll have to get used to the inconvenience."

She put her hands on her hips. "I'm starting back to work at the hospital next week. What'll we do then?"

"Whatever is necessary to ensure your safety."

"There haven't been any developments?"

"Just one, but you're not going to like it…it has to do with Marcus."

She lowered her hands to her side. "You've been investigating Marcus?"

The injured expression on her face tore at the very core of his being. Turning toward his table, he motioned for the captain to leave them alone.

He stood, offering his chair to Erin. "I'll give you a call tomorrow, Sinclair."

"Thanks, Captain."

"Take care, Erin."

She nodded.

Logan glanced around the cafeteria, thankful it was almost empty. Only a few nurses in green or blue surgical scrubs remained. He joined Erin at the table, took a deep breath to ease his nerves, and then told her what Detective Wilson had come up with.

Erin sat quietly, staring at the floor. He couldn't tell from her expression if she was surprised or upset with the news. "You have to understand, Erin, we have to look at all the angles. No matter how painful they may be."

She looked up at him. "Marcus isn't involved in this, Logan."

"You can't be sure of that."

"Yes, I can. I know Marcus better than I know myself. Yes, he did have a gambling habit, and yes, he was involved with some pretty dangerous people. But he never bet on sports, he played cards, and he hasn't done that in over four years."

"The past sometimes has a way of coming back and biting us when we least expect it, Erin."

She laughed dryly. "You're preaching to the choir on that one." She leaned across the table and took his hand. "Look, Marcus has done some things he's not proud of, but he's never hurt anyone, and the thought of him taking part in a conspiracy that could somehow harm me is asinine."

"You sure have a lot of faith in this guy."

"For the last two years he's the only one I had faith in."

"I hope you're right, Erin."

Chapter Twenty-One

"How is your friend doing?" Stephanie asked.

"They took him off the respirator yesterday. He's holding his own." Erin cradled the phone against her ear and settled back on the sofa. This made the fourth phone call in a week from Logan's sister. The first coming the night after Marcus was attacked. Being the same age and having similar interests, they'd never lacked for conversation.

The first two calls had been spent getting to know one another. Stephanie told Erin all about her life in Germany, her husband Danny, and her three children, Andrew, Aaron, and Alicia. In turn, Erin had told her about her children at the hospital and the kids at the shelter.

"I'm sure Marcus will have a full recovery."

Erin smiled at her optimism. It had gotten her through some very tough days in the past week. Spending most of her days at the hospital by his side, fearing he would never wake up, she'd looked forward to her phone calls. She suspected they were going to be very good friends in the future.

"So tell me, has Logan let you in on his secret project yet?"

"Not yet. He just keeps saying I'll find out soon enough." She thought about their daily routine. He would drop her off at the hospital shortly after breakfast, disappear till noon, join her for lunch, take her to her afternoon appointments, drop her back off at the hospital, and then pick her up at dark and take her to his parents' estate. At first, she thought he had returned to work, but when she'd grilled him about his absence, he promised he was behaving himself. "Are you sure you don't know what he's up to?" she asked, suspecting he confided in his sister more than he did anyone else.

"Sorry. He refuses to tell me anything. Probably afraid I'll spoil his surprise."

"Erin, you in here? There you are. I've been looking all over the place for you."

"Speak of the devil. I think I'll go have another piece of your mother's delicious cheesecake. I'll be back." She stood and met Logan in the middle of the library. "Talk to your sister till I get back."

Erin went to the kitchen, snuck another piece of dessert and was on her way back to the library when Marilynn stepped in from the veranda. "Ah ha, I caught you."

She grinned. "You keep making delicious desserts like this and you'll never get rid of me."

"Well, in that case, I'll just have to make more." She placed her hand on Erin's arm and gave it a gentle squeeze. "It's been such a treat having you here, Erin. I wish it were under better circumstances, of course."

"So do I. I appreciate your hospitality, though."

She leaned over and hugged her. "Any time, dear."

Erin was still smiling when she entered the library.

"It's too soon, Steph." Logan glanced up, his eyes widening. "To be planning a family vacation. Erin's back...looks like she brought me a piece of cheesecake."

Erin giggled as she held the dessert out of his reach. "No way, buster. Your mom caught me sneaking this one. I'm not chancing another trip."

"You heard her, I'm on my own...okay...love you too...I'll tell her."

She watched him hang up. "I wasn't done talking."

"Alicia's got an upset stomach. She said she'd call you Sunday."

Erin nodded, then carved off a fork full of cheesecake and stuck it in her mouth.

"That sure does look good. I don't suppose you'd want to share?"

She pretended to think about it, then joined him on the sofa. Carving off another slice, she fed it to him.

"You know, I could get used to this." He slipped his arm around her.

She recalled the tail end of the conversation she'd walked in on. "Is that what you and Steph were talking about...a future marriage proposal?"

He leaned back as if shocked. He didn't fool her. "Whatever gave you that idea?"

She laughed just as her cell phone rang. She handed him the cheesecake and retrieved her cell phone from the coffee table. "Erin Jacobs."

"It's Candice. Can you come to the hospital?"

Her smile faded. "What's wrong?"

"Marcus is awake. He's still a little groggy, but he's asking to see you."

"I'll be right there." She hung up just as Logan set the half-eaten cheesecake on the coffee table. She flung her arms around his neck, the tears already forming. "Marcus is awake; he wants to see me."

"CANDICE SAID YOU'VE been spending a lot of time here at the hospital."

Erin glanced over at her dear friend. The phone call she'd received last night had been the best news she'd ever gotten. They had only been allowed a short visit, though, and Marcus had drifted in and out of sleep the whole time. Today, he was wide awake.

She wrapped her hand around his and gave it gentle squeeze. "You gave me quite a scare." He looked much better now. He was getting his color back and the swelling in his face was almost gone.

"I know. I'm sorry."

"I'm the one who should be apologizing. You wouldn't be here if it weren't for me."

"None of this was your fault, Erin. Get that through your head right now."

"Was it Washington and Phelps that beat you up?"

He nodded. "I did manage to get in a few punches of my own, though."

She grinned. "Will you tell me what happened?"

"I stepped outside for some fresh air. You know how I get in enclosed places. Anyway, I saw them standing near the back entrance." He paused to take a drink of water before continuing. "They both had on security uniforms, but I recognized Washington right away. I went berserk, started hammering away on him. Before I knew it, Phelps struck me with something from behind. When I came to, they were gone, and I could barely move. I half crawled to the parking lot and was finally able to flag down one of the cops patrolling the area."

"Have you told Logan any of this?"

"Not yet. He's supposed to be dropping in later."

"He thinks you're somehow involved because of your past gambling habits. That you set me up the night of the shooting."

"Do you believe that?"

"No," she said softly. She lowered her gaze to his swollen and bruised hand and thought back to the early morning phone call he'd made to her the day before the auction. "But I think you know more about what's going on then you've let on." She looked up at him. "Why else would you cut loose on Washington and Phelps instead of going for help?"

"Because of the hell they've put you through in the last two months." He hesitated briefly, as if choosing his words carefully. "Someone picks on my best girl, they're going to pay for it."

"Well, if you ever pull a stupid stunt like that again, I'll kick your butt myself."

He squeezed her hand. "All right. Now why don't you go on and get out of here? Find that boyfriend of yours and make him buy you lunch."

"Get some rest." She leaned over and hugged him the best she could without disturbing the IV. "I'll see if I can't postpone giving your statement till tomorrow."

"Thanks."

"YOU DON'T BELIEVE HE'S not involved?"

Logan gave a heavy sigh. For the past ten minutes, he'd sat in the parking lot of the hospital listening to Marcus's version of what had taken place the night he had been beaten up. "That isn't what I said, Erin. I said, my instinct is telling me there's more going on here than meets the eye."

"You don't know him the way I do. He'd never hurt anyone, especially me."

"I want to believe that, Erin. Really, I do. Look, right now, I don't want you to think about any of that. I just want you to relax and enjoy the day."

"Why, what's so special about today?"

"I have a surprise for you." He reached into the glove box and took out a red bandana. "Here, put this over your eyes."

"You're blindfolding me. I don't know that I like this, Logan."

He laughed. "Just do it, Erin."

She did as he asked. "Does this have to do with the special project you've been working on?"

"No, but I think you'll like it just the same."

Five minutes later, he pulled up in front of the two-story brick building with new double glass doors. He smiled at the makeshift banner stretched across the front of the building. *The future site of the Green Acres Youth Center.* "Okay, you can remove your blindfold."

Erin laughed. "You did this?"

"I only suggested the title, the kids made the banner. You're welcome to change it."

"Are you kidding? I love it." She turned in the seat and threw her arms around his neck, hugging him.

He reluctantly ended the embrace and took her hand. "Come on, there's more."

Using the key Andy had lent him; he unlocked one of the glass doors and held it for her to enter. The smell of lumber filled the interior of the building, the cement floor covered in sawdust. Guiding her through the reception area and a wide open space that would later be petitioned off into classrooms, they came to the rear exit.

"A basketball court," she squealed before he could even get the glass door unlocked.

He followed her into the courtyard. The old cement had been replaced with new and two basketball hoops had been added. "The kids have been very busy in the last two weeks. That Joey is some motivator. I think you're rubbing off on him."

"The kids from the shelter did this?"

He nodded. "Along with your old youth group and Andy and Bobby. Andy thought they'd appreciate it more if they took part in the construction."

She turned and looked at him. He saw tears trickling down her cheeks. "This wasn't Andy's idea. It was yours," she said softly.

"Okay, it was our idea. But the kids did most of the work." Watching them in action had confirmed their love for this woman. A woman he knew he could not live without.

She closed the distance between them and wrapped her arms around his waist. "Logan, you don't know how much this means to me."

"I think I have a pretty good idea." He lifted her chin and gazed into her tear-filled eyes. "I know how much these kids mean to you, Erin...I know how much Joey means to you."

"They're the children I can't have." The words seemed ripped from her soul.

She started to pull away, but he wouldn't allow it. He pulled her back into his arms and hugged her tight. He'd known from the beginning that she couldn't have children. He'd sensed it from the longing in her eyes whenever she was around them. Wade had confirmed it for him. It didn't matter to him, though. Having her in his life, growing old with her at his side, was all he cared about.

She pushed against him and he released her from his arms. She stepped back, still looking at him. "I've longed to have a large family since I was a kid. After the accident, I feared I never would. God fulfilled my desire before I even asked. He's given me more children than I ever dreamed of."

"You and Joey have a unique bond, though. More so than with the other children."

Crossing her arms in front of her, her smile faded. He'd touched on something very personal to her, more delicate than her not being able to bear children. "What is it Erin? What makes Joey so special?"

She walked to mid court and picked up the basketball. Rolling it around in her hands, she stood quiet. He was considering changing the subject when she turned to him. "I see a lot of myself in Joey. Neither of us have ever known a place where we felt we actually belonged. Or a place we could really call home."

"What about your life with Ben?"

She shook her head slowly. "The closest I've ever felt to belonging anywhere is when I'm with the children. That's why this center is so important to me. I want these kids to know that their circumstances don't make them insignificant in this world. I want them to know that they are loved, and that it doesn't matter if they grew up on the streets or in a home. That God has a purpose for their lives."

He reached out and took her hand, giving it a gentle squeeze.

She tossed him a welcoming smile. "You made me realize my purpose. You've made me realize a lot lately."

"What else have you realized, Erin?"

She gazed lazily at him. "That by not trusting in God, I could be missing out on one of the greatest blessings he's placed in my life...you."

He pulled her back into his arms and kissed her. The taste of her lips was like sweet honey. Her passion was so sensual he could get lost in its euphoria. He knew he could live to be a hundred and never grow tired of the sensation of just having her in his arms.

The kiss ended at the sound of a ringing cell phone. He reached for his at the same time she did hers.

"It's yours," she said.

"Sinclair."

"It's Connelly. Washington has been picked up in Iowa by the highway patrol. Even though he looks like a raccoon that's been run over by a Mack truck, he's denying everything. Said he was mugged. So, unless Wheeler can ID him, they're gonna have to turn him loose."

"He already has. Erin talked to him earlier. He identified both of them."

"When were you planning on telling me that?"

"As soon as I got an official statement, which I'm on my way to get just as soon as I drop Erin off."

"All right. I'll start extradition, and issue a news release."

"Good news, I hope," Erin commented as he hung up.

"Washington's been picked up in Iowa. He's denying everything."

"What about Phelps?"

"No sign of him yet. He's looking at the attempted murders of two police officers, armed robbery, and attempted kidnapping. If he's smart, he'll turn himself in."

"You need to go?"

"I'm afraid so. I'm sorry, Erin. I was planning to take you out for a nice dinner."

She smiled. "That's okay. We'll do it tomorrow or next the day."

"Tomorrow...somewhere very special."

"It's a date."

LOGAN ENTERED MARCUS'S room and found him asleep. He was considering going to the cafeteria for a cup of coffee when he heard the man clear his voice.

"I'm not asleep." Marcus punched a button at the side of his rail and the head of his bed rose. "Erin called. She told me Washington had been picked up, and that you were on your way."

"Figures." Her loyalty to the man was disturbing, to say the least.

"You don't like me much, do you?"

His arrogance was even more disturbing. "I like you just fine. I'm just curious as to how you're involved in all this."

Marcus let out a heavy sigh and placed his free arm underneath his head. "I can't prove any of it, but I think Washington was trying to grab Erin so he could demand a ransom."

"A ransom from who?"

"Her brother."

"But she doesn't have a brother."

"Not one that she's aware of. I'm her brother, Logan. I didn't know for sure until a few weeks ago. The night we had dinner, the night you were shot, I stole her hairbrush from her purse. I had her DNA run against mine." He motioned toward an envelope on the table. "See for yourself."

Logan opened the envelope and glanced at the DNA report confirming that they were siblings. He blew out a mouth full of air. He was both relieved and confused by the news.

"Washington must have figured out what I was up to and decided to make some money before I exposed him for the louse that he is."

Logan sat down in the chair next to his bed. "Washington knows you're siblings?"

"Gage Washington is our uncle, our mother's brother. He took custody of us just long enough to wipe out our inheritance, then handed us over to the courts."

Logan thought back to the conversation he'd had with Erin about the fire that had claimed the lives of her parents. "Erin was told that her whole family was killed in the fire."

"I know. I was told the same thing after waking up from a three-month coma. By then Washington had left the state and I guess the courts never took the time to verify whether or not he was telling the truth. At least, that's what my attorney has managed to come up with so far. He's still looking into our records, but it's going to take some time to figure it all out."

Logan let his news sink in. Marcus Wheeler was Erin's brother. It explained a lot. Marcus was one of the highest paid wide receivers in the NFL, would have no trouble coming up with ransom money. And the fear of exposure was more than enough motive for Washington to do something this stupid. Phelps had probably just gotten caught in the middle of it.

"How did you find out the truth?"

"After my football injury, they had me on morphine, notorious for giving a person some wicked nightmares. Mine consisted of being trapped in a burning house. In a couple I remembered going into my sisters' room and trying to get them out onto the roof. I only managed to rescue one, though. As I went back for the other, a section of the first story collapsed, causing the roof to disappear underneath us. I remember seeing her rolling over the edge before everything went black.

"The images seemed too real to be a figment of my imagination, so shortly after my release from the hospital I petitioned the courts for my records and learned that I had a sister out there somewhere."

"But Washington used to be your agent. Are you telling me he didn't know who you were? That you didn't know who he was?"

"Wheeler is my adopted name. Canton is my real name. It's also Erin's maiden name. The best I can figure is that, when I was injured, Washington figured out who I was after I shared the dreams I was having. That was the reason he resigned as my agent. He was afraid that, sooner or later, I might remember who he was."

"How long have you known that there was a possibility you were Erin's brother?"

"Several months ago she had me over to help her move some stuff up to her attic. Her wedding album just happened to be sticking out of one of the boxes. Curious, I looked. Her maiden name was listed on the marriage certificate. I didn't want to say anything until I was certain, though. She's been through so much; I didn't want to cause her any more heartache." He reached for the glass of water on the table and took a sip.

"I'd planned on telling her the truth the night of the fundraiser. I knew it was a special night for her, and I was hoping the news would make it even more special. I paid off the printer to add her name to the bill, knowing the winner would have her undivided attention all evening. I wasn't counting on you, though."

Logan smiled. "You'll get the chance to tell her soon enough."

"I had the chance earlier and couldn't do it."

"Why not? She needs to know."

"This is the happiest I've ever seen her, Logan. I don't want to spoil it."

"I just imagine she'll be pretty ticked off that you didn't tell her sooner. But afterwards, I'm sure she'll be thrilled."

"You think?"

"Without a doubt," he assured, recalling their conversation earlier. "I have to admit, this news has sure taken a load off my mind."

Marcus chuckled. "She told me you were a little jealous of our friendship."

"I'm sure she did." He took out his notebook. "I'm going to need your statement as to what happened at the auction if you feel up to it."

"Fire away."

Chapter Twenty-Two

The following day, Logan stepped outside the hospital for some fresh air. Two hours had passed since he left Erin with Marcus. He hoped things were going well. He had reservations later this evening at a restaurant Marcus had suggested. Depending on how well Erin took the news that she had a brother, he was going to ask her to marry him. He'd been struggling with whether or not it was too soon for a marriage proposal, but after their conversation at the youth center, he felt fairly certain she would say yes. He'd already asked Addison to be his best man, and thought he'd suggest Andy perform the ceremony. Or if she wanted to elope, that was okay too. He didn't care one way or the other; he just prayed she'd say yes.

Pausing under the awning, he saw Candice approaching. "Have you seen Erin?" she asked. "I've been trying to reach her. She's not answering her cell or her pager."

"She's in with Marcus. They're talking."

"Is everything okay?"

"Yeah, I think so. Can I give her a message?"

"Just tell her to give me a call. I might need her to help out in the ER next week a couple of nights."

"I'll tell her."

"You know there's nothing going on between them."

He fought the temptation of telling her the good news. "I know, Candice. Thanks."

"Sure. See you around, Logan."

"You can count on it." He glanced at his watch again, and wondered how things were going.

"I WAS TEMPTED TO TELL you when I first suspected it, but I wanted to be sure. And I was afraid of how you would react."

"You didn't think I'd be happy about it? Marcus, you're one of my best friends."

"I was afraid of the repercussions. You made the comment once that you hoped you'd never remember the fire."

It wasn't so much the fire she didn't want to remember, but her life following the fire. Marcus had been subjected to physical abuse in the foster care system; she had suffered mentally.

"Well, according to your memories, I was unconscious throughout most of it so perhaps there won't be anything to remember. Either way, I'm glad you told me." She squeezed his hand, her smile widening. "You're my brother…we're a family." She thought about the car he'd given her. "Is that why you gave me the Jag?"

He grinned. "I was afraid you were going to get yourself killed on that stupid bike."

"Okay, let's get something straight right now. Just because you are my brother, doesn't mean you can start telling me what to do. I have enough people trying to run my life as it is."

"Honey, I wouldn't dream of it. Besides, I know you well enough to know you're going to do what you want to do no matter what anyone else says."

She leaned back in the chair and smiled. All these years, she thought he was dead. It was a lot to digest. Not only did she now have a brother, she had an uncle who had nearly destroyed her life. She took a deep breath and let it out slowly. She wasn't going to think about any of that right now. "There is something you should probably know now that you are my brother."

"What's that?" He leaned his head to one side, smiling.

"I think Logan is going to ask me to marry him."

"Seems logical, he does love you. What's your answer going to be?"

She grinned. "I want to marry him." It was the only thing she was sure of.

"Him being a cop doesn't frighten you anymore?"

"I don't like it, but I'm willing to accept it because that's who he is. And I can't imagine my life without him in it."

"Well, I have to admit, he's brought about quite a change in you."

"He isn't the only one."

"No, I don't suppose he is."

LOGAN GLANCED UP AT the opening of the elevator doors. An elderly couple and two small children stepped off. He glanced at his watch. What could be taking so long? Were they discussing their entire childhood?

"Logan."

He turned to see Erin coming down the hall. He zeroed in on her face. As usual, he couldn't read her. "You okay?"

"I'm fine. Sorry it took so long. I stopped off at the chapel."

He was glad of that. Though she still hadn't returned to church, he sensed the relationship between her and the Lord was on the mend. "You ready to go?"

"I'm ready, but would you mind terribly if I took a rain check on dinner?"

"Of course not," he answered, trying not to sound too disappointed. There would be no marriage proposal tonight.

He slipped his arm around her shoulder as they left the hospital. "How'd it go with Marcus?"

"Okay. He told you yesterday, didn't he?"

"Yeah. I would have told you, but I thought it should come from him. Are you okay with it?"

"Of course I'm okay with it. Why wouldn't I be?"

"You just seem upset."

"I'm fine."

She didn't sound fine. She sounded almost angry. When they reached his truck, he opened the passenger door for her. "Are you sure you're okay, Erin?"

"I just learned that I have a brother, and that my own flesh and blood threw me into a system that almost destroyed me, Logan. It's going to take some getting used to."

He went still at her words. She'd never offered much information about the foster homes she'd been in except for the couple that had adopted her. Judging from her words, there was good reason for that.

"Can we just go, please?"

He closed her door. *Lord, help her through this. Please give her the strength and courage to face her past and put it to rest once and for all. Help me to be there for her. Give me the patience and wisdom to help in any way I can.*

She was silent on the drive home. Pulling up in front of her house, he turned to her. "Please don't shut me out, Erin."

"I'm not shutting you out, Logan. I just need some time to sort through some things."

"Okay. But if you need to talk, I'm just a phone call away."

His offer won him a beautiful smile that set his apprehensions to rest.

Chapter Twenty-Three

"I thought I might find you here."

Erin looked up and saw Logan walking across the makeshift basketball court on top of the hospital. She hadn't seen him in two days. Not since the day Marcus had told her they were siblings. "Sorry I haven't been returning your calls."

"That's all right. I figured you needed your space."

She had. Marcus's news had brought back some painful memories of the past, memories that wouldn't be with her had it not been for the evil actions of one man.

"Do you mind if I join you?"

She tossed him the ball. He dribbled a few times, took aim, and made the basket cleanly.

Ten minutes of silence lapsed between them before she got the nerve to ask about her uncle. "What's going to happen to Washington?"

"Don't worry; he'll be going away for a very long time." He passed her the ball. "As will Phelps, who according to the captain, turned himself in day before yesterday, along with his brother. They were the two who robbed the restaurant, and the ones who shot Addison and me."

She took aim, shot, and missed.

Logan caught the rebound and followed up with a clean shot from the sideline. "Placing you and Marcus into the system was the best thing he could have ever done for you. He had no business being a parent."

She caught the rebound. "Neither did some of the people I was placed with."

"You were abused?" he guessed.

"Not as bad as Marcus. For me, it wasn't so much physical as it was mental abuse. I was placed with some very cruel and heartless people. To them,

I was only a means of getting more money from the state. And when I was placed with a good family, it seemed I'd just get settled in when something would go wrong and I would be yanked out and placed somewhere else. After a while, instead of taking the risk of getting too close, and being let down, I would just take off, run away.

"Then I met the Brannons." She took aim and shot. The ball hit the backboard and dropped through the net. "They taught me the true meaning of love by introducing me to Jesus, and He led me through the healing process." She retrieved the ball and tossed it to him. "It wasn't until college, though, that I could bring myself to get close to anyone my own age. That's where I met Miles and Candice, and they taught me the meaning of true friendship. I was in my second year when Walter and Julia passed away within months of one another. Miles and Candice were there for me.

"I'm still going through that healing process, Logan. One day at a time."

He tossed the ball aside, stepped forward, and placed both hands on her shoulders. "Well, you won't be going through it alone. You'll have me."

She smiled. "Are you sure you're up to it? I can be a handful...just ask any of my friends."

"Take a drive with me, Erin. There's something I want to show you."

She thought of the special project he'd been working on. "Do I have to wear a blindfold?"

"No blindfolds, I promise."

THE GRAVEL ROAD THEY traveled down was familiar, only she hadn't been down it in several weeks. She glanced over at him and smiled. He was taking her to his farm.

"There's still a lot of work to be done, but what do you think?"

She got out of the truck and looked around. The grass and shrubs had been cut, the barn painted, the corals fixed, and the house was getting a new addition added on. "Looks awfully big for one person."

"Yes, but perfect for six or seven."

Her smile faded. He was talking about children. Children she couldn't give him. She thought he'd understood that after their talk the other day, but evidently, it hadn't sunk in. "Logan, we need to talk."

"Just hear me out, okay?" He wrapped his hands around hers. "We both love kids, and have a good rapport with them. I thought we could…"

She stopped him by placing her fingers to his lips. Tears welled in her eyes. She wished she'd told him sooner, but she'd never counted on falling in love with him. "Logan, I can't give you children. The accident I had in college…the damage that was done to my pelvis…the doctors said it would be impossible."

"Erin, you've already given me children." He turned loose of one hand to wipe the tears from her cheeks. "I was talking about Joey, and other kids like him. I figure, if we finish the basement and add two bedrooms, we could take in four or five kids."

She grinned deliriously. "You want us to be foster parents?"

"Or we could adopt. What do you think? I know Joey would love the idea."

"You're really serious about this?"

"I've never been more serious about anything in my life. I love you, Erin, and I want to spend the rest of my life with you." He reached into the front pocket of his jeans and took out a small, blue box.

Her heart fluttered as he let go of her other hand to remove the ring. "I had planned on giving this to you the other night at dinner," he said.

She let out a nervous laugh as he took her left hand. It trembled as he slipped the ring on her finger. More tears welled in her eyes.

"Will you marry me, Erin?"

"Yes," she barely managed. She wrapped her arms around his neck and met his lips in a fervent kiss.

He ended the embrace seconds later and took both her hands into his. She gazed down at the ruby surrounded by smaller diamonds. She'd never seen anything more beautiful.

"Mom gave it to me; she wanted you to have it. It belonged to her mother. But she said if you didn't like it…"

She choked back another sob. "I love it."

"Good." He kissed her hand, gazing lazily into her tear-filled eyes. "So, would you like to see the renovations?"

"I'd love too."

THEY WERE MET AT THE front door by his orange tabby.

She knelt and petted the tomcat. "Hi Boris. I certainly hope you're a good mouser." Her heart swelled at the thought of sharing a home with Logan and Joey. And not just Joey, a whole house full of kids. So what if they weren't hers naturally? It didn't matter. They would still be a family.

Logan took her hand. "Watch your step through here. The guys I've got doing the work don't clean up after themselves very well."

"You haven't been helping, have you?" She still couldn't believe this was the project he'd been working on all this time. It proved even more just how much he loved her and wanted to spend the rest of his life with her.

He grinned sheepishly. "Just a little...I promise I'm not over doing it, though."

He led her through a maze of sawhorses and stacks of lumber toward the back of the house. "This is the master bedroom. I'm having that wall taken out to allow space for a whirlpool. It might help with your back pain. Oh, and I'm extending the closet."

She looked around the room, still amazed he'd done it all for her, and for Joey. "You've thought of everything."

His eyes leveled on her. "I want you to feel comfortable here, Erin. I want it to be a place you can call home."

Tears welled in her eyes and her heart felt like it was going to explode. She doubted she could ever love him more than she did right now. "How long have you been planning all this?"

"My first thought was to turn this place into a group home, and hiring house parents. You gave me the idea that first day I brought you here. When you told me about the work program you wanted to start. I thought, why not just have the kids live here and take part in its upkeep? But then, my plans started to evolve the closer we became. After that, everything just sort of fell into place."

"It's funny how that happens sometimes."

He grinned. "Yeah, it is."

In that moment, she'd never felt more loved. Not just by Logan, but by God. "You know, your mother called me this morning."

"Oh yeah?"

"She invited me to church this Sunday. I told her I'd love to come."

"Really? Does that mean you've graduated your anger management class?"

She laughed. "Thanks for not giving up on me."

He pulled her into his arms. "The thought never crossed my mind."

The End

ABOUT THE AUTHOR

Anne Patrick is the author of more than a dozen novels of Romance, Mayhem & Faith, including the award-winning and best-selling Wounded Heroes Series, Fire and Ash, and Ties That Bind. When she's not working on her next novel she enjoys spending time with family and friends, and traveling to foreign countries to experience new cultures and adventures. She makes her home in Kansas.

Other books by Anne:
Dark Alliance
Lethal Dreams
Ties That Bind
Out of the Darkness
Fire and Ash
Sabotage
A Familiar Evil
Journey to Redemption
Renegade Hearts
Fire Creek
Kill Shot – Wounded Heroes Series, Book One
Trespasses – Wounded Heroes Series, Book Two
Betrayal – Wounded Heroes Series, Book Three
Secrets – Wounded Heroes Series, Book Four – coming soon
Vengeance – Wounded Heroes Series, Book Five – coming soon

To learn more about Anne, please visit her website: http://www.annepatrickbooks.com. She loves to hear from her readers!

Made in the USA
Columbia, SC
14 September 2021